The Raven␣ Daug␣

A Victorian Historical Murder Mystery

Book 1 of
The Field & Greystone Series

Lana Williams

USA Today Bestselling Author

To Brad, Brandon, & Jordan,
for always believing.
Love you

Mysteries by Lana Williams

One

London, 1883

Heart rattling against his ribs, Aberforth Pritchard held his lantern aloft to fend off the eerie night. He glanced about with no small measure of trepidation.

Bartram had picked a terrible time to escape.

Fog had risen from the Thames like a ghostly shroud and cast odd shadows over the grounds of the Tower of London this cold October evening. Thick tendrils of the stuff bellowed before the coat that flapped against his shins as if in protest at his passage.

With a firmer grip on the lantern, Aberforth fixed his gaze on the Middle Tower gate just ahead, fearful it might soon disappear in the mist. What should look familiar did not. Even the air smelled strange this frosty evening, a damp, brackish mix of sulfur and soot.

"Damn ravens," he muttered as he withdrew a ring of old iron keys from his pocket when he neared the gate. "Never staying where they're supposed to. Prying me from the comfort of my warm bed."

His words created puffs of steam. Whether he talked to reassure himself or to keep any restless spirits at bay on this dark night, he couldn't say. Few people would argue that the Tower didn't have a ghost or two. He certainly wouldn't.

Aberforth was a superstitious man despite—or perhaps because of—his seven and forty years. A Yeoman Warder, after serving a quarter of a century in the military and continuing his service as a guardian of the Tower, shouldn't fear the dark.

But something about the night unsettled him.

There was no problem, he reassured himself. He intended to keep his wits about him as he always did. His daughter of a mere seven years waited for him at home in the casements across the Green. He was all she had, after they lost her mother when she gave birth. Hopefully Maeve remained in bed where he'd left her sleeping soundly.

If only the damned raven would've done the same. Bartram was a rebel of sorts and too smart for his own good. Ava, his mate, had caused a ruckus, which was the reason Aberforth had awoken to investigate. Ava didn't like it when Bartram was out at night and made certain Aberforth knew about it. Someone had been messing with his charges of late, and he had a suspicion as to who and why.

Guarding the ravens at the Tower was no easy task. They were clever and had minds of their own. Not all the Yeoman Warders liked the birds, but Aberforth wanted to believe the creatures respected him as much as he did them. Why, just this morning, Ava had brought him a rat's tail. If that wasn't a sign of affection, he didn't know what was.

The ravens were good judges of character and just didn't take to some people. They didn't like strangers, nor did they like to be looked in the eye. Heaven forbid the birds sensed fear in a person. Their bite was powerful, and Aberforth had his share of scars from moments he hadn't been paying attention.

Legend said that Charles II decreed at least six ravens should always live in the Tower or the Crown would fail and England along with it. Bartram was one of those six, hence the reason Aberforth was searching for him. Night was a dangerous time for ravens. It was when the most harm could befall them, from sly foxes and the like. The darkness made it damned difficult to locate a black bird.

Clipping the ravens' wings didn't mean they wouldn't wander when the urge struck. He'd already searched the Tower Green to no avail. Time was of the essence as the fog would soon rise high enough to blot out the full moon, stealing any chance of finding Bartram before a fox did.

Aberforth unlocked the iron gate and eased through, leaving it unlocked behind him. Hopefully it would not be long before he returned with Bartram.

The bird had escaped a few times before. Twice Aberforth had found him on the bank of the Thames where the tide tended to kick up bits and bobs, leaving them along the river. Bartram liked shiny things, as did most ravens, and the glittering objects would've been visible until the fog rolled in.

The gentle swing of his glowing lantern was of some reassurance as he moved along the walkway and down the slippery stairs toward the river. He kept his focus on it, rather than the shadows that crept forward the second he looked away. The scent of the water was stronger as he neared the river. Not much farther now.

He only hoped little Maeve didn't wake while he was gone. Thoughts of her quickened his pace, and he soon reached the riverbank. In his rush, he almost didn't hear the muffled voice floating down to him from above.

"She'll arrive by train."

Aberforth halted, startled by the voice that distracted him from his thoughts.

"Then what?" a different male voice asked.

Aberforth lowered his lantern as he realized the men speaking were on the walkway above him. He would have run into them if he hadn't come down the stairs.

Unfortunately, knowing he wasn't the only one out at this hour brought no comfort. In fact, chills prickled along his skin. He told himself their conversation was no business of his, but a sinking sensation in the pit of his stomach suggested otherwise.

"The carriage will take her from the station to the palace."

Heart pounding, Aberforth knew they were speaking of the Queen, though he couldn't explain his alarm, considering so little had been said.

"That is when we act." The conviction in the hushed tone was undeniable.

A raven's croak filled the air like a harbinger of doom. It had to be Bartram, but Aberforth did not move. How could he pursue the bird when something so foul was afoot?

Duty demanded he do something. But what? He'd noted two men meeting near the Tower twice in the past week and hadn't liked the look of them, even if one had worn fine clothes and was familiar. The bits of conversation he'd overheard now roused his suspicions, and he had to wonder if these were the same two.

Confronting them was too risky when he was outnumbered. Even more might be up the stairs. His best hope was to get closer to hear what else they said and try to catch a look to possibly identify them later.

He shut off the flame on his lantern then set it on the ground and straightened, his military training taking hold. With as much stealth as possible, he returned to the stairs and climbed upward, staying close to the wall. His heart thudded dully, his knees weak as a kitten's.

He reminded himself that well over a hundred people were nearby within the Tower walls, thirty-six of them soldiers. Yet they might as well have been across the Channel for as much good as they could do him at short notice.

"I'd prefer it if we didn't have to make Her Majesty's death quick." A hint of an Irish brogue colored the man's deep tone. "A painful end would send a clearer message."

"Only if you claim responsibility." The other man chuckled as if he'd made a jest.

"When the time is right, we will tell everyone who we are and what we stand for."

The snapping of a twig brought Aberforth's progress to a halt. It hadn't been him who caused the sound.

"Who's there?"

Aberforth waited, certain his pounding heart would give him away. If he could draw a little closer, he might be able to see the men while they were distracted by the noise and whoever—or whatever—had made it.

Identifying them was imperative.

He crept forward again, one step at a time, until his head was level with the top of the stairs. Then he peeked around the stone column that marked the start of the staircase.

A strong hand grabbed his upper arm and hauled him the rest of the way up, sending panic skittering through him.

"What do we have here? A spy?" The man's fine attire marked him as a gentleman though his strength suggested he led a far more physical life. His accent was crisp and succinct. An Oxford man, for certain. Someone Aberforth recognized...

"Release me at once," Aberforth demanded, his bearing erect like the soldier he was. He clenched his fists, prepared to fight.

"I'm afraid that's impossible." The man with the Irish accent joined them. He held a knife in one hand, the blade flashing in the fading moonlight that the fog was rapidly overcoming.

Aberforth swallowed hard and willed anger to lend him strength. "I'm a Yeoman Warder. Step away."

The Irishman chuckled, a thoroughly unpleasant sound that chilled Aberforth to the bone. "Why would that make any difference?"

"You overheard a private conversation." The gentleman shook his head, his tone one of polite regret. "How unfortunate."

"I didn't hear anything. I'm searching for a raven that's gone missing from the Tower." Aberforth attempted to jerk his arm free, to no avail. "Release me, and I'll be on my way."

"If only we could believe you. I saw you lingering near the Tower the other day as well. You and those pesky ravens." The gentleman nodded at the Irishman as if giving him permission to proceed.

Panic rushed through Aberforth, demanding he act. He plowed his free fist into the gentleman's stomach and gained his release. He shifted, balancing on the balls of his feet, and threw a wild punch toward the Irishman but only managed to graze his jaw. He struck out again, fighting as if his life depended on it—because he was certain it did.

The first slash on his arm caught him by surprise. The blade cut through his thick coat as if it were butter. The knife had come and gone before he felt a thing. A second slash then a third caused his breath to hitch. He looked down to see the blade hilt-deep in his chest before his attacker withdrew it.

Outraged at the audacity of the man, Aberforth landed a blow on the man's arm. Though the man grunted in pain, the blade flashed again. Then again.

Aberforth continued to fight but his blows lacked power, as if his strength were draining out, allowing pain in. He couldn't gasp a proper breath. What he thought had been mostly small pricks burned as though the devil himself had set them alight.

His vision started to fade, narrowing. Was the mist closing in or was it something far worse? He dropped to his knees, his legs giving way beneath him as he fought to stay conscious.

Then his gaze caught a figure in white across the walkway.

Maeve. Oh, dear God.

Tears filled his eyes even as his breath began to gurgle, blood burning the back of his throat. She must've come looking for him. His sweet, young daughter.

Run, he mouthed, praying she'd understand. Her eyes rounded with horror as he was stabbed yet again, his body jerking from the strike. She hunched her shoulders and eased back into the shadows.

Run, he silently cried again. Then all went dark.

Two

Amelia Greystone carefully scooped a white powdery substance—sodium bicarbonate, to be precise—into a measuring spoon and leveled it off with the back of a knife blade. She tapped the powder into a beaker filled with water and stirred, pleased when the liquid bubbled slightly.

The morning's experiment was a practical one, with the aim of finding a better method to clean soot from brick. Day after day, Amelia had witnessed the maid scrubbing with all her strength to remove the black stain from the bricks around the drawing room fireplace. There had to be an easier way.

Early morning light shone through the tall bank of windows behind her long worktable. The modest laboratory she had set up in the attic gave her great pleasure, with its neat rows of various-sized jars, a brass scale, a filter funnel, and a porcelain mortar and pestle set. A tall wardrobe made of walnut stood at the far end of the room and housed other supplies. The opposite end held shelves with glass vessels containing a colorful array of liquids and substances with which to experiment.

Though she knew chemistry was an unusual hobby for a woman, Amelia owed her love of it to her father, an apothecary who served a small village just outside London. Yet selling tonics and concoctions to the public was not where Amelia's interests lay. Her preference was dabbling in toxicology, though chemistry of any sort fascinated her.

The concentration needed to conduct experiments was a productive way to keep her thoughts from growing dark.

Despite being only nine-and-twenty, Amelia had experienced more than her share of grief. She and her husband, Matthew, had lost their one and only child, Lily, at the tender age of three to scarlet fever. That loss three years ago had nearly broken Amelia and threatened her marriage as well.

Matthew had thrown himself into multiple excesses—work, drinking, cards—while Amelia had spent far too much time abed, unable to function. It had taken months to crawl out and begin to live again. Though they'd regained a semblance of the friendship which had drawn them together, their relationship never recovered from the wedge of loss between them.

Then, nearly a year ago, Matthew had been killed.

His death had been a shock, though she supposed she had dealt with it better than she had Lily's passing. His murder remained unsolved, adding to the worry that still followed her.

But life demanded her participation, regardless of whether she agreed. The best coping mechanism she'd found was to stay busy.

The days had slowly become easier, but not all. Definitely not all. She'd learned to take each one as it came.

Today was a good day.

Four bricks with approximately the same level of sootiness were aligned in a row near her elbow. She intended to create four different solutions to see which one performed best.

The side of her that appreciated order and control thoroughly enjoyed these experiments. She could decide the variables and what she was willing to risk.

If only life were like that. If only love worked that way.

Amelia gently applied the wash to the brick, giving only a small scrub to the surface. After all, the purpose was to do little to no scrubbing.

Then she moved on to the next solution—crushed duck eggshells mixed with lemon juice. This seemed far less practical. The eggshells made a mess, even if they created an abrasive of sorts. Still, she applied the mixture to the next brick, already certain it wouldn't be the best option.

Ammonium carbonate came next, though the strong, unpleasant odor made it an unlikely option. Lastly, she used a combination of sodium bicarbonate and vinegar. The result of this one was nearly immediate, and she smiled in satisfaction. Though the smell was mildly unpleasant, its results were favorable compared to the others.

"Mrs. Greystone?"

Amelia looked up from the line of beakers and bricks to see Mrs. Fernsby, her housekeeper, in the doorway. "Yes?"

"I'm sorry to disturb you, but I'm afraid we have an unexpected visitor."

"Oh? Who is it?" Amelia knew it must be someone of importance or she wouldn't have been interrupted. The servants avoided doing so while she was in her lab unless absolutely necessary. They respected her need for quiet while she was conducting an experiment.

Mr. Fernsby served as butler and his wife as housekeeper. The pair lived-in along with a maid and the cook. The size of the staff seemed like too many servants for one woman who lived by herself but employing them gave Amelia the freedom to do the activities that interested her.

Her gratitude to Matthew for leaving her enough money to do as she wished, within reason, was enormous.

But it didn't lessen her grief or quiet her questions about his death. Nor did it bring comfort in the dark of the night when she couldn't sleep.

Mrs. Fernsby's brow puckered, but otherwise her expression was unreadable. "Perhaps it would be best if you saw for yourself."

Now Amelia was intrigued. She rarely had visitors, let alone at this early hour. The fact that it was Mrs. Fernsby who'd come to tell her rather than the woman's husband was also puzzling. But perhaps she was making too much of the small detail.

"Very well." She removed the white apron she wore in the lab and followed Mrs. Fernsby, pausing to hang the apron on the hook by the door.

The housekeeper was a short, stout, hardworking woman with gray hair and high standards. She expected much from the staff but equally as much from herself. Her husband wisely bowed to her suggestions. Together, the pair was indispensable.

Amelia followed the housekeeper down the stairs. Her bedroom was on the front side of the house with two guest rooms nearby. Mr. and Mrs. Fernsby had a room in the back. Amelia pressed a hand against her heart to ease the ever-present ache as they walked by the small bedroom which had been Lily's, now empty, the door closed.

They continued down the next flight of stairs. Amelia grew more curious by the moment as they passed the empty drawing room before descending another flight. They moved through the entrance hall and the tiny reception room where guests, if she ever had any, waited.

Yet Mrs. Fernsby didn't pause there. Instead, she led the way down the corridor toward the back of the house past Matthew's study.

Amelia glanced at the door as they walked by, thinking not for the first time that she should take the space as her own. She used it occasionally to write her articles and notes on her experiments, but Matthew's presence still overshadowed the space. While being surrounded by his things had at first been comforting, it wasn't any longer. Whether that was because she was moving through her grief or because of the questions she had not only about his death but the life he'd been living beforehand, she did not know. Perhaps both. As she too often told herself, now wasn't the time to worry over such things.

Mrs. Fernsby continued down the last flight of stairs that led to the kitchen and the cook's quarters, making Amelia even more curious.

Hoping her questions would soon be answered, she kept her silence but couldn't hide her surprise when the housekeeper strode toward the delivery entrance. Amelia noted the cook's worried expression along with that of Yvette, the maid's, then followed the housekeeper out into the crisp morning air.

Like all the redbrick houses on Bloomsbury Street, the service door was partway below ground level. The low wrought-iron gate that led down the stairs to the door where deliveries arrived was closed, and there—

A small form clothed in white huddled on the bottom step.

The realization that the figure was a girl wearing a long nightgown caused Amelia to catch her breath. For the barest moment, her mind tricked her into thinking it was Lily.

Of course it wasn't.

The child's head was buried in her folded arms on bent knees. Her mousy brown hair hung in a long, untidy braid just past her shoulders.

A vague sense of recognition filled Amelia. She moved past the housekeeper and joined the girl on the step, reaching out to touch a gentle hand on her shoulder. "Maeve?"

Why she bothered to say the girl's name, she didn't know. Maeve was deaf and mute.

At her touch Maeve stiffened, head lifting to reveal a tear-streaked face and brown eyes wide with fear.

Amelia's heart tugged at the girl's fright, and she immediately opened her arms, hoping the rather skittish child would accept her offer of comfort.

After a moment's hesitation, Maeve leaned toward Amelia and wrapped her arms tightly around her neck.

The unexpected show of affection pulled at Amelia even more, though she hardly knew the child—she had met Maeve only a week ago, while interviewing the ravenkeeper at the Tower of London for a magazine article. Engaging with the little girl had been bittersweet; she was about the age Lily would have been if she'd lived.

Because of that, a lump had lodged in Amelia's throat from the moment Yeoman Warder Pritchard had introduced her to the seven-year-old.

"I can't imagine what brought her here in this state," Mrs. Fernsby said.

"Nor can I. I suppose she remembered her visit to my lab." Amelia had felt sorry for Maeve, locked in a silent world, and tried to connect with her. She mentioned her workspace to Warder Pritchard during their interview, and he'd explained it to Maeve. The girl had expressed curiosity about it, so Amelia had invited the pair to her home the next day to give them a tour.

"Her face lit up when she saw the beakers, glass tubes, and such," Amelia added.

"The visit must've made quite an impression." Mrs. Fernsby kept her gaze on the girl.

Amelia had shown Maeve how to do a couple of simple experiments. First, they'd made water rise in a shallow bowl by lighting a short candle and placing a glass over it. Next, they'd made raisins dance in a glass of sodium bicarbonate and vinegar.

The girl's delight and her father's pride that she'd assisted with the experiments convinced Amelia she'd done the right thing.

"I can't imagine what's happened." Amelia held the crying girl for a long moment, her worried gaze meeting the housekeeper's, whose concern matched her own.

Maeve's guttural sobs wracked her thin frame, tightening a knot of worry in Amelia.

Reminding herself of the girl's inability to hear, Amelia tried to ease back to communicate with her, but Maeve held on tight. After waiting another minute or two, she loosened the girl's grip to look at her face, brushing a wisp of hair from Maeve's forehead. Amelia placed a finger under her small chin, hoping the girl would look at her.

"What happened?" She mouthed the words slowly so Maeve could read her lips, but the girl only shook her head, her face contorted as she continued to cry.

Amelia wrapped her arms around her once again, rocking back and forth, whispering "Shh" over and over, though she knew the girl could not hear, hoping her efforts comforted her enough so the child could somehow share what had happened.

After several minutes, Maeve drew a shuddering breath.

Amelia dearly hoped that whatever was wrong was something simple. Something that was within her power to solve. She pushed aside the memories of Lily and the fact that she hadn't been able to help her.

She blinked to dispel her own upset then drew back to look into the girl's brown eyes again. "Are you lost?"

Please let that be the problem. She would happily escort the girl back to her father at the Tower of London.

But the question only brought more tears.

Once the girl had calmed again, Amelia shifted to stand and pointed to the door. "Let's go inside."

She waited as the girl considered her request. Maeve slowly rose, revealing scuffed bare feet caked with mud.

The housekeeper tsked as she stared at the girl's toes. "She must have been walking half the night for them to look like that."

Amelia nodded. The same thought had crossed her mind. "Please ask Mr. Fernsby to send a message to her father. We'll clean her up and locate a change of clothes for her. She must be hungry. Then perhaps she can help us understand what happened."

Mrs. Fernsby nodded. "It seems to me that the faster we return her to her father the better. He must be worried sick." The housekeeper held open the door as Amelia escorted the girl into the kitchen.

"I'm sure you're right."

But Amelia feared that whatever had shaken the girl so deeply was far from over.

Three

S cotland Yard Inspector Henry Field walked beside Sergeant Adam Fletcher toward the Tower of London, wishing the body had been discovered elsewhere.

He wasn't overly fond of the foreboding fortress.

The Tower might be considered a green haven in the middle of London by some, but it made Henry uncomfortable. He blamed the feeling on his father's penchant for telling ghost stories when Henry was a lad, particularly the tale of the two princes locked in the Tower. The idea of boys his own age being murdered by those who were supposed to care for and protect them had given him nightmares as a child.

The hour was early and the air brisk even for October. Fog still lingered in the low areas like an old woman eavesdropping from the shadows.

"What do we know from the constable's report?" Henry asked. He would speak with the man eventually but was anxious to begin the investigation. This was the first meaningful case he'd been assigned in weeks, and his progress would be under close scrutiny. All the more reason to dig into the situation.

"A body washed up from the Thames and was discovered nearly two hours ago." The sergeant scowled. "A lad found it and alerted Constable Stephens. Sliced up pretty good, just to forewarn you."

Adam Fletcher was six years older than Henry's own two and thirty years, his time on the force, along with a decade in the military, made him an excellent officer. Little ruffled the man's feathers. Yet when Henry glanced at him, Fletcher's impressive brown moustache twitched again, suggesting the body truly was in bad shape.

Henry frowned but did not break his stride. He'd spent eight years as a constable in S Division in north London. Two years ago, he'd been promoted to inspector—a quick rise according to some. Still, he had seen his share of unpleasant sights.

He hoped his investigative skills had gained him the promotion, but when one's father and grandfather had been respected chief inspectors, chances were that more than his own abilities played into his promotions through the ranks of the Metropolitan Police.

"You're not worried, are you?" Fletcher asked after another look at him. "This one might be an open and shut case."

"One can hope." Though Henry doubted it. Not after his failure with the last case.

"One unsolved murder is nothing. Besides, there were no clues to follow. It was unsolvable. No one could've done any better."

"I have to think my father could've. My grandfather as well." He was the weak link in the line, and that was something for which he couldn't forgive himself.

His desire to be an inspector reached back for as long as he could remember. His larger-than-life grandfather, the famous Charles Frederick Field, well-known for not only his brilliant career but for his friendship with Charles Dickens, had inspired that yearning. Henry's father had followed in his father's footsteps, and both were elated when Henry had chosen to do the same.

"The trail went cold," the sergeant argued. "Frigid, in fact."

"Hmm." That much was true. Henry had done his best to warm it up and shake loose a clue with Fletcher's help, but to no avail.

"This case will be different," Fletcher added.

"Perhaps." He was anxious to redeem himself, and this could be his chance.

Blowing out a breath to clear his mind, he accompanied Fletcher's burly uniformed figure toward the Queen's Stairs only to pause as his gaze caught on the pavement a short distance away.

It had rained during the night, but that hadn't entirely washed away the stain of blood.

Henry squatted down and saw the faint traces of spatter on the stone wall that lined the pavement. How unfortunate that the rain had blurred it. Still, a pattern was visible, and it did not bode well.

"I suppose it's safe to say the man was killed here," Fletcher murmured.

"It seems so." Henry slowly stood as he studied the area but couldn't discern any footprints. "The rain took any clues left behind. I'll have a closer look after I see the victim."

A constable guarded the top step. As the young man, who looked to be all of twenty years, opened his mouth to give his report, Henry held up a hand. "Not until I've seen the body."

"Yes, sir."

Henry almost smiled at the careful way the man kept his back to the scene.

"The tide won't be low for much longer," Fletcher reminded him. "We'll have to make quick work of our investigation." As a former sailor for Her Majesty's Royal Navy, he was an expert in such things.

Henry slowed his pace as they descended the stairs. A few smears of blood remained on the stone steps, though they'd been mostly washed away as well.

He lifted his gaze to survey the area. The Tower loomed nearby. The fog had receded for the most part, a few tendrils still reaching toward the shore from the Thames as if clinging on for dear life. Clouds hung over the city and showed no signs of parting for the morning sun.

The faint scent of the sea caught his notice, a welcome relief from the ever-present stench of soot. As he reached the narrow shore where the water lapped gently, the *Belle of the Thames*, a steamship that ran between London and Ipswich, passed by.

How interesting that the victim had been dumped into the river so near to where he'd been murdered. Apparently whoever had killed him hadn't made much of an attempt to ensure the body didn't surface. That might be a clue in itself. Henry hated to think of those the river never relinquished and therefore never received justice.

"Here we are," Fletcher said after they reached the gravelly shore.

The victim lay face up, eyes closed, skin pale, mouth agape. His long brown overcoat had been cut in numerous places, the edges of it open to reveal an equally cut simple white shirt. Only when Henry neared did he see the man's throat had been slashed nearly ear to ear, a grisly smile of death.

"Recently killed, from the look of him," Henry murmured. He squatted for a closer inspection. "Perhaps late forties to early fifties in age." Lines marked the skin near the eyes and on his forehead. His brown hair was clipped short, his face cleanshaven other than long sideburns. "A military man?"

"That crossed my mind as well." Fletcher nodded, his gaze holding on the body, eyes narrowing. "So many cuts. To what purpose?"

"Depends on whether they were done before or after the slicing of his throat." The gaping wounds were made grislier by the lack of blood. Seeing the pink flesh beneath the skin was almost worse when the slices were deep enough to reveal the organs. One in his middle revealed a good portion of his intestines.

"Hmm." The sergeant frowned as if he were considering the possibilities.

Henry studied the slices, seeing a macabre pattern to them as if they'd been done with glee. He lifted the dead man's hand. A torn nail and a long cut on his palm ran from the base of the man's index finger to the opposite side of the bottom of his palm. "Looks like he may have tried to protect himself." He lifted his own hand, palm out, trying to imagine the scene.

"He faced his killer and defended himself."

"Yes. He must've landed a blow or two, based on the look of his knuckles." Henry shifted the body onto its side with Fletcher's help. "No cuts in the back of the coat other than what came through from the front."

"Makes you wonder what sort of knife the murderer used."

"A long blade. Must have been incredibly sharp."

Henry let the body return to its place and lifted what remained of the shirt to better view the chest. The cuts were indeed numerous, the depth of them suggesting the intent was to kill. Blood stained much of the fabric. Or rather, it had until the river washed it out, leaving pale red circles around the slits.

"He must've bled significantly given the number of wounds before he was tossed into the river." While he didn't always share his observations aloud, Henry liked to with Fletcher. The man's logic was helpful and doing so made certain they were both working with the same clues.

Fletcher moved to the man's feet. "Scuff marks on the heels of the shoes, as would be expected since he was dragged down the stairs to the water."

Henry scanned the decreasing shoreline, walking several paces up and down the area as he took inventory of the scene. A lantern sat high on the bank, but no footprints were visible in the gravel.

"A lad found him, you said?" Henry asked as he knelt near the victim again to study the ground, seeing nothing of interest.

"A street urchin told the constable where the body was." Fletcher grimaced. "The boy came down to the river to wash up and got more than he bargained for."

"A bad way to start his morning."

"We had best move him soon," Fletcher warned as he eyed the rising water.

"Yes," Henry agreed, then shifted to take hold of the man's shoulders and waited for Fletcher to lift the victim's feet.

Grunting with their load, they made their way up the stairs with their unwieldy burden, but it wasn't until they'd nearly reached the top when the constable hurried toward them.

"Need assistance?" Stephens asked. The fact that he remained a good foot from the body suggested he wasn't eager to help.

"Take a foot, will you," Fletcher ordered, amusement glinting in his eyes as his gaze caught Henry's.

"Um. Yes. All right." The constable reached out only to draw back his hands, before at last gingerly grasping the foot.

"Take hold of him and lift," Fletcher demanded.

Henry nearly shook his head at Fletcher's insistence, but such things were a rite of passage for newer officers. He'd experienced it himself. Stephens needed to become accustomed to tasks like this one if he wanted to remain in his position.

Stephens adjusted his grip and took some of the weight from Fletcher, all while carefully avoiding looking at the body.

After a few more steps, Henry decided the pavement was as good a place as any to set the body for now. The area was deserted at this hour and the trio lowered him to the ground. Henry resumed his examination, counting up to eleven entry wounds before deciding to allow the surgeon to find them all. Doing so would be easier once the clothing had been removed.

The coat the man wore was of common fabric and little could be discerned from it. The clothes beneath might have been thrown on hastily as the shirt was partially untucked but that could have happened during the struggle.

He raised the shirt again, noting the pattern and the diagonal direction of the slashes. Top right shoulder to lower left abdomen. Top left to lower right. The surgeon should be able to determine which blow had come first—and which had been fatal.

"A street urchin found the body?" He glanced at Stephens before returning to his inspection.

"Yes, sir." Stephens quartered away from the victim, swallowing hard. "He said he went down to the river to wash at dawn and saw the body partially on the shore. I pulled it the rest of the way out."

"Whoever dumped the body didn't get it into the water very deeply, or it would've been pulled downstream. And it doesn't appear they used any weights to keep him from being found," Fletcher said.

Henry nodded. Often something heavy was lashed to a victim to be certain they didn't surface. What that said about the killer—careless or confident—remained to be seen. "The boy didn't see anything else?"

"No, sir. I can find him again if needed. I see him regular like on my beat."

Henry patted the clothing and discovered a set of keys in an inner pocket of the coat. "We'll need to see what these belong to." The skeleton keys looked old, based on the size and shape. He tossed them to Fletcher. "They must be of importance considering where he kept them."

Moving his attention to the large outer pocket, he peered into it but couldn't tell if it contained anything. He eased his hand inside and found a piece of paper. Carefully, hoping the wet paper didn't tear, he drew it out and unfolded it.

"A news sheet of some sort?" Fletcher asked.

"*Justice*. Can't say I've heard of that one." Henry skimmed the few words of a headline still legible. "A political group, I would guess."

"Perhaps we'll be able to read more once it dries." Fletcher took the paper gingerly when Henry handed it to him.

Henry finished searching the pocket but found nothing more so stood and walked around the body to check the other one. Again, looking into the dark pocket didn't offer any clues, so he reached in, pausing when his fingers touched something damp and lumpy. He knew he wasn't going to like whatever it was but pulled it out anyway.

"What *is* that?" Stephens asked, his voice raspy with revulsion.

"Meat?" Fletcher asked.

"F-From the body? Oh, God." The horror in Stephens' tone mirrored Henry's thoughts. Clearly overwhelmed by the idea, the constable managed two steps before bending over to empty his stomach.

The sound of retching was never pleasant, often tempting Henry to follow suit. But he wasn't an inexperienced constable and forced back the urge, doing his best to remain objective and stay focused on the details. The chunks of raw meat were small, about the size of a shilling, uniformly cut.

He lifted the shirt for a closer study but saw no wounds that matched the small pink chunks in his hand and drew a shallow breath of relief. "I don't think so." He returned his attention to the pocket, steeling himself to reach in and take out what remained. Soon he held a handful of the pieces.

"Can't imagine why someone would be carrying around those." Fletcher's narrowed eyes made it clear he was nearly as disturbed as Stephens by the sight.

"Perhaps he worked with animals or the like," Henry suggested. The meat bothered him less now that it didn't seem to have come from the body.

Fletcher, ever efficient, offered a clean handkerchief and Henry dumped the meat into it then stowed it in his own pocket, hoping he wouldn't have to leave it there overly long.

The nearby Tower caught Henry's notice again. It wouldn't open to the public for several hours, and the gates were closed, but surely they could catch someone's notice. "Stephens, why don't you see if anyone at the Tower can identify the man?"

"Of course, sir." Stephens hurried away, clearly grateful not to have been ribbed for being sick and to have something useful to do—thankfully far from the body.

"Any initial thoughts?" Fletcher asked.

"Whoever killed him was either angry or takes great pleasure using a knife. It doesn't seem like a simple robbery. That's for certain." Henry didn't say anything more, not wanting to make assumptions. That was how mistakes were made. He intended to take his time with this case and follow procedure, being as thorough as possible. He would not fail again.

Stephens returned shortly, bringing along a Yeoman Warder recognizable by his distinctive dark blue uniform with red trim and matching hat. The worry on the man's face suggested he might, indeed, be able to identify their victim.

"Oh, no." The man shook his head as he slowed his steps, gaze riveted on the body. A mix of shock and sorrow lined his face. "No."

"You knew him?" Henry asked, pleased to have an answer so quickly even as he was sorry for the man's loss. He'd witnessed plenty of grief, and everyone reacted differently.

For some, it descended slowly, like a cold rain on a spring day. For others, it took them under like a torrent, threatening to drown them. The weight of it could buckle even the strongest.

"Aberforth Pritchard. The ravenkeeper." The Yeoman pulled his Tudor bonnet off in a show of respect, revealing neatly combed wavy gray hair.

"Ravenkeeper?" Fletcher asked as Henry stood.

"A Yeoman Warder charged with tending the ravens at the Tower," the man supplied, his focus never shifting from the dead man. "He had help of course, but he is—was—the one responsible for them."

Henry knew of the ravens kept at the Tower but hadn't given much thought to who might care for them. That explained the meat, although it still seemed odd that he'd kept it in his coat pocket.

"May you never die a Yeoman Warder," the man muttered.

"I'm sorry?" Henry had heard him but wasn't sure of his meaning.

The man shook his head as if too grief-stricken to explain. "What happened?" he asked only to gasp when he took a step closer and caught sight of the slit in Pritchard's throat. It was impossible to miss. "Dear God in heaven." He grasped his own throat as if in defense.

"He was murdered." Henry stated the obvious. "Can you think of any reason why or who might have done it?"

The man blinked several times then turned his attention to the horizon and back again in disbelief. "No. H—He was a quiet man. A widower with a young daughter." He pressed a hand to his mouth in dismay. "Poor Maeve." He stared at Henry, eyes wide. "We've been searching for her and Pritchard for nearly half an hour."

"How old is she?"

"Only seven years. We can't find them—her—anywhere. This is terrible. No mother and now no father to watch over her."

It truly was terrible. Had she witnessed the murder and hidden because of what she'd seen? Or had she suffered the same fate as her father?

For now, he'd hold out hope that she would be located and could provide some insight.

"Your name, sir?" Henry asked.

"Christopher Wallace. Chief Yeoman Warder."

Perfect. Henry wouldn't allow his hopes to rise, but already the case was going well. "I'll need to ask you a few questions."

"Of course. Anything to help."

Henry moved closer to Wallace, which forced the Chief Yeoman to look away from the body. He wanted the man to focus on the questions rather than the sight of his friend.

After pulling out a notebook and pencil stub, Henry jotted down the man's name and title. "Where did Pritchard live?"

"In the Tower. We have homes in the casements along the outer walls, of course."

"When did you last see him?"

"Last night. At the pub on the Tower grounds. We gather there most evenings after work for a pint or two."

"Any idea why he would've left the Tower last night?"

Wallace frowned and shook his head. "It would've taken something urgent to make him leave Maeve. Perhaps it had something to do with the ravens. One escapes on occasion. He was devoted to them."

"And are any ravens missing?"

"I don't know. We'll have to check."

"Please do. And the sooner we find the daughter, the better." A sense of urgency filled Henry. She could be the key to solving the murder, but only if they found her.

Four

"Don't look them in the eye. They don't like strangers, y'know."

Henry jerked his gaze from the raven perched on the nearby fence to nod at Frank Daniels, a Yeoman Warder who occasionally helped Pritchard with the birds at the Tower, as they stood on the South Lawn where the ravens hopped about.

Chief Warder Wallace had departed to share the unfortunate news of Pritchard's death with the Lieutenant of the Tower, who would then advise the Constable of the Tower. Henry supposed he would have to visit one or both at some point. Wallace then intended to continue the search for Pritchard's daughter, leaving Henry to question the warders he came across. Daniels was the most recent one.

Pritchard's body had been taken by dogcart to St. Thomas' for the postmortem. Henry intended to learn as much as he could while he waited for the examination to be completed.

Daniels, a beefy man slightly taller than Henry's six-foot frame with a chest the size of an oak barrel, hadn't taken the news of Pritchard's death well. Whether that was because it meant more work for him or because he'd miss the ravenkeeper remained unclear.

The man kept shaking his head. "No wonder the birds were so upset this morning."

"How can you tell?"

He glanced at the ravens. "They're restless. They normally strut when they walk. Instead, they're bobbing and fluttering about. Definitely not themselves."

Henry risked another look. He didn't understand his growing fascination with the ravens. It wasn't as if he hadn't seen them before. Anyone who lived in London encountered the large birds. At least from a distance. Perhaps seeing them up close and thinking of Pritchard caring for them made a difference.

"We tend to think the Tower ravens are especially intelligent," Daniels said as he glanced at one with almost a fond look. "They were abundant in the city until 1800. But people considered them pests and spreaders of disease, so they were heavily hunted throughout England. They have slowly returned to London as the public became less hostile. Now they are one of the main attractions at the Tower."

"They are stockier than I realized." Perhaps the shagginess around their throat, which resembled fur, added to their bulky appearance.

"They are big birds. Their wingspan can reach four feet."

"Are any of them missing?"

"One. Bartram," Daniels said even as he glanced around in search of him. "This is Ava, his mate. They mate for life."

"If Pritchard knew the raven was missing, would he have gone in search of him?"

"More than likely. They rarely escape, but it's concerning when they do. Especially at night. More predators out then."

"How long had Pritchard been tending the ravens?" Henry asked.

Just then, sunlight pierced the cloud cover, and the rays struck the bird's black feathers, turning them iridescent—green, blue, and purple—making it difficult not to stare in fascination.

"Five years. He knew them well. They'll miss him."

"Why do they stay?"

"Their wings are clipped." Daniel fingered a place on his chin, rubbing a spot that appeared to be bruised. "We keep six here at all times. For the legend."

"Oh, yes. Else the kingdom will fall or something of the sort." Henry had heard it before but not paid much attention.

"People are superstitious, especially royals. If something happened to the ravens at the Tower, many would consider it a bad omen for all of England."

Henry wondered if Pritchard had believed that. "Did Pritchard mention any problems to you? Anything that was concerning him?"

Daniels considered the question for a long moment as if searching his memory. "Not in particular. Then again, he was always grumbling about something. He wasn't fond of the public visiting the Tower and messing with his charges."

Henry patted his pocket to make certain he reached into the correct one and pulled out the damp red handkerchief. "Did he normally carry bits of meat?"

Daniels frowned as he stared at the bundle that Henry opened to show him. "No. More often than not, we give them rabbits with the fur still on and rats, of course. We try to keep their food life-like, when we can. Then there are pig hearts, fish, liver, and the like. We don't chop the food as small as what you have."

Disappointed not to have an explanation for the damp bundle that was becoming more unpleasant by the minute, Henry rewrapped it and returned it to his pocket, still convinced the meat had to be important.

"Looks like you have a bruise." Henry tapped his own chin to indicate his meaning, remembering Pritchard's grazed knuckles. "What happened?"

Daniels shook his head. "One drink too many the other night led to a heated argument with a friend and a couple of punches. Nothing serious."

Henry nodded, allowing the explanation to stand for now. He cast a glance around the Tower grounds again, still hoping to catch sight of Pritchard's daughter, not that he would recognize her. He'd leave the task to Wallace for now, since he knew the grounds and the girl.

Meanwhile, Henry was speaking with as many people as he could. Fletcher was doing the same. There was always a chance the suspect lived at the Tower, or someone had seen something. He'd looked through Pritchard's small home but hadn't examined it thoroughly yet. At a glance, all appeared to be in place there.

Henry thanked Daniels for his time as the large man introduced him to another Yeoman Warder. He jotted down a few notes as he spoke with the man and the next one after that. Unfortunately, the conversations were similar to the ones he'd already had.

No, they didn't know who would have wanted Pritchard dead. The man was quiet and kept to himself.

No, they hadn't seen anything and had been at home in their beds last night.

No, they didn't know where his daughter could be.

However, one only need to look around to see how many places the Tower had for a little girl familiar with the grounds to hide.

Next Henry was introduced to Michael Blackwell, who oversaw the Armoury within the Tower walls. The well-dressed gentleman had a beard and dark hair dusted with gray at the temples and spoke in cultured tones. He expressed a rather detached response to the ravenkeeper's death. Henry asked him the same questions and noted his responses.

From there, Henry returned to other warders. The next one, Peterson, resented Henry's questions. Apparently, the man was irritated that the murder of one of their own was being investigated by an "outsider." Henry ignored his attitude. The Constable of the Tower was usually a senior military officer but not experienced in criminal investigation. Several decades previously, the Duke of Wellington had held the position.

After suggesting Peterson take his concerns to the chief warder for consideration, he continued with his questioning of the next warder.

While the man answered the same questions, Henry kept an eye on his surroundings. The grounds bustled with activity, mainly because of the search for the missing girl. Warders and their family members helped look for her.

The longer she was missing, the more Henry worried that she'd been killed along with her father. Perhaps they just hadn't found her body yet. He would send Constable Stephens down to where they'd found Pritchard to see if the girl's body had washed up as well.

A stranger approached in a modest brown suit coat, clearly puzzled as he glanced about with a frown. "What has everyone so busy this morning?" the man asked the warder even as he looked at Henry, who raised an eyebrow.

The Tower didn't open to visitors until ten, suggesting the man had business on the grounds.

"Terrible news, Mr. Elliott. A warder was killed last night. Murdered," the warder added as if to emphasize the point before looking askance at Henry as if wondering too late whether he should've told him the news.

No purpose would be served in keeping it quiet. However, Henry hadn't shared any details of how Pritchard had been murdered and had advised Wallace to avoid doing so as well.

At this point in the investigation, everyone was a suspect. The death of a yeoman warder was concerning and warranted a thorough investigation. Anyone who knew the details of the man's death would be thoroughly scrutinized.

"Inspector Field, this is Mr. Thomas Elliott, a manager at the Mint," the warder said.

Henry frowned. "I thought the Mint had been moved to the new building on Tower Hill."

"We still keep some operations here," Mr. Elliott advised. "In truth, I spend more time going back and forth between the locations than I'd like." He glanced between Henry and the warder. "Who was killed?"

"Pritchard. The ravenkeeper."

Henry watched closely as Mr. Elliott took in the news much like he had each time the information was shared. Though he didn't expect to see a telling reaction, one never knew.

"I'm sorry to hear that." The newcomer shook his head. His crisp tones suggested he was well educated. He appeared to be taken aback but didn't reveal any deep sympathy for the victim. "Do you know what happened?"

"We're working on that," Henry advised before jotting down Mr. Elliott's information and repeating his questions then thanking him for his time. "If you happen to have seen anything unusual over the past few days, I'd appreciate you letting me know."

"Of course." He dipped his head and strode across the grounds.

Henry looked back at the warder. "Be sure to send word if you think of anything else that could prove helpful."

With that, Henry walked toward the West Gate in search of Stephens—only to halt in surprise.

Amelia Greystone stood at the Tower gate, speaking with one of the guards, her hand holding a young girl's. Sergeant Fletcher hurried forward to greet her.

A mix of emotions rolled through Henry at the sight of the widow. Could it have been a whole year? A twelvemonth since he'd called on her to tell her of her husband's death. The fact that he had yet to solve Matthew Greystone's murder weighed heavily.

Despite his lack of progress, he visited Mrs. Greystone each month to inquire as to her wellbeing and provided an update on the case, not that there had been any developments for months. He had the faint hope she would come across something of her husband's that might provide a clue as to why the owner of an import-export shop had been shot dead.

His brief visits were painfully awkward, given the fact he had nothing to offer in the form of closure on her husband's murder. The failure was one he detested and was determined to right, yet each week that passed made that feel more impossible.

Learning she had also lost a daughter a few years prior made him question whether she knew who she was anymore without the black cloud of death hanging over her.

What had she had been like before grief had dimmed her light?

What bothered him further was that under different circumstances, he would have found the lady...appealing. She was intelligent and attractive with wide brown eyes and long, thick hair of a similar shade. However, the fact that he hadn't found her husband's killer in the last year was a crevasse across which he could never leap.

"Inspector Field?" Sergeant Fletcher reached him, surprise in his expression, something that rarely happened after his many years of experience. "You're not going to believe this."

Henry looked back toward Mrs. Greystone who had followed Fletcher, her attention shifting from Henry to the girl still at her side. Only then did he take a closer look at the small figure, noting the fear and upset on her face. "You found the ravenkeeper's daughter."

Fletcher smiled. "Mrs. Greystone did."

"Inspector Field." Mrs. Greystone glanced down at the child, the narrow brim of her black hat momentarily shielding her face from view before she looked back at him. "The guard suggested I speak with you."

"Good day, Mrs. Greystone." He nodded in greeting, his relief that the girl was alive and well immense. Surely, this was the break in the case he'd been hoping for. "This is Maeve Pritchard?"

"Yes." Mrs. Greystone's worried gaze held Henry's. "H-Has something happened to her father? You must tell me."

Henry glanced at the girl, not wanting to break the news too abruptly. She had precisely the same brown hair and slender frame as her father.

He was somewhat surprised Mrs. Greystone wasn't more concerned about the child's reaction, especially when the girl was already upset based on her pale, somber face.

"I'm afraid so," he began.

The girl turned toward Mrs. Greystone to bury her face in her skirts.

"I have...ah. Terrible news," Henry began slowly, his stomach tightening with unease as he watched the girl. How he detested this part of the job. But from the child's demeanor, she seemed to suspect something.

"Inspector, she can't hear you," Mrs. Greystone said as she gently drew the girl closer.

Henry pulled his gaze from the girl back to Mrs. Greystone. "Excuse me?"

"Maeve is deaf and mute."

Shock rolled over Henry at the disappointing news. Well, it would have been too good to be true to have a potential witness who could easily identify the killer.

Mrs. Greystone cleared her throat, as if attempting to keep her own emotions under control. "Do you want to take her somewhere private to explain the circumstances?"

Henry was still reeling from the news that the girl was unable to communicate when only a moment ago, he'd been hopeful they were about to solve the case.

"Of course." But he didn't move. "May I ask why she's with you?"

"I interviewed Warder Pritchard last week. For an article. You might remember that I took a position as a special correspondent for *London Life*."

"Oh, yes." She'd mentioned that during one of his recent visits.

"I met Maeve then as well." A flash of pain crossed her features as she looked down at the silent girl's bowed head. "She and her father came to my lab, and we did an experiment or two. Needless to say, I was surprised to find her on my doorstep this morning. I can't imagine how she came to be there."

Nor could Henry. Mrs. Greystone's house was a fair distance from the Tower. The idea of the little girl walking so far by herself was alarming. The widow must have made quite an impression on the girl for her to have remembered where her home was in the dark of night, fear pumping through her veins.

"I have to assume she already knows what happened to her father," Henry said slowly. Why else would she appear so upset?

Mrs. Greystone's gaze lifted to meet his, trepidation darkening her eyes. "Was it an accident?"

"No." He didn't miss the shudder that ran through her.

"I see. How?"

"A stabbing."

She hugged Maeve tighter as her chin trembled with emotion. "How terrible. I hope she didn't see it."

Henry refrained from expressing an opinion. What he thought didn't matter. Only the facts did. He considered the girl, wondering how best to proceed. He didn't have much experience speaking with children, especially not one who was deaf and mute. "Is it possible to communicate with her?"

"She can read lips, for the most part."

"I'm sorry to ask this of you, but she doesn't appear to have any relatives nearby. It's clear that she trusts you. Would you remain with her while I speak with her?"

Henry hated to ask when she'd already been through so much in recent years. If he hadn't been watching, he would've missed the way Mrs. Greystone's lips tightened. He had the distinct impression she wanted to refuse and couldn't blame her for wanting to distance herself from yet another death.

Unfortunately, he needed her assistance. "Please."

Five

Amelia's stomach tightened as she watched Inspector Field kneel before Maeve's chair in the chief warder's sitting room to tell her the terrible news. It was no surprise that the girl's gaze remained firmly fixed on the floor.

Amelia knew how she felt, knew the hope that if the tragic circumstances thrust upon one were ignored, they might go away.

Warder Wallace had offered his home to speak in private with the girl, though Amelia felt certain Maeve already knew what had happened to her father based on her previous upset and the stony façade she now presented.

Maeve had allowed Amelia and Mrs. Fernsby to clean and dress her earlier. Yvette, the maid, had a younger sister near Maeve's age, so had returned home to borrow clothes. Meanwhile, Amelia and the housekeeper had convinced Maeve to eat a bit of food and drink some milk.

But it was as if once the girl's tears stopped, she'd become unresponsive. She allowed them to wash her, change her clothes, and brush her hair but showed no reaction to any of their efforts. It was as if she were a loose-limbed doll. She'd only eaten what they'd fed her themselves, going through the motions of chewing and swallowing.

Since their arrival at the Tower, her reserve and distant expression had only grown. She held tight to Amelia's hand, but otherwise had retreated to where Amelia couldn't follow; a silent place where she blocked out the world and all the pain it brought.

Amelia's heart ached for the girl. Watching her vacant expression was nearly as painful as her throaty sobs earlier. Somehow, she didn't think that what Inspector Field was about to tell the girl would come as a surprise, but neither would it bring her back from where she'd escaped.

The day the inspector had told her of Matthew's death remained starkly clear in Amelia's mind. He'd pulled off his hat, revealing dark hair combed to the side in need of a trim. His brown eyes had filled with sympathy, yet he'd kept the same professional expression he wore now.

How many times had he given bad news to loved ones? What a terrible task that would be. One she did not envy.

"Maeve?" Inspector Field's tone was gentle, but Amelia frowned. Had he forgotten she couldn't hear?

Before she could remind him, he touched the girl's shoulder, clearly struggling to find a way to communicate his message.

Rather than step in to aid him, Amelia held back, her heart still tender and bruised from her own losses. Witnessing Maeve's grief had made it raw again, nearly more than she could bear. The girl's grief threatened the dam she'd built around her emotions to at least pretend she could go on with life.

Though she knew it was selfish, she wanted to return home to her quiet life; block out the morning's events and ignore them as best she could, much as Maeve was doing.

Despite that longing, Amelia remained in place, ready to offer comfort to Maeve if needed.

Inspector Field placed a finger under the girl's chin in an attempt to get her to look at him. Still Maeve's gaze remained fixed on the ground.

He tilted his head and bent lower to try to catch the girl's gaze as he took her hand in his.

Amelia's breath caught when Maeve's small fingers clutched the inspector's. The tell-tale movement sent a lump to Amelia's throat and suggested Maeve was more aware of her surroundings and the situation than they realized.

"Maeve, I'm sorry about your father," Inspector Field said, though the girl still didn't look at him. He tightened his grip on her hand. Her gaze shifted but still didn't meet his. "Maeve?"

After a long moment, Wallace cleared his throat. "Why don't I try? Perhaps speaking with someone she knows will make a difference."

The inspector nodded. After carefully pulling his hand from Maeve's, he stepped aside.

Wallace took his place and squatted beside the girl. He put both hands on the child's shoulders, but she showed no reaction. "Maeve?" He cupped his hand along her cheek. "I'm so sorry about your father. He was a good man."

Did the words bring him comfort as Maeve couldn't hear them? Amelia had found herself doing the same thing earlier, offering re-assurances the child couldn't hear because it seemed like the proper thing to do.

The rituals of mourning were for the living more than the dead.

Amelia drew a slow, deep breath, uncertain how much more of the painful exchange she could watch without succumbing to tears herself. "Does she have relatives in the area? She might respond to a family member."

Wallace sighed. "Pritchard has a younger sister who lives in Leeds. I will send word and ask her to come."

Maeve certainly needed family at a time like this. Amelia's parents had been a rock in a stormy sea when first Lily then Matthew had died, even if she hadn't always appreciated their well-meaning advice.

How ironic to think she wouldn't be here at this moment if not for their insistence that she find something to do that forced her out into the world where she could interact with others. They'd been pleased when she'd told them of the magazine correspondent position and thrilled when she'd gone to conduct her first interview a few months ago.

If not for their urging, she never would've met the ravenkeeper or his daughter. At the moment, she wasn't certain whether to be grateful about that.

"Does Maeve have a favorite toy or the like that we could get for her?" she asked quietly. "She might appreciate having something familiar to hold on to."

Wallace seemed uncertain as he stood, still watching Maeve. "We could take her into her home to see, I suppose."

"There's a rag doll on her bed," Inspector Field said. "I saw it when I looked around earlier."

Amelia nodded, unsurprised that the inspector had noted the detail. From the little she knew of him, he was quite observant.

Unfortunately, those skills hadn't helped him find whoever had murdered Matthew.

She quickly halted her thoughts before they took her down a rabbit hole from which it always proved difficult to emerge.

Pondering who had killed Matthew and why left her uneasy, because it led her to further questions—about their marriage, and whether she had truly known her husband.

Before Amelia could regain her emotional balance Maeve stood, walked to her, and took her hand in hers. Touched, Amelia glanced down at her, but the girl kept her gaze downward, her face a blank mask.

Wallace and Inspector Field both looked at Amelia in surprise, but she shook her head to indicate she didn't know what Maeve might be thinking. She still couldn't believe the seven-year-old had walked all the way to her house in the dark of night alone, barefoot, and terrified.

"I have the key," Wallace said as he led the way out. "Pritchard's home is a short distance away along the outer wall."

When they reached the door, Maeve drew to a halt several feet away from it, her hand trembling in Amelia's, her lower lip quivering with emotion.

Clearly, she wasn't certain whether she wanted to go inside.

Amelia bent down but Maeve's focus remained on the door that Wallace unlocked. Wishing she could do more to offer support, she placed a hand on the girl's shoulder to lend her strength.

Maeve eased forward with Amelia at her side and walked through the open door into the cozy interior. The girl's gaze darted around the rooms, her expression pinched with hope. It quickly faded when no one stepped forward. Tears filled her eyes and coursed down her cheeks as her shoulders shook once again with silent sobs.

Amelia held her tight and smoothed her hair as she swallowed back her own tears. The quicker they found what they came for and left, the better.

Maeve's home had brought no relief to the girl, only confirmation of the loss of her father. Perhaps a part of her hoped that what she'd seen had only been a terrible nightmare.

Amelia glanced at Inspector Field for direction, relieved when he led the way up the stairs and gestured toward the first open doorway, seeming to agree that the sooner the task was over the better.

Still holding Maeve's hand, she escorted the girl into her room, noting the unmade bed with its faded quilt, a cloth doll tossed to one side.

The image of the girl crawling from the warm bed to look for her father took hold of Amelia's thoughts. What had woken her?

Had she followed him or guessed where he had gone?

What had she seen that frightened her so?

And how could they possibly convince her to tell them?

Amelia gave herself a mental shake. This wasn't her concern. It was Inspector Field's. She glanced at him to see the detective watching the girl closely. No doubt the same questions were running through his mind.

Good. That meant he didn't need her.

Amelia reached for the doll and handed it to Maeve, pleased when the girl took it, closing her eyes and burying her face in the doll, seeming to breathe in its familiar scent.

Amelia had read once that those who lost one sense developed more heightened ones in other areas and wondered if that were true with Maeve. Could she see or smell better than other children her age? Or was it something less tangible, such as sensing the emotions of those around her?

Amelia bent to press a kiss on the girl's head, hoping the doll brought her some respite. A glance around the room showed a few dresses hanging on pegs along the wall and a scuffed pair of shoes neatly tucked below them. A small cloak and bonnet were there as well. Perhaps Maeve would be more comfortable in her own clothes than the borrowed ones she wore.

"What happens to her now?" Amelia turned to look between Inspector Field and Warder Wallace, who stood nearby. "Where will she stay?"

"I suppose she could stay with us," Wallace said with a frown. "She knows my daughter, Betsy." He held out his hand to Maeve.

Maeve eyed it over the top of her doll and after a moment's consideration, backed away and stepped even closer to Amelia.

Amelia's heart lurched, a part of her honored to think the girl preferred her. Another part had no wish to be involved in the situation any further. Not when she was only beginning to find her way after her grief.

"Mrs. Greystone." Inspector Field's deep voice had her meeting his gaze, reluctance in his expression. "Would it be possible for Maeve to stay with you? Just until her aunt arrives. She seems most comfortable with you."

Amelia looked down at the top of the little girl's head, her braid still neat and tidy from Amelia's fingers. How could she refuse?

Six

Henry arrived later that afternoon at the Metropolitan Police Force headquartered just off Great Scotland Yard. He nodded at a few fellow detectives as he entered the back hall amidst the uniformed constables who hurried past.

"Good afternoon, Field." Sergeant Johnson, who manned the desk in the small receiving area, glanced up from reviewing the thick stack of papers on his desk.

"Johnson. Is Reynolds in?"

"I believe he is. Haven't seen him leave, anyway."

Henry nodded then continued down the short hallway that led to the main office. Desks were lined up in rows, some bare, others stacked with papers in various stages of disarray. He always took it as a good sign that his was neither the worst nor the tidiest. His last name already made him stand out, and he preferred none of his colleagues found further cause to notice him.

He'd left Fletcher at the Tower to keep an eye on things and continue speaking with the warders and their families. There was always a chance that someone would remember a detail they hadn't shared when questioned the first time. If so, Fletcher would be there to hear it if they did.

Henry paused at his desk and saw another case had been assigned to him—a jewelry theft—and was relieved it wasn't anything more serious. That allowed him to focus on Pritchard's murder. With luck, they'd be able to convince the ravenkeeper's daughter to share what she knew and quickly solve the case.

The girl had to have seen something based on her distress when Mrs. Greystone found her on her doorstep.

The widow's reluctance to keep Maeve hadn't been a surprise. After all, she'd already been through so much. She hardly knew the girl and had no reason to become involved. That made him appreciate her agreement even more.

Henry hadn't considered how difficult it was to communicate with a little girl who not only couldn't hear but didn't want to. He didn't blame her. Why would she want to speak with a stranger who would only confirm that her father was never coming home?

He knocked on the open office door of the Director of Criminal Investigation, John Reynolds.

Reynolds looked up from a report. "Field. Any news for me?"

The Director had a round face with gold-rimmed spectacles that were eternally smudged. Though well into his fifties, his dark hair held no hint of gray and was neatly parted in the middle. Muttonchops covered his jaw and led to his thick moustache but left his chin bare. His no-nonsense manner suited Henry well. Reynolds' door was always open. He didn't hesitate to say what was on his mind but only after hearing what his men said first.

Henry took the chair Reynolds gestured toward, then gave a concise summary of the progress of the murder investigation.

"Mrs. Greystone?" Reynolds' eyes narrowed as if trying to place the name after Henry told him that she had brought the missing ravenkeeper's daughter to the Tower.

Henry cleared his throat, aware of how much of a coincidence the situation was. "The widow of Mr. Matthew Greystone, an unsolved murder case."

Reynolds blinked behind his smudged lenses as he processed the news.

"Mrs. Greystone serves as a correspondent for a magazine and recently interviewed the ravenkeeper in question," Henry added. "She met his daughter in the process."

"Is there a chance her article somehow plays into the murder of the Beefeater?" Reynold asked.

"Unlikely, but I've requested a copy of it to review."

"How did the daughter manage to get to Mrs. Greystone's residence?"

"I can only surmise that she must've awoken and followed her father out of the Tower. The Middle Tower gate was found unlocked this morning. It appears that he left the grounds in search of a raven that escaped and is still missing. Mrs. Greystone found the girl on her doorstep barefoot and clad in only her nightgown this morning."

"What does the girl say happened?"

"And therein lies the problem. She's deaf and mute."

Reynolds sat back in his chair with a scowl, clearly displeased by the news.

"She must've seen something, based on her fright," Henry continued. "But finding a method to communicate with her is a...challenge."

"Poor dear. How terrible if she truly witnessed the murder; she must've been terrified." Reynolds shook his head. "I can't imagine my own daughter experiencing something of the sort."

"Her shock is understandable but makes it even more difficult to communicate with her. She stares into the distance and won't make eye contact. Since she doesn't know how to read and write and can't speak, I'm not certain what steps to take next. She reads lips so I'm hoping she'll be of more help once her shock eases."

"You're sure she's comfortable with Mrs. Greystone? You know how important it is that she feels safe if we want to learn more."

Henry nodded, thinking of how tightly Maeve had held onto Mrs. Greystone's hand. "It was the girl's choice. I will call on them in the morning to see how they're progressing."

"Any word from the surgeon?" Reynolds asked.

"I'm headed there now." Henry stood.

"Excellent. Keep me apprised."

"Yes, sir." Henry turned to go.

"And Field?" He turned back. "We need to solve this quickly. Once reporters get wind of it, especially if the news gets out about the girl, the public will be clamoring for an arrest. Make no mistakes on this one. Follow procedure carefully."

"Of course, sir." Henry clenched his jaw as he took his leave. It wasn't as if he'd failed to follow procedure or made critical mistakes on the last case. He just hadn't solved it.

But Reynolds was right. He needed to handle this case with care for the sake of his career, for Aberforth Pritchard, and for Maeve. He intended to make certain whoever had killed the man was found and prosecuted. The ravenkeeper and his daughter deserved justice.

So did Matthew Greystone.

If only Henry knew how to provide it for him. Perhaps spending a little more time with his widow while he worked to communicate with Maeve would bring to light a new clue in her husband's murder.

His arrival at Mr. Taylor's examination room at St. Thomas', which wasn't far from the Yard, proved fortuitous as the surgeon was just completing his exam of the ravenkeeper.

"Field." Mr. Taylor looked up from the body on the table before him, scalpel still in hand, before returning to his work. "I thought you might arrive soon."

A nasty odor of chemicals and death struck Henry the moment he entered the room and quickly reminded him to breathe through his mouth. How those who worked here endured it, he didn't know. "Do you already have results?"

Often the postmortem report was delayed because numerous cases awaited Mr. Taylor's attention. Of course, potential murder victims received preferential treatment. That was one question that had already been answered in this case. The fact he was a yeoman warder in a royal residence further elevated the importance of the examination.

"Nearly done."

Mr. Arthur Taylor was in his late forties with an average build and dark blond wavy hair clipped short in the back with a lock or two tumbling onto his forehead. He spoke fondly of his wife, but she must only see him on rare occasions as he was always working.

A young man, undoubtedly a medical student, stood at the doctor's side holding a board clip on which he took notes as the surgeon stated his findings.

"Interesting case," Mr. Taylor said as Henry joined him near the body. "There are nineteen wounds, not including the one on the throat or those on the hands. Some were delivered after the victim fell to his knees."

That detail brought a wave of sympathy through Henry. Seeing the body unclothed made it even more clear how terrible the man's death had been.

"He has some interesting scars." Mr. Taylor lifted a brow. "Do you know what he did for a living?"

"He was a ravenkeeper at the Tower of London, and a soldier before that."

"Ah. A Beefeater. Contact with the ravens explains some of his scars. They have a powerful bite from what I understand."

Henry waited with as much patience as he could muster. Mr. Taylor didn't like to be rushed, nor did he like to be questioned. He preferred to share his findings in his own time and in the order he felt important.

The expression of the young man at his side held a combination of fascination and dread, pencil poised to jot down more observations.

"The time of death is difficult to pinpoint due to the time the body spent in the water, but I'd guess between midnight and two o'clock. Whoever caused the damage did so with abandon." Mr. Taylor stepped back, his gaze sweeping the entire body. "I would say that the jabs to his ribs came first then at that point, he must have raised his arm in an effort to protect himself which explains these slashes." He lifted the arm and held it across the chest in a position not so different than Henry had demonstrated to Fletcher earlier.

"This is the longest slash and runs from his raised arm to the opposite hip. It is not deep and didn't do much damage."

"No doubt it still hurt," Henry murmured as he stared at the long slice on the pale flesh, all too easily picturing the scene.

"True. The pain and shock alone would have done damage."

The assistant gave a slight shudder. Henry didn't blame him. Imagining how it felt was enough to make him shudder as well.

"This entry wound pierced a lung." The surgeon pointed to a narrow slit that didn't look nearly as harmful as the long, diagonal one. "Losing the ability to breathe would cause panic. The victim did his best to fight but those efforts would have been short lived."

"He was a soldier, so it makes sense that he would not only defend himself but fight back," Henry said.

"I'm certain you saw the scuff on his knuckles and damage to his nails. He definitely put up a fight." He leaned close to look at Pritchard's hand.

For a moment, Henry imagined the dead man's hand smoothing his daughter's hair. Holding her close when she'd had a bad dream. Comforting her if she scraped her knee.

Now who would love the girl?

He gave himself a mental shake. Such thoughts would help neither Pritchard nor Maeve. He needed to keep his focus on evidence, not emotions. That meant he had to stay detached and unemotional. To use logic and reason to his advantage.

"Any opinion on why the killer sliced him so many times?" Henry had a few ideas but always liked to hear Mr. Taylor's perspective.

"The blade had to be at least five or six inches in length. Fairly narrow and sharp. The killer moved from upper right to lower left. The attack would have been done quickly in a series of fast strokes except for the first two or three. I have to think that whoever did this did so with pleasure. He is skilled with a knife and enjoys it. If he had killed merely in anger, there would have been fewer wounds, but deeper ones."

Henry nodded. He'd thought the same.

"The killer is most likely shorter than the victim." Mr. Taylor turned to look at Henry. "Slightly shorter than your height, I would guess. It would take strength and quickness, suggesting someone who is strong. Perhaps of our age range, perhaps younger."

An image of the killer began to form in Henry's mind, as it did in most cases, but he'd learned not to allow the image to become too detailed for fear of overlooking a criminal who stood beneath his nose. He didn't want to twist the evidence to match who he thought should be guilty, something a few of his associates tended to do.

Finding someone to arrest regardless of guilt was hardly justice.

"I'll keep you apprised of any additional findings once I finalize my report." Mr. Taylor met Henry's gaze. "I believe you should proceed carefully with this case. The killer appears to have an impressive skill with a knife which could prove deadly to more than Pritchard, based on how much he apparently enjoys using it."

"I will certainly keep that in mind." First Reynolds, now Taylor. He didn't need to hear their warnings when he'd already intended to take care—but neither would he allow caution to guide his actions when he had a case to solve.

Seven

Fernsby stared in surprise at the little girl who held Amelia's hand when he opened the front door. "Good afternoon, Mrs. Greystone, Miss Maeve." He offered a stately bow, though his brow remained puckered with confusion.

"Good afternoon, Fernsby. We need to prepare a room for Maeve. She will be staying with us for a day or two." Amelia handed him the small bag that held the girl's clothes and a few personal items they'd collected from her home.

Amelia hesitated to explain the reason for their unexpected guest—there was no use in upsetting her—only to remember that she couldn't hear. It would take time to become accustomed to her deafness. "Her father has been killed. Murdered." She said the last word quietly, noting the alarm in Fernsby's expression.

To think that murder had touched her household not once but twice was upsetting to say the least.

A glance at Maeve showed the girl continuing to hold tight to her doll, her expression vacant as she stared straight ahead. In truth, Amelia wasn't quite sure what to do with her or how to reach her.

"I'm terribly sorry to hear that." Fernsby's dark eyes held on Amelia as if he wondered how she was taking the news.

In truth, Amelia wasn't taking it well. The heavy weight of loss draped over her like a thick veil, clouding her thoughts and actions.

She didn't need another reminder of the harshness of life. Not when she'd only started to feel herself.

But this situation wasn't about her. *Maeve was the one who mattered*. The thought had Amelia straightening her shoulders.

"Maeve has no other relatives in London, so she'll remain with us until her aunt and uncle arrive from the country," she advised the butler.

Fernsby bent down to Maeve's level and reached out a finger to gently touch the doll.

To Amelia's surprise Maeve looked at the butler, who smiled and nodded to show his approval of the treasured toy. The tension around Maeve's eyes softened and, for a moment, Amelia thought she might smile. Then the moment was gone, and somberness returned.

Still, the interaction, however brief, gave her hope. Maybe they could reach through her shroud of grief.

The butler straightened. "Which room shall I prepare?"

Amelia hesitated. The practical choice would be Lily's, for it held a small bed and was decorated for a young girl. Yet she couldn't bring herself to suggest that. Not when the idea brought a painful ache to her chest.

As if sensing her distress, Fernsby said, "May I suggest she share Yvette's room in the attic? We wouldn't wish her to be alone during this difficult time. As the maid has younger sisters, I'm certain she'd be happy to help watch over the girl."

With a deep breath of relief, Amelia agreed. "Excellent idea. Perhaps you could bring tea to the sitting room while preparations are made?"

"Of course. Nothing like cake and biscuits to provide comfort." His sympathetic gaze fell on Maeve again.

"Thank you, Fernsby. I don't know what I'd do without you." She truly didn't. The servants had been with her through the painful years, always offering a steady hand and words of encouragement.

"My pleasure, Mrs. Greystone."

While the butler saw to her request, Amelia took Maeve's hand and gestured toward the stairs. The small sitting room off her bedroom was cozier than the more formal drawing room. Perhaps Maeve would be more comfortable there.

They walked up the stairs together and entered the room. Amelia was pleased when Maeve looked around, taking in the room with its slate blue walls, paisley drapes, and warm wood tones. It was certainly better than the empty look her face had previously held.

Amelia released the girl's hand, removed her own gloves and cloak, and set them aside. Next she took off Maeve's cloak, running a hand along the girl's hair, hoping her touch brought reassurance.

They'd settled on the settee when Fernsby appeared. "Yvette will be along after you've had tea to show Miss Maeve to her room." He put more coal on the fire and adjusted the damper, the fire welcome both for its heat and cheeriness. "The air is chilly today."

Maeve stared at the coals, and Amelia found herself doing the same thing after Fernsby departed. She took hold of Maeve's hand, noting her cool fingers, and set about warming them as they sat in silence.

The butler soon returned with the tea tray, setting it on the low table before them.

Maeve perked up, her eyes wide at the sight of the plates stacked with individual iced cakes, various sandwiches, and several kinds of biscuits.

"Shall I pour, Mrs. Greystone?" Fernsby asked.

"I will, thank you. Please tell Cook she has outdone herself. I have no doubt our guest will be tempted by the offerings."

"She'll be pleased to hear you think so." Fernsby departed with a smile and a lingering glance at Maeve.

Amelia poured the tea, then used the tiny tongs to lift a sugar cube, certain Maeve would prefer her tea sweetened. She held the cube above the cup and looked at her.

The little girl gave a single, cautious nod, and Amelia dropped in the cube then retrieved another. Again, Maeve nodded. Amelia smiled as she complied. Maeve nodded at the addition of a dollop of cream as well. Amelia handed her the spoon to stir it.

Though they were only communicating about tea, they were still communicating.

The girl set her doll to the side and took the teacup gingerly. She sipped twice before setting it down, her gaze holding on the tiny, iced cakes.

With a smile, Amelia used a slightly larger set of tongs to place two of the petit fours on a plate and then handed it to her. Maeve hadn't eaten much at breakfast and luncheon had come and gone without notice. Seeing her eat anything was welcome.

The two cakes were gone in the blink of an eye. Amelia pointed to the selection of sandwiches only to see Maeve's brow pucker. Amelia held up one finger to convince the girl to try one before she ate more cake.

Though her lips twisted with displeasure, Maeve pointed to one and soon finished it before trying yet another cake and a biscuit in between sips of warming tea.

A knock on the door had Amelia looking up to see Yvette enter the room.

"I'm ever so sorry to hear the terrible news, ma'am." Yvette's brown eyes filled with sympathy as she spoke.

"As was I. I hope we can provide Maeve some comfort until her family arrives."

As if sensing the topic of conversation, Maeve set her plate with its half-eaten biscuit on the table, her appetite apparently departed. She reached for the doll and held it tight.

Yvette bent over and held out a hand to the girl with a smile. "Shall we take a look at where you'll be sleeping?"

Maeve's shoulders hunched as she drew back.

Amelia set her teacup on the table and rose, holding out her hand as well. "Why don't we all go?"

Maeve reluctantly took it and stood, expression wary.

Yvette's room shared the attic with Amelia's lab and had two narrow beds with room for a third. Amelia led the way with Maeve's hand firmly tucked in hers and opened the door, pleased to see the girl's bag already on the end of a bed.

Maeve paused in the doorway to look around the sparsely furnished space before her focus latched onto her bag.

Following her instincts, Amelia brought her closer to it. Maeve released her hand to touch the bag as if needing to reassure herself that it was hers.

Yvette joined them. "Let us get you unpacked."

Amelia eased back while the maid opened the bag, drew out a dress, and laid it on the bed. "This is pretty," she said as she smoothed the small pink flowers embroidered along the neckline.

Maeve's small finger followed the maid's over the colorful thread.

"Pretty," Yvette repeated when Maeve glanced at her.

The girl nodded and Amelia smiled. Surely any interaction the girl responded to was a good thing, whether it was sugar in her tea, petit fours on her plate, or her belongings under her fingertips.

With luck, they'd find a way for Maeve to share what she'd seen when her father had been killed. The sooner whoever had done it was caught, the better.

As the two continued to unpack Maeve's bag, Amelia moved to the attic window to look out where a narrow slice of the street was visible along with part of the garden. The garden had lost the lush green and vibrant colors of summer and now boasted shades of brown and gold, a reminder of autumn. The gray sky promised rain, though it had yet to fall. The street was relatively quiet, only one hansom cab passing by.

Or not passing by. The cab drew to a halt a short distance away, near the street corner. A man in a dark jacket with a bowler hat alighted. After a few words with the driver, the cab pulled away, leaving the man standing on the opposite side of the street, looking about himself. He reached a gloved hand to adjust his hat, his attention seeming to settle on her house.

With slow steps he walked past, his focus remaining on the house until he disappeared from sight.

Unease crept over Amelia as she watched. A few minutes later, the man walked back to the corner and the cab returned to collect him before departing.

She didn't know what to make of the curious sighting, but she did not like it.

Eight

The next morning, Henry returned to the Tower with Fletcher at his side. He shared what Mr. Taylor had told him as they walked toward the gate where a Yeoman Warder stood guard in his customary dark blue uniform with red trim.

"Not much to go on, is it?" Fletcher shook his head.

"Every clue could prove helpful." Henry was determined to stay positive. Thinking otherwise might bring bad luck—though he wasn't overly superstitious, he wasn't willing to take the risk.

"Yes, of course. I suppose I was hoping for a bit more."

The hour was too early for visitors to be allowed entrance, but the guard recognized them from the previous day and opened the gate.

"Mr. Taylor suspects the killer is more than likely a man of some strength and about my height or slightly shorter."

"Now we're getting somewhere," Fletcher said. "Except for the fact that the description matches a good share of the yeoman warders."

"I can't deny that." Henry glanced at the White Tower as they walked, a turreted keep famous for its dungeons. It refused to be ignored, casting a long shadow over the grounds, much like the reputations of Henry's father and grandfather.

Always present and impossible to ignore.

"Perhaps one of the Beefeaters will have remembered something useful," Henry mused. "I have a few more questions for the Chief Yeoman Warder."

"Is there someone in particular with whom you'd like me to speak?"

Before Henry could answer, the croak of a raven caught their attention. The bird leaped from the ground and flapped its wings, managing a short flight to land on the nearby wall. It cocked its head back and forth as if considering their worthiness.

"Do you think that's the one that was missing?" Fletcher asked as he closely watched the bird.

"Don't look it in the eye," Henry advised as he shifted his own gaze to the sergeant, tracking the raven with his peripheral vision.

"What?" Fletcher stared at Henry as if he'd lost his mind.

"Daniels, the other ravenkeeper, told me they don't like direct eye contact."

"Why do we care what they like and don't like?"

"I, for one, don't want a raven displeased with me." Henry risked another look. "That beak could break a finger—or worse. You saw the scars on Pritchard's hands."

"Hmm. Good point." Fletcher frowned as he glanced away from the bobbing creature. "Maybe the raven saw what happened. Too bad it can't tell us."

"They're intelligent, but not that intelligent." Henry continued forward but couldn't bring himself to completely turn his back on the raven. It seemed unwise. "At any rate, we need to confirm the whereabouts of everyone on the grounds during the hours Pritchard may have been killed, starting with the Yeoman Warders. We asked many yesterday, but let's do it again and see if anyone's story changed. I'll find you after I talk to Wallace again."

"Very well." With a dip of his head, Fletcher walked toward three warders who stood watching nearby.

Henry continued to the Gate House where Wallace had his office and knocked.

"Enter."

Henry opened the door, intrigued to see a small octagonal room. A set of old iron keys rested on a wooden peg near the door. A display of ceremonial axes adorned one wall. Another door stood open on the opposite side of the room which led to a spiral staircase. The old walls of the office were steeped in history. One could feel it.

"Good morning, Inspector Field." Wallace wore his uniform, the matching bonnet on his desk. His gaze caught Henry's, clearly hoping he had good news to share.

Henry wished he did.

"I'd like to ask you a few more questions if you don't mind." Henry pulled out his notebook.

"Of course. Anything to help." He set aside the letter he'd been reading with a jerky movement. "I sent a telegram to Pritchard's sister yesterday. She and her husband live farther north than I remembered, so it may take several days before they can make the arrangements to travel to London. How is Maeve?"

Henry would check on her later but assumed she was fine since he hadn't heard otherwise from Mrs. Greystone. "As well as can be expected."

Wallace nodded, rubbing his forehead as if a headache brewed there.

"There's hardly a square inch in here that doesn't reflect history," Henry remarked, hoping to put Wallace at ease. People tended to remember more details when they were relaxed.

"If these walls could talk." Wallace attempted a chuckle at his own jest.

"I'm not sure I would want to hear all the stories they have to tell. After all, the Tower is not a cozy palace but a walled fortress where many dark events have occurred."

"As fascinated as I am by its history, I would have to agree," Wallace said. "Yeoman Warders have been in service at the Tower of London since 1485. Throughout the centuries they were glorified jailors, guarding everyone from spies to political prisoners to royalty, escorting some of them to Tower Green for execution."

"Even the warders themselves have a checkered past, from what I have heard." Henry glanced at Wallace to see if he agreed.

Wallace nodded. "Early warders were often corrupt. They could buy and sell their positions for a significant sum of money, as much as 250 guineas."

Henry whistled in surprise. "That's a sizeable amount."

"The Duke of Wellington ended all that, for which I am grateful. Now one must have twenty-two years in the military, achieve Warrant Officer rank, and leave the military with a good conduct medal before being considered for the position of Yeoman Warder. Those changes discouraged the scoundrels amongst us. The goal used to be to sell one's position before dying as a way to provide for any family left behind. People are all too often greedy. Despite the reforms, we continue to use the toast, 'May you never die a Yeoman Warder.'"

"Unfortunate that Pritchard did," Henry murmured.

"Yes. Fortunately we can offer a bit of a pension to the family if needed. I'll see if Pritchard's sister and her husband require assistance when they take in Maeve."

"Pritchard was not always well thought of." Henry waited to see Wallace's reaction.

"There are a few who didn't care for him. He could be difficult and prickly, at times." Wallace sighed. "I'm sure you've spoken with some already."

"Can you think of anyone in particular who made his dislike of Pritchard clear?"

"Yes, though it saddens me to say it." Wallace rose and reached for his Tudor cap. "Let us find McClintock. He was never fond of Pritchard and made no secret of it."

Reaching for the keys on the peg, he led the way out of his office and locked the door behind them before perusing the grounds.

"Did the missing raven return?" Henry asked.

Wallace nodded. "He came back before dusk last night. I'm sure Pritchard went in search of him. That's the only reason he would leave the Tower grounds in the dark of night."

"Did he often check on the Ravens at such a late hour?"

"No, but if a raven is missing the others will kick up a fuss. Especially its mate. We've tried keeping the birds in an enclosure, but they always manage to escape. They are good with tools and can use a stick or a rock to unlock a gate."

"They want to escape so badly?"

Wallace shook his head and smiled. "Nothing of the sort. They just want to be here on their terms rather than ours. Clever beasts. I wonder if the ravens were happier back when the Tower used to be a zoo and other animals were nearby. Then again, some of the more exotic creatures kept here might have upset them. Anything unusual or out of the ordinary distresses them."

Henry thought again of the bits of meat he'd found in Pritchard's pocket which he'd left in his landlady's cellar for safekeeping, still uncertain if they had any bearing on the case. They seemed an unlikely clue, but he would hold onto them until he knew for certain.

In short order Wallace located McClintock, who appeared to be close to Pritchard in age. It wasn't a face he recognized; evidently Henry had not encountered him the previous day.

Wallace introduced them. "I will leave the two of you to talk while I see to my other duties."

Henry nodded and Wallace strode away.

McClintock shifted on his feet and looked around the grounds as if wishing he were somewhere else. Several inches shorter than Henry, his uniform made his stout form all the more obvious.

Henry decided it best to get directly to the point. "Wallace tells me you didn't care for Pritchard."

"Can't say as I did but that doesn't mean I wished him dead." Alarm filled the man's dark eyes. "Surely you don't think I had anything to do with his murder?"

"We are speaking to everyone."

"Well, I'm not the only one who didn't like him. He was nosy, always listening to other people's private conversations. Makes me wonder if he heard something he shouldn't have."

"Such as what?"

"How would I know?" The man's frown suggested impatience rather than guilt. "Thirty-seven of us, plus our families, make our homes here, true. But during the day the Tower is open to the public. All sorts of people come through our gates, from royalty to the aristocracy to chimney sweeps and everyone in between."

As they spoke, visitors filed through the entrance a short distance away. One need only take a look at the variety of clothing to see that McClintock was right. Some had clearly never been on the grounds before, based on the way they looked about with wonder. Others didn't look twice but proceeded about their business as if their visit was a daily occurrence.

Trying to determine if Pritchard had heard anything of import seemed impossible given the number of people who passed through the Tower every day. It wasn't only like looking for a needle in a haystack but wondering if he was even in the right field.

"He spent most of his time tending the ravens, of course. Or with his daughter." The man's voice softened as he spoke of Maeve.

That remark alone made McClintock seem an unlikely suspect.

"Which other Beefeaters didn't care for him?" Henry asked.

"We prefer not to be called that, you know," McClintock said with a frown.

"Oh?" Henry asked, hoping he'd explain. The term was commonly used by many.

"There are several stories as to where the name came from. Some insist our predecessors were fed well to make certain they had the strength needed to guard the royal family. Others say they were paid wages in beef."

"Interesting." Henry waited to see what more he'd say. Sometimes an awkward silence drew out something akin to a confession...

"As for Pritchard, I'm not certain who else didn't like him." McClintock shrugged as if unwilling to cause any of his fellow warders to become a suspect.

"Surely you can name one or two," Henry pressed.

"Andrews, for one," the man said reluctantly. "Check with him."

Henry noted McClintock's whereabouts at the time of the murder and that his wife would vouch for him.

The warder turned to go only to look back at Henry. "It's not as if I had any words with the ravenkeeper. I just didn't care to hold conversations with the man. That's not a crime."

"No, it isn't." Henry held McClintock's gaze. "But whoever killed Pritchard did so brutally. We need to find out who did it and make certain it doesn't happen to anyone else."

McClintock's eyes widened in surprise. After a moment's pause, he nodded. "Agreed. I still can't believe it was one of us."

"That's good to know. But someone might have seen something that was unimportant at the time. The more of you I can speak with, the better. Where can I find Andrews?"

His conversation with the man a few minutes later didn't result in anything of interest, though the warder also mentioned that Pritchard tended to eavesdrop.

Had that been because people didn't notice him because of his job as ravenkeeper? Had he enjoyed stirring trouble based on what he heard? Or because he was a lonely widower who tended to live vicariously through others' experiences?

In his line of work, Henry had met all types.

After several more conversations with others who'd known Pritchard, including several wives of warders, he spotted Fletcher and strode toward him.

"Anything of interest?"

"Not particularly." Fletcher's scowl suggested he'd had a similarly disappointing morning.

They compared notes and Henry was unsurprised to discover Fletcher had heard much the same things Henry had.

"There are twelve acres of Tower grounds, yet we've discovered little." Fletcher shook his head. "It's frustrating. What's next?"

"Let's take another look at Pritchard's home."

"Anything in particular that we're searching for?"

"I'd like to see if there's anything related to the news sheet we found in his pocket. It might help to tell us if he was interested in that political organization or merely rubbish that he picked up on the grounds."

Fletcher fetched a key from Wallace and soon they were standing in the entrance.

"Rather cozy for a man, considering he was a widower," Fletcher remarked.

It was true. A sketch of a farm was on one wall and faded decorative pillows were tucked in the corners of chairs in the sitting room. Though small, the place was tidy. "Perhaps the domestic touches were made by his wife before her death."

"Must be," Fletcher agreed.

Henry had walked through the rooms twice the previous day but hadn't taken the time to do a thorough search. Now he tried to imagine Pritchard and Maeve there, what their life was like.

"I'm going to have another look upstairs," he told Fletcher, leaving the sergeant to search the lower rooms. The narrow stairs led to two small rooms that could have been cells at one time in their history.

In Pritchard's room the covers on the bed were tossed back as if he'd just risen. His uniform hung on pegs near the door. A book on the history of the Romans sat on a stool beside his bed. There wasn't much else in the room to hint at more of the man. Clearly he slept there and little else.

Henry looked out the narrow window, but the view was only of a brick wall. Still, he opened it and took a moment to observe. The croak of a raven sounded from the near distance.

Had Pritchard heard a similar sound the night he'd died? One of distress? If he'd cared so much for his charges, it made sense that he'd rise, dress, and leave his little girl sleeping soundly to discover what caused it.

Following his instincts, he shut the window and went down the stairs. "I'll return directly," he called out to Fletcher.

Once outside again, he walked to where the raven's call had come from and found Daniels near the birds.

"Good morning, Inspector," Daniels said.

"Morning. What gate would Pritchard have departed through at night to search for the missing raven?"

"Probably the Middle Tower Gate. He has—or rather, had—a key."

"Thank you." Henry remembered he'd given the keys found on Pritchard to Fletcher and made a mental note to ask if he'd returned them to Wallace.

He walked to where Daniels had pointed, imagining the area quiet and dark and covered in fog as it had been that night…Maeve crossing the grass barefoot in her nightgown in search of her father.

Outside the wall, not far from the gate, was the place where Pritchard had been killed. Where blood had stained the pavement despite the rain. He'd examined the area thoroughly the previous day, but no clues had been left behind other than a few blood spatters.

What had happened while Pritchard was searching for the raven? Had he stumbled upon a thief? The idea didn't sound right to Henry. If that had been the case, wouldn't he have stabbed Pritchard and hurried away when he realized the man had nothing of value?

Or was it something more sinister?

Given the extent of the wounds, he had to think that might be the case.

Nine

B y the time Amelia woke the following morning and prepared for the day, she'd convinced herself that the man she'd seen standing on the street had been visiting someone in the area. He hadn't been there because of her or Maeve.

After all, it wasn't the first time since Matthew's death that she'd seen someone outside her house who'd caused her unease—yet none of those sightings had amounted to anything. Her imagination was no doubt running away with her again.

To reassure herself she pulled aside the drape of her bedroom window, relieved to find the street below empty. Matthew had been gone for nearly a year. If someone had intended her harm, they would have already acted. And if someone wanted to hurt Maeve, it seemed unlikely they could know the little girl was staying with her.

With a calming breath at her sound, logical reasoning, Amelia finished the letter she was writing to her parents, deciding against mentioning the situation with Maeve. Not yet, anyway. She didn't want to worry them.

Yvette had assisted her to dress earlier and reported that Maeve had slept fitfully, to be expected when sleeping in a strange place and grieving her father. If she truly had seen what happened to him, those images would most likely play in her mind over and over.

Amelia made her way downstairs, greeted Fernsby then continued down to the kitchen where Yvette had taken Maeve. Amelia had planned to work in her lab that morning, as well as determine her next interview for the magazine, but those tasks could wait for the few days Maeve was with them.

Comforting the girl was all that was important. While she wasn't quite sure how to manage that, keeping her in the company of others was a good place to start.

"Good morning," Amelia said, breathing in the mouth-watering scent of freshly baked bread that filled the air of the warm room.

Maeve sat at the table with a coddled egg and toast untouched before her, her doll tucked under one arm. The girl didn't acknowledge her greeting, but of course she hadn't heard it.

Mrs. Appleton, the cook, was stirring batter briskly in a bowl and offered a smile. "Good morning, Mrs. Greystone. I hope it finds you well."

"It does," Amelia replied. "And you?"

"Quite well, thank you."

Yvette smiled as well as she pumped water into a basin. Her gaze fell to Maeve. "I'm sorry to say I haven't been able to convince her to eat anything as of yet."

Amelia nodded. "I will make an attempt." She pulled out the chair next to Maeve, running a hand over the girl's hair. The vacant look on her face had returned. Amelia sighed, wishing she knew better how to reach her.

"Would you like an egg and toast as well, ma'am?" Mrs. Appleton asked.

"Yes, please."

In short order, Yvette placed her breakfast before her along with cutlery and a napkin.

"Let us eat together, Maeve," Amelia said, touching the child's shoulder to catch her attention.

Amelia set the napkin on her lap. When Maeve didn't follow suit, Amelia did it for her. Then she handed the fork to the girl. When she didn't take it, she took the girl's hand and placed the fork in it.

Maeve held the utensil but stared across the room, seemingly oblivious to Amelia's efforts.

Refusing to accept defeat, Amelia wrapped her own hand around the girl's to scoop up a bit of egg. She tapped it onto the corner of the toast and held it to Maeve's mouth. To her surprise, the girl took a bite and slowly chewed, though she showed no reaction to the process.

"Would you like me to try that with her?" Yvette asked, her brow wrinkled as if she worried that she hadn't tried hard enough.

"We'll continue as we are, won't we, Maeve?" Amelia tipped her head to try to catch the girl's gaze without success.

The maid went back to her duties, and Amelia managed to get Maeve to take another bite before turning her attention to her own meal.

She placed a forkful of egg on her own toast and ate it, certain she saw Maeve watching her out of the corner of her eye.

To her delight, Maeve forked some of her egg and did just what Amelia had done.

Amelia shared a pleased look with Mrs. Appleton and Yvette. Maeve ate most of her breakfast before sinking back into her chair with both arms wrapped around the doll.

"Thank you for breakfast," Amelia told the cook as she stood, hand held out for Maeve.

The girl didn't look at her but took her hand and scooted off the chair.

"Shall I take her back to the room, ma'am?" Yvette asked.

"No need. She can accompany me to the lab for a time." Maeve had been so interested in it during her last visit that Amelia hoped she'd enjoy going there again.

They slowly climbed the stairs to the attic. Maeve's shoulders straightened when Amelia turned toward the lab rather than the girl's temporary room.

Releasing the child's hand to open the door and reaching for the apron hanging on the peg inside the room, Amelia hesitated for a moment's consideration, then offered a spare apron to Maeve to see what she'd do.

Maeve took it and put it on over her head, still holding the doll, then turned her back to Amelia to allow her to tie it. Obviously, the girl remembered from her last visit to the lab.

Amelia smiled. Hopefully this would provide a little distraction for Maeve to ease her through the day.

Having experienced her own battles with grief, Amelia knew to take each day as it came. At several points during her darkest days, Amelia had only been able to focus on one hour at a time.

Though it was impossible to believe it while aching with grief, time did help to heal all wounds.

Or at least, made them bearable.

After securing both of their aprons, Amelia moved to the table where the brick cleaning experiment was still spread out. She hadn't returned to empty the glass beakers or tidy her work area the previous day. Before she did so, she examined the bricks, pleased to see two showed promise for a solution to the cleaning problem. Next she would repeat the experiment with those two solutions, using different concentrations of the compounds to see what was most effective.

However, a glance at Maeve showed that she didn't seem particularly interested in brick cleaning. That came as no surprise.

As Amelia pondered what other experiment they could do, she emptied the contents of the beakers into porcelain bowls which Fernsby would discard later then rinsed out the beakers with water from the basin.

She wiped them dry with a linen cloth. Starting with clean vessels was important to gain accurate results.

Remembering how much Maeve had enjoyed watching bicarbonate of soda fizz, Amelia pulled out the powder along with a measuring spoon. She selected a wide-mouthed beaker and retrieved some food coloring from the wardrobe. After finding red, green, and yellow extracts, she set them on the table and glanced at Maeve.

Though the girl hadn't moved from where Amelia had helped her put on the apron, her gaze shifted from one object to another on the table, which was preferable to the emptiness she'd shown earlier.

Amelia leaned down to look in Maeve's face then pointed to the colors. "Which one?" She held up one finger, hoping that between reading her lips and her gestures, the girl would understand.

Except Maeve wasn't looking at her.

Amelia tapped her on the shoulder and tried again, pointing to the colors then holding up one finger. She couldn't force the girl to make eye contact. Her father must have been most patient. The two had had an excellent relationship, from what Amelia had witnessed. She could only hope Maeve would meet her partway so they could communicate in a basic fashion.

The girl seemed to grasp Amelia's meaning and pointed to the red vial. Amelia smiled, pleased Maeve had done that much.

Amelia retrieved the small step stool she'd had Maeve stand on during her last visit and placed it beside her so she could better watch the experiment. Working with a child was a challenge when so many of the compounds in her lab were potentially harmful. She would need to watch Maeve closely to make certain she didn't try to taste anything.

Amelia measured out the bicarbonate of soda, offering Maeve a spoonful to empty into the beaker. Maeve didn't take it. Instead, she watched Amelia while holding tight to her doll, making no move to participate.

Perhaps Amelia was trying too hard too quickly. With a disappointed sigh, she mixed some citric acid with the soda then carefully added a few drops of the cochineal extract to turn the concoction red. Moving quickly, she mixed the ingredients until they formed a thick paste.

After retrieving a muffin tin from the shelf beneath the table, she dropped a spoonful of the paste into each circle of the tin. The mixture would need to dry to be truly effective, but she hoped she'd made it dry enough to work immediately.

Next, she poured water into a basin then took a spoon and lifted one of the red paste balls. She turned the spoon handle to offer it to Maeve.

The girl's brow puckered, and her lips twisted as she considered the offering. To Amelia's relief she released one hand from the doll and took the spoon.

Amelia gestured for her to place it slowly into the water. Much like her last visit, Maeve did as Amelia instructed with careful movements.

The paste showed no reaction to the water for a moment, then began to fizz, creating hundreds of bubbles and foam as it dissolved in the water.

Maeve's eyes rounded with wonder as she watched it disperse, coloring the water red.

Amelia smiled. If her efforts allowed Maeve to set aside her grief for even a few minutes, she'd be pleased. She would need to think of a few more experiments that would be safe for the girl to help with.

Maeve held a finger above the bubbling solution then looked at Amelia, clearly asking if she could touch it.

Amelia nodded and Maeve almost smiled as the bubbles popped against her skin.

Almost. But not quite.

Amelia resisted the urge to embrace her, uncertain whether the gesture would be welcome. Losing a loved one was a difficult experience. Not being able to talk to anyone about it would make it doubly so. Amelia might be a familiar face to Maeve, but she was still a stranger.

That made it even more important that Amelia continue to try to connect with the girl until her family came. Hopefully, they were experienced in communicating with Maeve but meanwhile, Amelia intended to keep trying.

She puttered in the lab for a bit longer, but Maeve's waning interest had her cleaning up and removing their aprons before long.

Maeve looked tired, probably a combination of her restless night and the exhaustion that accompanied grief. Amelia remembered that all too well. She knew that weakness, a fatigue that made the smallest task seem monumental.

Amelia opened the door of Yvette's room, but Maeve held back, clearly not wanting to rest on the bed. Perhaps she thought Amelia would leave her.

The sitting room would be comfortable enough for her to nap if she wished. Amelia retrieved a few magazines that had pictures and sat beside Maeve, slowly turning pages and pointing to some of the more interesting images. Sketches of birds and other animals, as well as the latest fashion designs for women, filled the pages. The variety in magazines these days never failed to amaze Amelia, and she liked to think her own articles added to the appeal. The editor had been quite pleased with the positive response to her articles thus far.

Soon the girl's head drooped against her shoulder and Amelia felt her body relax. A quick glance showed Maeve's eyes had drifted closed. Amelia remained still, pleased Maeve felt comfortable enough to rest alongside her.

She wasn't certain what else they could do to fill the days until her family arrived. Perhaps Yvette had some ideas to keep the girl occupied.

Would Inspector Field come by? He'd want to speak with Maeve to see if he could learn what she'd witnessed, surely. But how?

Considering how challenging Amelia had found it to work with Maeve in her lab without the child's father present, asking Maeve to describe what she'd seen seemed impossible. She didn't envy the inspector the task. Hopefully he could find another way to discover what happened to Warder Pritchard.

The day passed slowly while she and Yvette took turns sitting with Maeve in one room of the house or another. Mrs. Fernsby escorted the girl to the kitchen for an hour or so to "help" the cook make biscuits for tea but reported that Maeve had shown only mild interest in the project.

Amelia was torn between letting her sit with her thoughts and keeping her busy. Neither option seemed ideal. A combination might be best.

The afternoon was waning when a knock sounded at the front door. It echoed through the quiet house, startling Amelia. She rarely had visitors. It must be Inspector Field calling to check on Maeve.

As she listened from where they sat in the drawing room with Maeve napping against her, Fernsby greeted the caller and a male voice answered.

Inspector Field. He was a bit of an enigma, rarely showing any emotion, perhaps because of his work. He had surely seen the worst in people.

Amelia appreciated his efforts to keep her apprised of any developments about Matthew's case. She was torn whether she wanted to know what her husband had been involved in prior to his death. His numerous absences, sometimes furtive behavior, and the money he'd left behind suggested he hadn't been completely innocent.

Each time Inspector Field visited, he looked at her expectantly as if hoping she had uncovered a clue that would allow him to solve the case. And she'd tried. She had been through all the papers in his desk several times, and while a few of them raised questions in her mind, none pointed to an answer.

She glanced down at Maeve, hoping Inspector Field could find justice for her father.

Fernsby showed the inspector in and anticipation filled Amelia. But it took only one look at his face to see that he had nothing of importance to share.

The way he looked between her and Maeve suggested he wondered if she had managed to discover what the girl knew. Surely he didn't think it would be that easy to communicate with a deaf and mute child.

"Good afternoon, Mrs. Greystone." The inspector held his hat in his hands and gave a nod, always polite and respectful.

"Inspector."

Maeve woke and immediately stiffened at the sight of him.

Amelia put a hand on her shoulder, hoping to reassure her. "Do you have news?" Though she already knew the answer, she couldn't help but ask.

"Not yet. However, we are continuing to follow up on clues."

"Please have a seat." She gestured toward the wingback chair nearby.

"Thank you." As was his custom during his visits, he sat on the edge of the chair as if to make it clear he wouldn't stay overlong. His gaze held on Maeve. "How is she faring?"

"As well as can be expected, I suppose. It has been a challenge to convince her to eat. Little holds her interest." Amelia offered a one-shouldered shrug. "Needless to say, communication has been limited."

The inspector's lips tightened as his focus returned to Amelia. "I was hoping she would find a way to share what she saw."

"As was I, though I am not sure how she would do that."

"The concern crossed my mind as well. I confess to having little experience with children, let alone one who can't hear or speak."

"Perhaps once her emotions have calmed, she might find a way to tell us. I must say that my respect for her father has grown. It can't have been easy to raise a child on his own, certainly not one who presents such unique challenges." Amelia smoothed the girl's hair, surprised at the protectiveness rising within her.

"You mentioned that they came to your house not long ago."

"Yes. I offered to give them a tour of my lab when Maeve showed interest in my hobby, after the interview."

His eyes narrowed as if trying to imagine it. "How did she learn about your lab?"

"A combination of reading her father's lips and mine. He acted out a few things as well, pretending to pour and the like. Apparently, that was enough to help her understand. Much like a game of charades, I suppose. But that's impossible when she won't look at you."

Inspector Field considered the silent girl. "Have you seen her gesture to show what she wants?"

"Not other than pointing or staring at an object. Warder Pritchard seemed able to anticipate her wishes easily. In truth, I have hardly been able to convince her to look at me. I'm not sure which is worse—her terrible cries when we found her on the doorstep or the empty look she wears now."

The inspector's brow furrowed as if he wondered the same. "I hate to ask it of you, but if you could continue to work with her..."

"Of course." Amelia wasn't certain how, but she was willing to try. "Is there any word of when her family will arrive?"

"Not as of yet. Wallace thought it would take a few days for them to make arrangements to travel to London."

Amelia nodded, wishing they would come sooner. Surely Maeve would be more comfortable with them, and they would know better how to converse with her.

Inspector Field cleared his throat, his brown eyes full of sympathy. "Maeve."

Amelia touched the girl's shoulder and pointed to him, hoping to direct her attention to the inspector.

But as she had so often already that day, the girl stared into the distance as if she didn't see either of them. Or didn't want to.

He shifted off the edge of his chair with one knee on the floor, so he was at her level. "Maeve, did you see who hurt your father?"

Still the girl showed no reaction.

"Did you," he pointed at her, "see," he pointed at his eyes, "who hurt your father?"

They both waited a moment to no avail.

"I wish I had a suggestion." Amelia shook her head, feeling helpless.

Inspector Field sighed and returned to the chair. "As do I."

Ten

Henry departed from Mrs. Greystone's with disappointment weighing on him. While he knew his hope that the widow could use her connection with the girl to learn what happened to her father was unlikely, it had been his best lead since so few clues had been discovered thus far.

His own efforts to speak with Maeve had yielded no results either.

One look at the girl and the way she stared into the distance, showing no reaction to what was going on around her, made it clear that wouldn't happen any time soon.

How unfortunate to have a witness who couldn't share what she'd seen.

He hated to press her harder when she looked so empty.

He and Fletcher had spent a second day interviewing Pritchard's fellow warders, along with a few of the warder families, with little results. Other than eavesdropping, Pritchard didn't appear to have many unpleasant habits. He didn't have any close friends. He and Maeve had kept to themselves for the most part.

Everyone had remarked on how quiet Pritchard had been. Perhaps that was a force of habit from living with a deaf and mute child.

Henry was grateful Mrs. Greystone was willing to continue to watch over Maeve. Though more than one of the families at the Tower had offered to keep her, Henry preferred she not be near the place. It seemed safer, perhaps even healthier, for Maeve to stay at a different location.

Where was the line between being comforted by the familiar and constantly reminded of what had happened?

Did Mrs. Greystone find solace in being surrounded by her husband's things?

There wasn't much of Matthew Greystone in the house other than in his study, which she might have changed by now. It had been some time since he'd been in the room as he normally met with her in the drawing room.

Henry shook off his thoughts and found a hansom cab. Then, with care, he pulled out the news sheet that had been tucked in Pritchard's pocket. He hadn't locked it away at the Yard because he wanted to study it. The paper was fragile and only parts of the headlines were legible. The rest had faded completely.

From what Henry had learned, the paper was produced by a new political organization whose views aligned with that of Karl Marx. Henry was no expert on the latest in politics, but he knew someone who was—his father.

Thurmond Field had been born and raised in the Metropolitan Police Force. At least, that was what Henry's mother liked to say. To Henry's thinking, his father hadn't had much choice when it came to his career, but Thurmond had embraced his father's legacy.

Henry's grandfather, Charles Field, had been the son of a pub owner from Chelsea. With a dramatic flair and a charismatic personality, he'd hoped to become an actor. Instead, for financial reasons, Charles had joined the Metropolitan Police when it had first been established in 1829. Not many could brag of being among the first to join the force.

His grandfather hadn't stopped there.

He'd made the best of the situation and charmed the skeptical public who viewed the newly formed police force with suspicion, certain they were little more than spies. After starting as a constable, he quickly rose to the position of sergeant then inspector and eventually chief inspector before retiring.

As if that wasn't enough, early in his career, he'd managed to catch the attention of Charles Dickens and become good friends with the man.

Henry wished he had even one of his grandfather's qualities, learned if not inherited. Alas, not only did Henry not resemble him, but he'd been told he lacked charm and any hint of charisma. That was no surprise to Henry.

However, Henry's father had shades of Charles Field in him. He, too, was well liked and had enjoyed a successful career which ended as a chief inspector. Thurmond had an abundance of logic and common sense along with an appealing smile which had gotten him far during his time on the force.

Henry had grown up wanting to be an inspector just like his father and grandfather. As he'd grown older, he realized he didn't want to simply follow in their footsteps. He wanted to—needed to—forge a path based on his own merits.

After all, it was pure chance that his last name was Field. His adoption into the family was something he'd learned by accident at the age of twelve. To this day, his parents still didn't realize that he knew the truth.

It answered the question of why he was so different but also created a wall between them that he didn't seem able to scale.

If only he didn't want to be a true Field with every fiber of his being. To know that he belonged rather than merely being a member of the family by happenstance.

But the feeling made him all the more determined to prove his worth. Henry's superiors either expected him to outperform his co-workers or thought his quick rise through the ranks was solely due to his name. Everything he did was evaluated and compared beneath a magnifying lens.

Having an unsolved murder was a strike against him that some viewed as a tell-tale sign that he wasn't anything like his father or grandfather. It didn't matter that unsolved cases were a common occurrence.

Henry's determination to follow in his family's ill-fitting footsteps was slowed by doubt. There had been times in the last year when he'd questioned his career choice. But the middle of another murder investigation wasn't the time for uncertainty.

Though he wanted to stand on his own, he wasn't above using his father's knowledge, especially when it might help to solve the case and bring justice to the victims and their families. They were the ones who mattered more than Henry's bouts with insecurity.

His family home on Glentworth Street just off Marylebone Road was in a good neighborhood that experienced little of the crime his father had so often been knee-deep in while working.

Stubbs, the butler, greeted him with a welcoming smile and directed him to the drawing room where his mother was.

"Henry. How lovely of you to drop by." His mother's customary warm greeting as she set aside her embroidery always helped to ease any trouble on his mind. "How are you?"

"Mother." He bent to kiss her soft cheek, catching the faint scent of rosewater. The smell alone was enough to bring back pleasant memories from his childhood. His mother had been a steadfast presence in his life, something he still appreciated. "I am well, and you?"

He didn't miss how her gaze lingered on his face to determine how he truly fared. She worried too much. No doubt that came from having both a husband and now a son on the police force.

Despite that worry, Katherine Field was aging gracefully. Her warm brown eyes always sparkled with interest as if she were fascinated by everything he had to say. Her brown hair held only a few touches of gray, her figure was still trim, and the fine lines around her eyes and mouth were barely noticeable unless one looked closely.

Henry didn't. He preferred to think she wasn't growing older, that she'd always be there for him.

"Quite well. Thank you. How is work?"

He sat in one of the comfortable wingback chairs that she'd recently had recovered in a blue slate floral pattern. "Busy at the moment." He was careful not to share too much. Worrying her would hardly help. "I like the new fabric," he said as he smoothed a hand over the chair arm, trying to relax and enjoy the time with her despite the feeling of urgency simmering inside him.

"Thank you." She smiled. "You always notice any changes I make."

"I try." He returned her smile. "What have you been doing of late?"

"Yesterday was our monthly book club meeting. We are to read another mystery by Michael Shaw."

"I've enjoyed several of his books. He always has a twist or two in his stories." He appreciated the way the author included unconventional criminals or settings.

"What brings you by today?" she asked with a knowing look.

Guilt speared through him. Then again, the hour was still relatively early. No doubt she surmised he was working. His father wasn't the only one who had excellent observation skills.

"I hoped for a word with Father but wanted to speak with you first."

"How nice, he'll be pleased to see you. We can visit another time since I can tell you're anxious—you must come for dinner soon. Your father should be in his study." As Henry turned to go, she asked, "Is this about a new case?"

He looked at her, aware she had mixed feelings about him following in his father's and grandfather's footsteps. Police work could be dangerous at times. "Yes."

She nodded but didn't ask anything more, so he continued to his father's study and knocked on the open door.

Memories filled him of times from his youth when he'd done the same thing, always finding a warm welcome and a steadying hand. His parents meant the world to him. That was one of the reasons he'd never told them that he knew about the adoption. Knowing them, whether to tell him had been a decision they'd wrestled with, and he didn't want them to think they'd chosen wrong.

"Henry. Good to see you." Thurmond smiled as he removed gold-rimmed spectacles and set them on his desk and leaned back in his chair. His body was a slightly slimmer version of the stout figure his grandfather had enjoyed. "What brings you by today?"

His father had never been one for idle chitchat. It was a quality they had in common.

"I wondered if you'd heard of this." Henry withdrew the delicate news sheet from his pocket and handed it to him.

His father's brown hair had lightened with gray. Deep creases lined his forehead and mouth, probably from the constant strain of his career over the years.

His father reached for his spectacles and put them back on as he took the paper. "*Justice*. I do believe this is a publication from Hyndman's organization."

"Hyndman?" Henry didn't stay abreast of politics the way his father did. While he took the time to study candidates and issues so he could vote, that was as far as his interest went. The rest seemed beyond his control, and he felt his time was better spent elsewhere.

"Henry Hyndman. He was a conservative but converted to socialism and now follows the ideas of Karl Marx. He recently founded the Democratic Federation, a political party that promotes social equality."

"I see." That made it seem even more unlikely that Aberforth Pritchard would've been a follower of those views. Few military members appreciated the ideas of socialism.

"The paper has seen better days," his father observed as he looked over the faded sheet.

"It was in the pocket of a murder victim who was tossed in the Thames."

"Oh?" His father's interest perked up even more at that news. He turned on the lamp that sat on his desk to examine the paper more closely.

Retirement had sounded more appealing than it actually was, according to Henry's father. Finding ways to spend his days that didn't drive his wife to distraction was more difficult than he'd anticipated. Henry's grandfather had experienced the same problem and dabbled with serving as a private detective until the income he generated resulted in the temporary halting of his pension.

Henry's mother made it clear to her husband that he was not going to follow that path. She was done with having him in danger. He had begrudgingly agreed but was always more than willing to discuss a case if asked. Henry was careful not to do so too often lest his father decide he couldn't bear retirement and return to investigating. His mother would not be pleased if that were to happen.

Besides, Henry preferred to figure out as much as possible on his own. Consulting his father felt a bit like cheating. He didn't want his superiors to think he couldn't solve a case without his father's help, though the worry they believed it anyway kept circling in his head.

"Was the victim anyone of interest?" his father asked.

Henry hid a smile at the forced casualness of the question. "A ravenkeeper from the Tower of London."

"Ah. I see. I believe I saw a note about that in the news sheet." His father frowned at the paper. "A military man, then. It seems unlikely that he would have socialist tendencies."

"Agreed. Perhaps he simply picked it up and put it in his pocket, not realizing what it was."

"He wouldn't want the ravens to get hold of it. From what little I know, they like sorting through the refuse bins if given the chance."

That made sense yet didn't completely dismiss the potential clue from Henry's mind. "It wasn't crushed but rather folded neatly, as if kept with care."

"Any wrinkles could've eased from being wet." Despite sharing the thought, his father continued to study the paper. "If it's of interest, I believe I read somewhere that Hyndman was so intrigued by the ideas Marx presented in his book that he called on the man. Hyndman later handed out his own summary of Marx's ideas without giving Marx credit for any of it. Marx didn't appreciate that."

"I don't suppose so." Henry frowned. "Seems like a rather bold move on Hyndman's part. Surely he realized Marx would discover what he'd done."

"Quite shortsighted of him. Marx is well known and respected. Not someone to make an enemy out of unnecessarily."

"Certainly not when you supposedly share the same ideologies."

"Exactly." His father tapped a finger on the desk as he sorted through his mental files. "From memory Hyndman attempted to run for office a few years ago but received limited support so withdrew from the election. He seems to be easily influenced by others' beliefs. His new party has attracted a few radicals that limit the chances of its success, in my opinion."

The paper therefore seemed an unlikely clue. But Henry had so few that it wouldn't do to overlook this one.

"How was the ravenkeeper killed?"

"Stabbed. Multiple—or should I say—numerous times."

His father's eyes narrowed. "That might be a clue in itself. Why numerous when one or two would be enough to gain the same result?"

"I thought the same and intend to find out. It seems the killer is more than adept with a blade." He didn't share further details as he still had a lead or two on which to follow up, including the paper. Henry pushed to his feet. "Thank you for the information, Father. I appreciate it."

"You're leaving already?" His father rose, clearly disappointed Henry didn't want to discuss the case further.

"I must be going. Fletcher and I are meeting to review our progress."

Thurmond heaved a sigh but nodded. He knew Fletcher well and respected him. "Do let me know if I can be of additional help."

"Of course." Henry smiled. He couldn't deny the appreciation he felt for being able to ask his father's opinion.

"Do take care, Henry," his father added. "The press will have a field day with such a brutal stabbing, let alone of a yeoman warder, when they learn the details."

Henry nodded. "I would guess they've discovered it by now and come the morning, the reports will speculate on who did it and why."

He sighed, aware of the clock ticking on the case. "Thanks again, Father."

A third warning? Henry mused as he took his leave. If he were the superstitious sort, he might have cause to worry.

Eleven

Henry entered the Three Pigeons on Stafford Street to find Fletcher already seated at a table with a pint before him. The pub was bustling, the workday ended for many who stopped by for a drink and a chat before going home to their families.

After a quick glance around, Henry ordered a pint and joined his colleague. Places like this made him more aware of his solitary existence. Most days, he liked his life just as it was, but seeing friends and couples greet one another created an unwelcome knot of loneliness difficult to untangle. It almost made him grateful to have a murder investigation on which to focus.

While he had friends on the force, gathering with other detectives meant an evening speaking about work. He was a private person and preferred not to discuss details unless there was a specific reason to do so. The long hours he spent on the job made finding friends outside of it difficult. He enjoyed the occasional dinner with his parents, but otherwise tended to be alone.

"Come across anything of interest today?" Henry asked after he took his first sip.

He liked Fletcher for many reasons, one of them being that he was a man of few words and said what was on his mind. Henry didn't like to waste time when on a pressing case.

Then again, all of their cases were pressing. At least, they were in the victim's view. He did his best to keep that in mind when he put in long hours with little to show for it.

"Someone tried to poison the ravens this morning." Fletcher's announcement had Henry setting down his drink abruptly, causing it to slosh over the rim.

"What?" His heart raced at the news.

"Daniels found me shortly after I arrived. He thinks it was done soon after the gates were opened to the public."

"Were any of the birds harmed?"

Fletcher shook his head. "He found the meat before they got a hold of it."

"Why does he believe it contained poison?"

Fletcher's grim smile had Henry even more curious. "He said the ravens acted oddly around it. It looked remarkably similar to the pile you found on Pritchard that you showed him yesterday, which made him think it had to be poisoned."

Henry blew out a breath as he considered why on earth Pritchard had the meat in his pocket. "Perhaps Pritchard found the meat, suspected it was dodgy, and put it in his pocket to keep the ravens from getting into it?"

"That seems the most logical answer," Fletcher said. "The birds fluttered around the stuff but weren't eating it. As smart as those damned ravens are, I have to wonder if they realized something was off."

Henry shook his head. "Glad he caught it."

"Why would anyone want to harm the ravens?" Fletcher asked quietly. "I can't say as I care for them as they're rather creepy in my opinion, but that doesn't mean I want them dead."

"Perhaps to stir the legend," Henry mused. That was the only thing that made sense. Pritchard was already dead. The killing of a raven would no longer hurt him.

"Humph. You mean the one about the ravens remaining at the Tower lest the Crown, along with the country, will fall?"

"That's the one. You know how superstitious people can be." Henry turned over the possibilities in his mind. "The question is whether it is somehow tied to Pritchard's murder."

"Hmm. The ravenkeepers aren't part of the legend, but it seems too much of a coincidence."

"Agreed." Henry's instincts told him the incidents were connected. As his grandfather had often said, coincidences were to be viewed with suspicion. "You collected the poisoned meat?"

Fletcher's huff boded bad news. "No. Daniels tossed the pile. When I asked him for it, he looked in the dustbin to retrieve it, but it was gone."

"Blast it." The news only further roused his suspicions. "Is he certain?"

Fletcher shrugged. "It wasn't where he'd put it. He couldn't say whether some other animal got a hold of it or where it might have gone."

"Or whoever left the meat didn't want it found."

"That seems likely."

"Did you speak with the other warders to ask if they'd seen anything suspicious?"

"Yes, but with little success. Daniels is the one who feeds them now. He'd already done so before he found the meat, which was shortly after the gates opened to the public. Of course, there's a chance it was left on the grass before that. As small as the pieces were that he described, it would've been impossible to see from a distance."

Henry sighed. "It's difficult to narrow down a list of possible suspects when the place is open to the public."

"Very true. I also spoke with Mr. Elliott, the Mint manager, and Mr. Blackwell, from the Armoury, again. They didn't have any further details to share. Both say they were home when the murder took place."

"Stay in touch with them. Something might yet come to their minds," Henry advised.

Fletcher took another sip, eyeing Henry over the rim of his glass. "Knowing you, you kept the first batch of meat you found."

"I did. Whether anything can be discovered from it remains to be seen." Luckily, he knew who might be able to help him find out.

"Inspector Field is calling again, madam," Fernsby announced from the drawing room doorway where Amelia worked that evening.

"Show him in." She set down her pen on the desk where she'd been documenting the results of her brick cleaning experiment. Night had fallen but it wasn't yet time for dinner, which made it an unusual hour for callers. Inspector Field's visit must have a specific purpose.

Nerves tingled along her skin. Did he bring news on Maeve's father's death?

"Mrs. Greystone." Inspector Field dipped his head politely as Amelia stood. "I'm sorry to bother you again, but I wondered if I might ask for your assistance."

As per usual, he still wore his coat and held his hat as if he didn't intend to stay long.

"Of course." She gestured toward the group of chairs before the fire.

The inspector glanced about the room, undoubtedly looking for Maeve.

"She's in the kitchen with the maid."

He nodded but still did not sit. "I am in need of a chemist."

Amelia's interest was roused. "Oh?" He was asking for her help? Her cheeks heated at the thought.

She rarely had cause to apply her knowledge for anyone other than herself. Her father had always encouraged her hobby while Matthew had been amused by it. He'd agreed to the laboratory in the attic but little else.

"We have reason to believe someone tried to poison the ravens."

"How terrible. Are they all right?" She could imagine Pritchard's upset if he had discovered that. The ravenkeeper had been quite protective of the birds.

"Thus far." He frowned. "I considered waiting until morning to call on you but worried that the longer we waited to check the sample, the less likely we would be able to find anything."

Good heavens. He *was* asking for her assistance. She had to keep from pressing a hand to her heart which raced with excitement. She needed to act as a professional rather than reveal how flattered she was. "You're right. The more time that passes the less reliable the results can be."

He cleared his throat as if uncomfortable. "I'm afraid the...the sample is less than appealing to view."

"You'll find I have a strong constitution." She drew closer, her curiosity getting the better of her.

Inspector Field reached into his coat pocket and carefully withdrew a bundle wrapped in a pink cloth. Only as he started to pull one corner aside did she realize why the fabric was pink and just how unsavory the sample was going to be.

He paused as his gaze met hers before revealing the contents. "Perhaps I should have warned you—it's chunks of meat."

She nodded.

"Pritchard had it in his coat pocket when his body was found. It wasn't in the handkerchief. Just the pocket." He peeled back the damp cloth to reveal small bits of discolored meat. "The Thames may have washed away anything that was on it, but it's worth a try. I should've thought to ask you to test it yesterday, but it didn't occur to me that it might be poisoned until a short while ago."

"What makes you think it is?" she asked as she studied the unappealing mound.

"A similar offering was left near the ravens this morning, but they didn't eat it. Or at least, they were hesitant to do so. The warder who took over Pritchard's duties discovered it and threw it away."

"Can a sample be retrieved?" she asked. "Given that this meat was stuffed in a coat pocket and soaked in the river, it's doubtful we'll find anything."

"Unfortunately, something—or someone—seems to have taken it." He grimaced with obvious regret as he spoke.

Amelia lifted a brow as she studied the inspector, sifting through the information he'd shared. "The matter grows more curious by the minute."

"It does." He lifted the bundle, acting uncertain for the first time since she'd met him. For some reason, she found his hesitation endearing. "Can we try to detect poison on this?"

"Yes. I suppose arsenic would be most likely." Amelia frowned, not liking the idea of failing the first time he asked for her assistance. "As I said, it's doubtful any of it remains given where it's been." She reached for a small decorative silver tray on a nearby table and held it out. "The less we handle it the better."

"Of course."

"Would you prefer to join me in the lab, or shall I send a message with the results of my findings?"

The inspector blinked in surprise. "You...you intend to test it now?"

"I'm sure you're anxious for an answer." She only hoped she could provide one. In truth, she was pleased he'd thought of her.

"I should very much like to join you." The flash of admiration in his eyes warmed her.

"Very well. Come along."

Many men frowned on women involved in the sciences, certain they couldn't perform as well or be as knowledgeable as men. She rarely told others of her interest. Matthew had discouraged her from sharing it, something that had both hurt and puzzled her on more than one occasion.

She wouldn't have told Inspector Field, except that she'd been working on one occasion when he'd called, and she'd had Fernsby show him to the lab since she was in the middle of something. He had been intrigued, especially upon seeing her workspace.

Ignoring the fluttery feeling in her stomach at once again allowing this man into her private sanctuary, she led the way up to the attic, mentally reviewing what she needed in order to test for arsenic.

Amelia turned on the gaslight lamps in the room but knew they wouldn't be sufficient to see what she was doing in the gloom of night. After setting the tray of meat on her worktable, she donned her apron and lit several candles, giving the room a strangely intimate glow.

"Do you have the supplies required to do the test?" Inspector Field asked as he watched with blatant interest.

"I do. All that is needed is zinc and sulfuric acid to see a visible trace of the poison."

"I confess that I'm fascinated you know such things."

Amelia looked up from the worktable in surprise. Though they'd had numerous conversations since Matthew's death, it was the first personal remark he'd made. "I studied James Marsh's findings on the matter."

Among other inventions, James Marsh, a British chemist, had devised not one but two highly sensitive tests to detect arsenic.

"Ah, yes. He used his newer method for the Lafarge case in France. I'm familiar with it."

Amelia smiled in response. "I was certain you would be."

For too long, arsenic had been used to kill without a trace and sometimes called "inheritance powder" in France.

"It's interesting that arsenic can be both beneficial and harmful, depending on how it's used," she added as she set up the area.

"Didn't I read that it has been successful in treating some forms of cancer?"

Amelia was surprised once again. "Yes, that's right. I know a considerable amount about the health benefits of such things, because of my father's work. He is an apothecary," she added. "And in very small amounts, of course, arsenic can be beneficial."

But the inspector hadn't called to hold a discussion on the advantages and disadvantages of arsenic. Sadly opportunities to discuss such things with others were few and far between. In her experience, only her father enjoyed sharing that sort of information. The few friends she had weren't interested in science, only in their families, fashion, or the latest gossip.

Still, as she plucked three glass beakers from a shelf and retrieved the acid and a small vial of zinc from the wardrobe, she wondered about Inspector Henry Field and his background. She knew little about him as a person.

The first few times he'd called had been like a punch in the stomach—a terrible reminder of Matthew's murder. That feeling had slowly faded as the months passed.

But the death of Pritchard as well as the arrival of Maeve on her doorstep had shifted Amelia's perspective on the detective. He'd transformed from being the inspector investigating her husband's death to a person with other cases and concerns. To think of him outside of his work changed her view of him yet again and would take time to adjust to.

Setting aside her thoughts, she placed the items on the worktable then used tweezers to take two pieces of meat from the pile and place them in a beaker. Next she added the zinc and acid then attached the beaker to a stand above a candle flame to heat the contents. The entire time, she was well aware of Inspector Field's close regard.

"If arsenic is present, we should see a silvery substance appear." She waited, studying the beaker closely for several minutes.

Inspector Field moved closer to view the contents as well. "Anything?"

"No." She eyed the remaining mound of meat. "Allow me to try another sample from the center of the pile."

"Excellent idea. Those pieces might have more on them."

"If they ever did," she added.

"True." He gave a single nod to acknowledge that possibility.

He waited patiently as Amelia repeated the experiment. It didn't take long for the results to become clear.

"Arsenic." She held up the beaker for him to see for himself. "Someone *is* trying to poison the ravens."

His eyes fixed on the silvery substance visible in the beaker, brow furrowing at the sight.

"Do you know why?" she asked curiously.

"Not yet. But it has to be connected to Pritchard's murder. This makes me think the killer might intend to stir the public with the legend about the ravens, casting doubt on the Crown." He glanced over to meet her gaze, his brown eyes dark with worry. "The case is becoming more sinister by the moment."

Twelve

The next morning when Henry checked in at the Yard, Reynolds waved him into his office.

"Did you see this morning's headline?" The Director held up a folded copy of *The Standard*.

Henry smothered a groan, not wanting to hear whatever it said. Based on Reynolds' grim expression, it wasn't good. "No, I didn't."

This was the third day of his investigation, too much to hope that the press had found more interesting news to report.

"'A Slasher Strikes at The Tower.'" Reynolds scowled. "It's only going to grow worse from here. Tell me you have some developments."

"We think there was an attempt to poison the ravens yesterday."

"You think? You don't know?"

"The yeoman warder now tending the birds threw away the meat he discovered, and it disappeared soon after. He says it matched the meat found on Pritchard. I've had that tested, and it contains traces of arsenic."

"What does this have to do with the murder?"

"I'm still determining that." Henry hated to admit he didn't have anything more to add. Nothing that could be proven anyway. Conjecture didn't count. "I'm also looking into the news sheet found on the victim to see where that leads."

Reynolds considered his answer for a moment. "What of the girl?"

Henry shook his head. "I remain hopeful that she'll be of assistance but at the moment, she's not able to communicate anything."

"Just our luck that the only possible witness is deaf and mute. Keep after it, Field. Don't let this one slip away from you."

"Yes, sir." Frustration filled Henry. Such reminders weren't particularly helpful.

He departed without looking at the papers on his desk and headed out, even more anxious to begin his day. He wasn't far from the Tower when he caught sight of a man picking pockets. Annoyed, he caught the thief, hailing a passing constable to take care of the situation.

By the time he arrived at the Tower, a queue of people waited to go inside. Between the hours of ten in the morning to four in the afternoon, a massive number of visitors paid a shilling, except for Mondays and Saturdays when entrance was free, to tour the grounds. They came to see the regalia, the Armoury, the crown jewels, Beauchamp Tower built in 1281 where many famous prisoners were held, and the ravens.

Henry was certain some hoped to glimpse a ghost or two or at least to feel their eerie presence. It was impossible not to sense something when walking the grounds and hearing the yeoman warders share stories of the past.

His grandfather had told him of the danger visitors in the 1850s faced. After purchasing tickets, they waited in the refreshment room where ginger pop and buns were offered with two water closets nearby. However, the stench from the water closets combined with the number of people crammed into the small space made for an unpleasant delay. Pickpockets found easy targets since many visitors were from the country and were unused to being on guard against thieves.

Luckily, the situation was much improved these days, allowing for a better experience for those wanting to view the Tower and all the history it had to offer.

Henry was pleased he didn't have to wait as the warder at the entrance remembered him and waved him through. He wanted to tell Chief Warder Wallace that arsenic had been discovered on the meat. Then he intended to speak with Daniels. The fact that the new ravenkeeper had tossed away the meat when they were in the throes of a murder investigation made Henry wonder, not for the first time, if Daniels could somehow be involved.

Mrs. Greystone's efficiency in testing for arsenic had been impressive. Finding a chemist willing to complete it so quickly would've been a challenge, let alone one who allowed him to wait for immediate results.

How fortunate that she was well versed in such things. Perhaps he should offer to procure a payment for her services. He'd mention it to the Director to see if it was possible to pay her for her expertise and the supplies she'd used.

Henry slowed as he studied the walkways, wondering how difficult it would be to drop a pile of poisoned meat where the ravens might see it, but the warders wouldn't. The men were all clearly visible in their distinctive uniforms; it would be relatively simple to avoid them when busy with people who clamored around them to ask questions about the Tower. The trouble was, he didn't have any idea where Pritchard had picked up the meat Henry had found in his pocket.

"Inspector Field."

Henry turned to see a familiar face striding toward him. It took a moment for him to remember the Mint manager, given how many people he'd spoken to during the past two days.

"Mr. Elliott." Henry nodded, waiting to see what he wanted since it was clear he had something on his mind.

"Any progress on the investigation?" The man glanced about the grounds as if hoping to see someone being arrested as he spoke.

"Slowly but surely," Henry replied.

"It's terrible to think a murder could take place right here with so many guards about."

"Actually, the crime took place outside the Tower wall."

Mr. Elliott lifted a brow. "Is that supposed to make us feel safer?"

Irritation stirred in Henry, but he ignored it. He should be used to questions and criticisms. "We are working as quickly as we can to find who did it."

"I suppose." The man scowled. "Meanwhile, the killer is walking among us, possibly ready to strike again."

"We don't know whether he lives or works in the Tower, nor do we have any reason to suspect that he has another target in mind." Yet Henry would be the first to admit that an attempt to poison the ravens boded ill. "Even so, I would urge you to take care and remain vigilant."

Mr. Elliott leaned close as if to speak in confidence. "Do you think it was one of the warders? Given their military experience, surely they're all capable of killing."

"We are considering every possibility."

"That's good to hear. I, for one, won't rest easy until the murderer is caught." Mr. Elliott nodded to emphasize his point. "Good day."

Henry watched him disappear into a group of passing tourists as he considered the conversation. Fletcher had mentioned that Elliott had spoken with him the previous day as well. It was surprising how often the man came to the Tower. Clearly he was taking an active interest in the investigation.

Then again, the public in general was fascinated by murder. It never failed to amaze Henry to hear of previous crime scenes that had become tourist attractions. The very idea!

The thought had him looking more closely at the visitors nearby, wondering if they'd read the morning headline and hoped to catch sight of the 'slasher' at the Tower.

He knocked on Wallace's office door and received a muffled reply to enter.

"Good morning," Henry removed his hat as he greeted the man, once again admiring the octagonal office and the historic feel of the room.

"Inspector." Wallace stood to shake his hand then gestured toward a seat. "Do you bring news?"

"Of a sort." Henry sat. "The meat found in Pritchard's pocket contains traces of arsenic."

"Truly?" Wallace sank into his chair as he processed the news. "That's terrible."

"I assume Daniels told you about the meat he found that looked similar to that which was discovered on Pritchard."

"Yes, he did." Wallace frowned. "Though I don't understand what could've happened to it. Daniels said he disposed of it but when he went to retrieve it, none of the meat was there."

"So I understand." Wallace didn't seem to suspect Daniels of anything, but Henry wanted to make his expectations clear. "If something in that vein is found again, it should be kept, and word sent to me. Anything in the least suspicious or out of the ordinary."

"Of course. I can't imagine what Daniels was thinking to throw it away."

Nor could Henry. "The ravens have remained well?"

"Yes. While they are suspicious creatures, if left to their own devices for too long, they might have eaten it."

"We must hope their restraint isn't tested again."

"I don't understand what the point of poisoning them would be."
Walters frowned. "Surely you don't think it's related to Pritchard's
death."

"I don't know yet. Has anything of the sort happened in the past?"

"Not to my knowledge." Wallace shook his head. "One or two of
the ravens have escaped before, but none poisoned."

To Henry, the effort required to tend the ravens seemed a high cost
to satisfy a legend. "Has anyone reported new information to you since
we last spoke?"

Oftentimes, once people had gotten over the shock of an unexpected death, they'd remember something out of the ordinary. A turning
point. That's what he needed.

"I made a point of speaking with several of the warders who had
the most contact with Pritchard last night in the pub." Wallace paused
to glance at Henry. "I believe I mentioned that most of us gather
there each evening to share a pint and a few stories. No one seemed
to have anything new to add. While not everyone held a fondness
for Pritchard, all expressed sorrow, especially for little Maeve. How is
she?"

"As well as can be expected, I suppose. She seems comfortable at
Mrs. Greystone's."

"I still can't imagine how the girl made it all that way in the dark of
night by herself—clothed only in her nightgown and with bare feet no
less."

"It couldn't have been easy." The fact that she had managed it
showed a strength of spirit. It was a grit that would serve her well in
the coming years. It also revealed how big of an impression Mrs. Greystone had made on the girl. That she'd decided to go there suggested
she hadn't felt safe returning home.

Why? If only the girl could speak.

Wallace lifted a brow. "Has she been able to share any of what she knows?"

"Not as of yet. How has she communicated in the past?" Had Wallace witnessed the lip reading and motioning that Mrs. Greystone had mentioned?

Wallace started to reply only to frown. "Well. Hmm. Let me think. She points and gestures, of course."

Henry nodded, hoping there was more.

"Pritchard seemed able to guess what she wanted. She was adept at reading his lips, though not as able to read others. I suppose familiarity helps."

"She never speaks?" Henry had to ask, though the answer seemed clear.

"No." Wallace shook his head, seeming to understand how much Henry wanted him to answer otherwise. "Not that I've heard. Nor did Pritchard ever mention it."

"I assumed as much. Perhaps she'll find a way to share what she saw that night if she truly witnessed anything."

He intended to call on Mrs. Greystone again to visit with Maeve later in the day. Perhaps he could create a series of yes and no questions that she could respond to and help point him toward a suspect.

But the memory of Maeve staring across the room during his last visit came to mind. As Mrs. Greystone had said, convincing her to make eye contact was a challenge in itself. Once her grief wasn't as fresh, maybe they could get through to her, although he wondered if the girl would ever truly overcome what she'd potentially seen.

Henry stood. "I'll have a word with Daniels to see if he has any other information."

"Of course. He should be on the South Lawn with the ravens at this time of the morning."

After bidding Wallace goodbye, Henry made his way in that direction, only to come upon another person interested in the investigation.

"Inspector Field." Michael Blackwell, the man in charge of the Armoury whom Henry had spoken with the day Pritchard's body had been discovered, tipped his hat in greeting. "How is your investigation proceeding?"

"As one might expect. We continue to pursue all avenues."

The man's brown wool suit fit him well and was of fine quality. Apparently managing the Armoury paid well. He was clean-shaven and looked to be in his late thirties or early forties with dark hair and a restless manner, often shifting his weight.

"How frightening to think one of our own was murdered." Blackwell's brown eyes perused the grounds as if trying to imagine who might have done it.

"Do your duties bring you to the Tower daily?" Henry asked.

"Indeed, they do." Blackwell gave an amused smile. "Am I a suspect?"

Henry did not return the smile. "Everyone is at the moment."

"How exciting." Blackwell's droll tone belied his words. "I can't say I have ever been one before."

"Tell me again where you were the night of the murder?"

"As I said before, at home in bed, most likely."

"Is there anyone who can confirm that?"

"My wife. The servants." The amused smile returned. "Do you wish to speak with them as well?"

"Yes, at some point." Henry didn't care for the man's attitude. He doubted anyone had shown this sort of flippancy to his father or grandfather. "I'll be in touch."

"I look forward to it."

Henry nodded. Blackwell's reaction to his questions struck him as odd, and he made a mental note to look into the man's background, along with that of Elliott from the Mint.

He continued to the South Lawn, pleased to find Daniels still there. The Yeoman Warder was watching his charges as they moved along the grassy expanse, to the delight of a small gathering of visitors. A young boy released his mother's hand and ran toward the ravens, sending them fluttering into the air as they croaked in displeasure.

Daniels immediately stepped forward to speak to the boy. Based on the words that drifted to Henry, he advised him not to chase the birds. The warder sent a stern glare to the mother as if to emphasize his point.

Daniels' protectiveness of the ravens when he didn't know Henry was watching suggested he took his duties seriously. So why had he discarded the poisoned meat instead of giving it to Fletcher?

As Henry approached, a reserved look came over Daniel's expression. Did he comprehend the mistake he'd made?

"Inspector."

"Sergeant Fletcher mentioned you found more meat chunks." Henry didn't bother with a greeting, given his frustration with the man.

"Yes." He turned and gestured toward the lawn to where the ravens had returned. "Right over there. Strewn about."

"Show me," Henry said, his tone sharp.

Daniels led the way across the lawn, scattering the birds much like the boy had done moments ago. "It was left all around here."

"Before visitors were allowed entrance?"

Daniels' lips tightened at the question. "I found it after the gates were open."

"Did anyone else see the meat?"

"No. I shooed away the ravens and hurried to pick it up before any of them ate it."

"In your hand?" Henry wanted as many details as possible.

"I put it in my handkerchief. The chunks were about the same size as the ones you found on...on Pritchard."

"Then you placed it where?" Henry glanced around for the nearest dustbin but there weren't any visible.

"Just inside the Bloody Tower. I only thought to make certain the birds wouldn't get into it. It wasn't until...oh, probably a half hour later that I realized I should've kept at least some of it to show you. By then, it was gone." He shook his head in disbelief. "I can't imagine why someone would have taken the stuff."

"If anything of this sort happens again, I expect you to collect any potential evidence and alert me as quickly as possible."

Daniels nodded, face flushing at his error. "I will. My mind was on keeping the ravens out of it."

"You didn't notice anyone nearby?"

"Many people were in the area." Daniels shrugged. "But no one struck me as suspicious."

"The meat found on Pritchard was poisoned."

Daniels' eyes went wide. "With what?"

"Arsenic."

"Pritchard didn't mention anything to me about finding it."

"Tell me again when you last spoke with him." Henry pulled out his notebook. It often paid to ask the same question more than once to see if the person gave the same answer. He turned to the page he'd written his notes on Daniels and added a few more details but for the most part, the warder's answers didn't change.

"Are there any people other than the warders who walk past this area on a regular basis?"

"Mr. Elliott is always passing through. I've seen him watching the ravens on several occasions. Seems suspicious to me."

Henry nodded but wasn't it possible that Daniels was anxious to cast blame on someone other than himself? "Anyone else?"

Daniels thought for a moment then gave Henry the name of two other warders and pointed to where they could be found.

Unfortunately neither of them, nor any others who Henry asked, had seen anyone putting the meat on the lawn. Whoever had done it appeared to be invisible, if it had happened at all.

Already the day was proving to be frustrating, and the clock continued to tick. The time had come to pursue the particulars of the news sheet with the hope it would lead somewhere.

Thirteen

A melia waited until after breakfast before deciding to question Maeve again. The girl only ate a few spoonfuls of porridge, even with cinnamon and sugar sprinkled on top.

Yvette said Maeve had slept a little better than the previous night. At least that was a positive sign.

Once again, Amelia offered her hand and Maeve took it. Amelia led her to the lab, deciding she would distract her with an experiment and attempt a few questions while they worked. Of course, that would only be successful if she could convince Maeve to look at her.

They climbed the steps to the attic and entered the lab to don their aprons. Maeve turned to allow Amelia to tie hers just like before. The doll remained tucked beneath her arm or held tight against her chest.

Lily had liked to carry a doll as well, though she had several to choose from and switched them often.

When Amelia would ask where the other one was, she'd say, "She's resting, Mama."

The memory warmed Amelia even as it pinched her heart.

Amelia retrieved the beakers and a few supplies, uncertain what experiment might hold Maeve's interest. The girl stepped up on the stool and watched Amelia's preparations.

Deciding this was as good a time as any, she bent down to look at Maeve and took hold of her hand. "Maeve, can you tell me what scared you the other night?" She spoke slowly with the hope the girl could read her lips.

Maeve shook her head, lower lip quivering.

"Did you see something?"

The girl shook her head adamantly. Did that mean she had witnessed what happened but didn't want to talk about it?

"It's all right." Amelia brushed a hand over her hair. "You don't have to be scared now. You're safe. You can tell me."

Maeve shook her head even harder, sending tendrils of hair flying from her braid. She leaped off the stool and pulled the apron over her head as if she couldn't remove it quickly enough.

"Maeve." Amelia reached for her arm only wanting to comfort her, but the girl jerked away.

Her small chest heaved as sobs threatened. She ran out the open door of the lab and across the hall into the bedroom she shared with Yvette, shutting the door behind her.

Amelia sighed, almost wishing she hadn't asked. Yet they had to keep trying to find a way to convince Maeve to share what she knew.

One thing was clear. She'd seen something that still frightened her. That made it even more imperative that they continue to persuade her to share it.

After waiting several minutes, Amelia started to knock on Yvette's door before remembering Maeve wouldn't hear her. She opened the door to find the girl curled in a ball on the bed, holding her doll with her eyes squeezed shut.

Amelia's heart ached at the sight. She'd done much the same thing when first Lily had died and then Matthew, wanting to shut out the world because it hurt too much to remain a part of it.

But life continued, whether she'd wanted it to or not.

She sat on the edge of the bed and ran a hand over the girl's thin shoulder. How she wished Maeve could hear her.

However, there were other ways to offer comfort, and she continued the soothing motion for a minute or two then cradled the girl to draw her onto her lap. To her relief, Maeve stiffened but allowed Amelia to pull her close.

"I'm sorry, Maeve." While she knew the girl couldn't hear what she said, the words made Amelia feel better. "I'm so sorry. For everything." She rocked her back and forth, holding her tight.

Fourteen

Henry directed Fletcher to remain at the Tower to inquire whether any of the warders or the others who worked there were familiar with the news sheet *Justice*.

Meanwhile, Henry made his way to the office where the news sheet was printed.

It seemed likely that Pritchard wouldn't agree with the publication's beliefs. If the ravenkeeper had merely been picking up debris from the grounds as any Yeoman Warder might do, however, why wouldn't he have simply tossed it in a dustbin rather than fold it and place it in his pocket?

Of course, there was a chance he hadn't been near one or had been too busy to do so. There could be a perfectly innocent explanation. But it was still a clue Henry would follow to see where it led.

The shop on Fleet Street was unassuming. Small gold letters painted on the glass in the front window declared it Hyndman Publishing. Apparently, Mr. Hyndman made no secret of who was behind the news sheet.

Henry opened the door and was assailed by the clackety clack clamor of a printing press. The sharp scent of ink permeated the air. Not one but two printing presses took up most of the narrow space, along with two men working the presses while a third moved bundles of paper.

The third caught sight of Henry, set down the paper, and dusted off his hands as he walked forward. "Can I help you?"

"I wondered if you could tell me about this." Henry retrieved the paper from his pocket and held it out.

The slender man, who appeared to be in his thirties, reached to take it with ink-stained fingers. "*Justice*. That's one of our publications. Hard to say which edition when it's so faded. What is it you want to know?"

Why it had been in Pritchard's pocket—but the man was unlikely to have that answer.

"I'm Inspector Henry Field of Scotland Yard. We're investigating a murder."

The worker stiffened. "Who was killed?"

"Aberforth Pritchard, a ravenkeeper at the Tower. Did you know him?"

"No." He glanced over his shoulder at his fellow employees. "Do you want me to ask them?"

"Please." Henry watched as he walked to the first worker who leaned close to hear him over the rattle of the machine.

The worker shook his head, his gaze shifting to Henry as if curious. The man repeated the process with the other worker who also shook his head.

The man returned to Henry. "Sorry we can't be of assistance."

"Can you tell me about the news sheet?" At the man's blank look, Henry prompted, "How often is it printed?"

"Weekly."

"Who writes the articles?"

"Mr. Hyndman has several journalists and thinkers who supply them."

"And their focus?"

The man shrugged. "The advantages of Socialism, I suppose. I don't read it. I just print it."

"Does Mr. Marx provide articles as well?"

The man smirked. "Not directly."

"How do you mean?" Henry's curiosity was piqued, despite himself.

"Mr. Hyndman is an admirer of Marx and often summarizes some of his writings."

"Oh?" Henry waited, hoping the man would share more.

"If that's all, I need to return to work." The man glanced at the tall stacks of packets as if they were calling his name.

But Henry wasn't finished. "How is the paper distributed?"

The man shrugged. "The usual way. After they're printed, boys pick them up and either hand them out on street corners or leave them at newsstands."

"How much do they cost?"

"The publication is free to anyone who wants it."

"Who pays for the printing?"

"Mr. Hyndman and several of his associates."

It was an expensive way to spread an idea. "Do you have a list of subscribers?"

"That's something you'd have to ask Mr. Hyndman. We don't have it." The man raised a brow, clearly ready to be finished with the conversation.

"Is *Justice* the only publication printed here?"

"No, we print several along with other items."

Perhaps Hyndman funded his efforts with those.

Henry glanced toward the back of the space, noting what looked to be an office. "I'd like to speak with Mr. Hyndman."

The man shook his head. "He doesn't spend much time here. You'd have better luck trying his home."

Henry took down the address. "Thank you for your time." With a dip of his head, he took his leave, thoughts circling to find a connection between Pritchard and the news sheet with little success. A conversation with Hyndman might help provide a connection.

Hyndman's home was only a few streets away in a well-to-do neighborhood, but the man wasn't home. The servant who answered the door couldn't say for certain when he'd return.

With a sigh, Henry paused outside to study the surrounding area as he considered what action to take next.

Thus far, it was clear that Pritchard had left the Tower grounds in search of a raven. He'd most likely been alerted by the other birds that something was amiss. The ravenkeeper had left the gate unlocked and his daughter had woken and followed him. Fine. That was all logical.

What happened after that was less clear. Who had he encountered outside the gate in the middle of the night? Why had that person thought Pritchard a threat? Why did he carry the poisoned meat and the news sheet in his pockets?

He'd been killed near the top of the stairs, but his lantern—identified by Wallace—had been found on the bank of the Thames. That either meant he'd been on the bank with the lantern in search of the raven, then set it down and returned up the stairs for some reason...or whoever had killed him had taken the lantern down to the bank when they'd dumped the body in the water. Perhaps they'd meant to toss it in with him or maybe they'd needed light to see what they were doing.

It was unlikely that Pritchard had meant to poison the ravens, so he must've found the meat, along with the paper. That he'd kept both items had to mean something, but what?

The ravenkeeper's daughter remained the best potential source of information. He had to find a way to communicate with the girl.

If anyone could get through to Maeve, it would be Amelia Greystone. He had every reason to believe what she'd said the previous evening: that she had a strong constitution despite—or perhaps because of—all she'd been through.

The woman might be reluctant to press Maeve for information given the child's upset, but they couldn't wait. He needed to solve this case quickly for her sake, her father's, and his own. Having another unsolved murder on his hands placed his reputation into question, given his last name. He couldn't bear to think what his father would say if that came to pass. The concern had his stomach burning.

Just over a quarter of an hour later, he was waiting for Fernsby to announce him at the Greystone residence. She was proving to be quite helpful on the case. His respect and admiration for her continued to grow. How ironic that the reason he knew her was because of her husband's unsolved case.

The lady who'd conducted the test with skill and efficiency was quite different than the brittle shell she'd been in the days following her husband's murder.

"Mrs. Greystone is awaiting you in the drawing room," Fernsby advised when he returned.

"Thank you." Henry hurried up the stairs.

"Good morning, Inspector." Mrs. Greystone stood near the window with Maeve beside her.

The greeting jolted him. *Morning?* It felt as if the day should nearly be over rather than still before noon. "Good morning."

The lady wore a gray gown that flattered her slender figure. He was relieved to see she looked well rested and in good spirits. He'd hate for the situation to wear on her.

His focus shifted to Maeve, disappointed to see the same distant look on her face as she stared blankly across the room, her doll under one arm.

Mrs. Greystone followed his gaze. "I attempted a few questions this morning. Suffice it to say that it did not go well." She put her hand on Maeve's shoulder as she spoke.

Disappointment rolled through him at the news. "How unfortunate."

"Yes. Very." She gestured toward the chairs. "Would you care to join us?"

"Thank you." He sat in a chair, searching for a way to learn what she knew. "May I ask how she reacted?"

She shared the details, explaining how it had taken nearly an hour to convince Maeve to leave the bedroom.

"Clearly, she saw something," Henry began.

"I thought the same." Mrs. Greystone worried her lower lip. "If only she could tell us what."

"The longer we wait, the less chance we have of solving this."

"I know." The understanding in her eyes was reassuring. "You're welcome to try to see if she reacts differently to you."

"Very well." He studied the girl again.

Only three days had passed since her father's murder. That was hardly enough time to lessen Maeve's grief, but he hoped it had at least eased the sharp edge of shock. "I wish we didn't have to press her."

"So do I." Though Mrs. Greystone seemed resigned to the fact. "No other clues have surfaced?"

"None that have yielded results as of yet."

"How unfortunate." She raised a brow at him expectantly.

Henry rose to kneel before Maeve and placed a hand on her shoulder, willing her to look at him.

It took a full minute but at last she did. The somberness in the brown depths of her eyes tightened his chest. "Maeve, did you see someone hurt your father?"

Tears filled the girl's eyes, and her face crumpled.

The ache in his chest sharpened. Henry placed both hands on her upper arms, partly to provide comfort and partly to encourage her to continue to meet his gaze.

"Did you see who hurt your father?"

Maeve hesitated as tears ran down her cheeks. Then she slowly nodded.

A rush of relief followed by regret flooded through him. How terrible for her to see the only person she loved in her small world violently killed. But if it was possible for her to identify the person, he could bring him to justice.

"Do you know who?"

At that, the girl turned her head away and drew back. Henry released his hold and watched helplessly as she ran from the room.

"Oh dear." Mrs. Greystone pressed a handkerchief to her nose, her eyes rimmed with red as if she were on the verge of tears. "Poor Maeve."

"Indeed."

"That's more than she told me. Perhaps she's starting to realize we're trying to help."

"I hope that as well." He stood and looked around. Should he go?

"Would you care to join us for luncheon?"

Surprised by the invitation, Henry hesitated. "If it's not any trouble."

"None at all. Perhaps if you spend a little more time with her, she'll share more." Mrs. Greystone glanced toward where Maeve had disappeared. "If she'll leave her room. I'll see how she's faring."

Henry watched her hurry out then released a breath, wondering how best to proceed.

Had Maeve seen whoever had killed her father well enough to recognize him? After all, it had been a foggy night. That she hadn't returned home the night of the murder could suggest that she recognized whoever had done it.

He needed another clue. There was a chance that whoever had tried to poison the ravens would make another attempt since the first two had been unsuccessful. He'd warn Daniels to keep a sharp eye out as another method might be used to harm them. Unless of course, it was Daniels himself who was the poisoner.

It might prove helpful to look into the political party that the publication represented. Surely they held meetings. Perhaps they kept a list of members he could obtain—the list of subscribers that the printer had mentioned.

He turned from where he stood at the window to see Mrs. Greystone in the doorway.

Without Maeve.

He lifted a brow, and she shook her head. "Maeve won't be able to join us. She's still too upset. The maid is sitting with her for a time."

Henry nodded, unsurprised but disappointed all the same. "I hope we can convince her to help us."

"As do I, the poor dear."

Fifteen

That evening after dinner, Amelia settled with a book by the fire in the drawing room. The day had been a long one with emotional pulls difficult to navigate. While tired, she needed to unwind before turning in for the night. She'd written another letter to her parents to share the basics of the situation but remained restless.

Maeve was with Yvette in the kitchen, who was finishing her chores for the evening. The girl seemed to enjoy watching the servants go about their work, helping when requested. Perhaps the busyness provided a distraction from her thoughts.

She and Maeve had spent the afternoon in the drawing room. Amelia had an interview scheduled with the oldest clockmaker in London in two days' time and had worked on the questions she wanted to ask about the history of clockmaking, and the family behind the small shop that had been in business for over one hundred years. Meanwhile, Maeve had drawn with paper and pencil and looked through some magazines. Amelia wondered if she might sketch something from the night her father had been murdered but instead, she'd drawn pictures of the ravens he'd tended.

Watching over the girl created a tumult of emotions hourly testing Amelia's fortitude. She was reminded time and again that Lily would nearly be Maeve's age. Thoughts of the moments she'd never share with her daughter made her ache. Normally, she did her best not to dwell on such things but being with Maeve made that nearly impossible.

Maeve hadn't known her mother and now she'd lost her father. Her life would've been difficult enough, given her inability to speak or hear, but now it would be doubly so. Amelia's heart—what was left of it—went out to the girl.

The highs and lows of the last few days had been something Amelia had tried to avoid since losing first Lily and then Matthew. Even Inspector Field's eyes had held shadows after trying to talk to Maeve that morning.

Amelia appreciated how patient he'd been with the girl. He was kind but also authoritative. Too much sympathy wouldn't help Maeve.

It hadn't helped Amelia when Lily had died either.

Mrs. Fernsby bustled into the room with a tray in hand, a welcome interruption from her thoughts. "I took the liberty of bringing you a bit of the chamomile tea you like so well, Mrs. Greystone."

"How thoughtful of you." Amelia smiled as the housekeeper placed the tray with its teapot and cup on the table. "That is just what I needed."

"Nothing like a good book and a cup of tea before the fire on an autumn evening." The housekeeper's gaze swept the room to make certain all was in order.

"Indeed." Amelia didn't want to admit that the book she'd started the previous week had failed to keep her interest this evening. She'd read the same page twice without remembering what it said. But the book wasn't at fault.

Seemingly satisfied with her inspection, the housekeeper returned her attention to Amelia. "I suppose we can expect Inspector Field to return tomorrow?"

He had spoken to Maeve again before he'd left after luncheon. He'd smiled at the girl and knelt before her to tell her that he would speak with her again soon. Amelia thought it wise of him to prepare her for his return. Hopefully, she understood that meant more questions about what she'd witnessed. Hopefully they'd receive more answers.

"Yes. He's anxious to determine what she saw the night her father was murdered."

Mrs. Fernsby shook her head, her expression sympathetic. "Poor dear. As difficult as the situation must be for her, I hope she can communicate something that will help find who did it."

"As do I."

"Well, the inspector seems proficient at his job. We shall hope he can solve it."

Amelia appreciated her confidence in Inspector Field but wished he'd found Matthew's murderer. How could she ever move forward with it still hanging over her?

"May I get you anything else?"

"No, this is lovely. Thank you."

Mrs. Fernsby departed, leaving Amelia to the tea and her thoughts. She closed the book and set it aside to pour herself a cup, allowing her thoughts to drift as she stared into the fire.

The cheerfully burning flames never failed to soothe her. The combination of a fire's warmth and a cup of hot tea had seen her through many difficult days.

Thank goodness Maeve had family. Amelia hoped she was close to them, yet worried they'd want to take Maeve away before they'd learned what she'd seen the night of the murder.

It wasn't long before Amelia felt the tight knot of worry that had settled in her shoulders loosen and her body relax. Hopefully she'd be able to sleep now.

She finished her tea then picked up the book and rose. Fernsby would see to the fire before he retired. Amelia walked to the window to adjust the drapes, pausing to look out.

Her heart sped at the sight of a man standing on the opposite side of the street just visible in the faint glow of the streetlight. She was careful not to open the drapes too far as she stared at him.

Though it was impossible to know, she had the distinct impression that he was watching the house.

"Mrs. Greystone?"

She jerked at the sound of Fernsby's voice and spun to face him, one hand pressed to her pounding heart. "You startled me."

"My apologies, madam." He frowned. "Is something amiss?"

She drew a breath to help calm her nerves. "There's a man across the street. It almost looks as if he's watching the house." She glanced over her shoulder at the window, wondering if she'd imagined it, almost hoping she had.

"Oh?" Fernsby joined her and peeked through the parted drapes. "That is rather suspicious."

She shared a worried look with him, uncertain what action to take. *Someone watching the house? Why?*

"May I suggest that we let him know that he is not doing so unobserved?" Fernsby asked.

"Excellent idea."

Fernsby nodded and drew back one side of the drapes with a bold swish. The movement must've caught the man's attention for he looked up at the window.

The outline of his bowler hat was visible but little else. He stared at them for a moment and then tugged the brim of his hat and walked away.

Unease crept along Amelia's spine as she shared a concerned look with Fernsby.

"I will make doubly certain the doors are locked and bolted. More than likely, his presence has little to do with us." The butler turned to go only to look back, his brow furrowed, an unusually serious expression for the man who had served her so long. "Perhaps we should advise Inspector Field of this tomorrow."

Amelia nodded. "Yes, we should."

"Meanwhile, we shall remain on guard, Mrs. Greystone. You may rest easy."

"Thank you, Fernsby. I appreciate it."

He took his leave, but Amelia remained to peer out the window one last time. There was no sign of the man, but he could easily have hidden in the shadows.

The locks had been replaced soon after Matthew's death, something Inspector Field had suggested. Amelia had been terrified then at the idea that whoever had killed her husband might attempt to break into the house.

The fear had weighed on Amelia's mind in the weeks and months following his death. But her worry had been for nothing. No one had tried to break in, though she had felt certain someone watched the house on more than one occasion.

Amelia forced herself to stop looking only a few months ago. It had felt a foolish notion—though foolish no longer. She stretched her shoulders, unsurprised to sense the tension from earlier in the day had returned. Did whoever was out there have an interest in her or Maeve? In truth, it didn't matter as it concerned her either way.

Amelia closed the drapes, telling herself that she and Maeve were safe. She only hoped it was true.

Sixteen

The morning started earlier than normal after Henry slept poorly. Unanswered questions regarding Pritchard's murder and how to communicate with Maeve circled his thoughts. Rather than continue tossing and turning, he rose and headed to Scotland Yard.

Despite the early hour, other inspectors and constables were already coming and going. Clearly, he wasn't the only one who wanted to accomplish more than a normal workday allowed.

He settled at his desk to read through the information on the stolen jewelry case he'd been assigned. Solving a murder took precedence, but he couldn't ignore his other assignments for long. Juggling numerous cases was one of the many challenges of being a detective.

Another crime always waited in the wings to claim his attention. Perhaps he could continue his inquiries into Pritchard's murder as well as the theft if he was careful with his time.

Henry carefully read the notes provided by a constable who reported that an entire jewelry box filled with valuables had been taken from Lady Somerset's bedroom during a dinner party. Lord Somerset wanted the box and its contents returned but did not care to offend his guests by having them questioned about the theft.

Unfortunately, there wasn't a way to avoid doing so unless the jewelry made a sudden reappearance.

Henry would speak with the servants, of course. But the guests would need to be questioned sooner rather than later if another clue didn't emerge.

Lady Somerset had provided a sketch of three of the pieces when she'd spoken to the constable. A stop by a few better-known pawnbrokers might turn up a clue as several of the stolen pieces were distinctive.

When he and Fletcher called on the pawnbrokers that morning, Henry could also speak with one or two of his regular contacts in the area to see if they'd heard anything helpful about the ravenkeeper's death.

There was always the chance whoever had killed him would tell someone else. It never failed to amaze Henry how quickly the rumor mill spread across London, especially when a grisly murder was involved. Little thrilled the public more.

He reviewed several other case files and jotted down instructions for three constables, certain they could deal with initial inquiries.

"Morning, Field." Joseph Perdy, a fellow detective, sauntered up to Henry's desk a short time later. "Director Reynolds wants to see you. Are you in trouble again?"

Perdy was nearly five years his senior and had just that much more experience. He considered himself wiser as well, although Henry had doubts as to the man's claim of that particular trait. The detective was quick to point out any mistake Henry made, real or imagined. It wasn't always easy to ignore the jabs the other inspector made.

"Let us hope not." Henry said curtly, rising to his feet. Since he didn't care to continue the conversation with Perdy, the sooner he saw the Director, the better.

Perdy chuckled. "Better you than me, Field. No need to worry though. I'm sure your father can put in a good word for you."

Henry didn't bother to respond. He'd heard the comment too many times before.

But as Henry knew, no one could 'fix' an unsolved case. Perdy couldn't have found Matthew Greystone's killer either. Not when the few clues had led nowhere, and the trail had gone cold.

However, a quiet voice in the back of his head suggested that his father and grandfather would have.

Would he ever feel he compared favorably to them?

Doubtful.

But that wasn't his purpose, he reminded himself. His goal was to be the best detective he could be, to bring justice to those wronged.

To make certain good prevailed over evil.

It sounded ridiculous, but the sentiment was how he felt. He supposed it was ingrained in him since he was a third-generation detective, even if his skills were learned rather than inherited.

He liked thinking of himself as a guardian of good, someone who helped to tip the scales in its favor.

Henry had prided himself on not becoming emotionally involved with the people connected to his cases. Doing so hindered objectivity and swayed views, keeping one from seeing the truth even when it became clear.

Yet he found that goal difficult when it came to Amelia Greystone and now Maeve Pritchard as well. They lingered in his mind at all hours of the day and night. That was even more motivation to solve their cases.

He knocked on the open door of Reynolds' office and stepped inside. "You wanted to see me, sir?"

The Director looked up from the paper he'd been reading to study Henry, his spectacles already smudged despite the relatively early hour. "Field. How's progress on the death at the Tower?"

"I intend to visit the owner of the news sheet to see where that leads. And I'll speak with the victim's daughter again today as well."

"Who did the test on the poisoning you mentioned?"

"Actually, Mrs. Greystone performed it."

"What are her qualifications?" Reynolds asked with a frown.

"She has significant knowledge in chemistry and her own laboratory." Why he bristled in her defense, he did not know.

"Hmm." Reynolds looked less than convinced. "We'll hope her results aren't a key component of the case. It's doubtful that testing by a woman whose hobby is chemistry will be sufficient."

"I would argue she's more than a hobbyist based on what I saw. She clearly knows what she's doing. Her lab is impressive as well."

"All the same, you'd better confirm the presence of arsenic with a reputable chemist."

"Yes, sir." A waste of time, when it was clear to Henry that Mrs. Greystone was more than competent.

"Anything new from the daughter?"

His shoulders straightened. "She has confirmed she saw her father killed. Whether she can identify the killer is questionable given the darkness and fog that evening, not to mention her fright. But we will continue to encourage her to share what she saw." Unfortunately, he didn't yet know how.

Reynolds nodded, though the twist of his lips suggested he wanted more. So did Henry. "Anything else?"

"Not at the moment."

"As you know, anything that happens at the Tower gains the public's attention. I would prefer not to receive a message from the Home Secretary asking why we haven't made an arrest."

"Agreed." Henry's stomach tightened at the thought. The Home Secretary had been acquainted with his grandfather and his father as well. Heaven forbid if the man asked his father to assist with the case. That was something Henry would never live down.

His grandfather's advice had always been "feet on the ground" as if walking the streets long enough would yield results. Sometimes it did, but that was only one method to gain information.

"Did the postmortem report confirm the weapon used?"

"A six-inch blade, most likely a dagger of some sort. A smooth blade rather than serrated. The excessive number of wounds suggest anger or frustration by the murderer. Or perhaps enjoyment."

"Hmm. More than likely wielded by someone who knows how to use it," Reynolds suggested.

"Yes. The slices were precise with no hesitation in the strokes."

Henry hoped that would help lead to the man's identity, though many trades required expertise with a knife, including butchers, glovers, hatters, and tanners to name a few.

Reynolds stared into the distance for a moment before looking back at Henry, his expression one of concern. "I look forward to hearing more results soon."

"As do I, sir." Henry dipped his head and took his leave.

The mention of the Home Secretary increased the pressure to solve the case when he already felt enough as it was. He needed to set aside the concern and focus on the next steps to take. Once he determined a motive, the identity of the murderer would follow.

He returned to his desk to retrieve his notes on the jewelry case, pleased when he looked up to see Fletcher standing before him.

"Morning." The sergeant skimmed the paper Henry held out and lifted a brow. "We're switching to a new case?"

"No." Henry huffed with irritation that his attention was being pulled away from the murder investigation. "We're combining efforts."

"How efficient of us." Fletcher's eyes twinkled.

"Shall we?" Henry nodded toward the door.

"Lead the way."

Soon they were walking toward Victoria Street where one of the more popular pawnbrokers was located. A hansom cab might be quicker, but Henry saved his money for times when speed was of the essence. The twenty-five-minute walk would give him and Fletcher time to discuss both cases.

While shops like T.M. Suttons were unlikely to purchase stolen jewelry, they might've been approached by whoever had taken it. Perhaps they would recognize the sketches Henry had tucked in his pocket.

"Let us review what we know about the murder," Henry said. Building a story around what might have happened often proved helpful to develop possible motives. Sharing it with Fletcher tested his logic and allowed them to fill in any holes, or at the very least, confirm what they still needed to discover.

Fletcher nodded.

"So. Pritchard was murdered not far from where he exited the Tower grounds at the top of the stairs."

"While searching for one of the damned ravens." Fletcher's tone suggested he thought that a shame.

"Yes. Most likely he heard them causing a fuss. He threw on his coat, collected his keys and a lantern, then left the grounds leaving the gate unlocked. His daughter woke and followed him."

"How is the girl?" Fletcher asked.

"Still too upset to share what she knows."

"If she knows anything."

"She's confirmed that she witnessed the murder. Whether she knows who did it or could recognize the person remains to be seen."

Henry shook his head as sympathy for the girl rose once again. "I will speak with her again later today. Yesterday's attempt did not go especially well."

"Unfortunate. It's difficult enough when children are involved in a crime, let alone one who's deaf and mute."

"Quite." Henry returned to his mental list. "We have the meat laced with arsenic."

"Attempted not once but twice, we think. Assumedly to kill a raven or two."

"But why?" Henry had an idea but wanted to hear whether Fletcher had others.

Fletcher lifted one shoulder in a half-hearted shrug. "Other than the legend, no reason I can think of."

"Have there been any reports of them harming a visitor?"

"No. I suppose there's a chance it wasn't reported, or that a raven killed someone's favorite pet, and they wanted revenge." Fletcher's audible doubt made it obvious he thought that unlikely.

"In which case, the meat has nothing to do with the ravenkeeper's death?" Henry waited to see if Fletcher's opinion on that matched his own.

"I don't think so." Fletcher scowled as he kept pace with Henry. "Too much of a coincidence."

Henry hid a smile. That was exactly what he thought. "Then why did someone try it again *after* Pritchard's death?"

"Because...because while related, one isn't dependent on the other."

"Agreed." Henry paused as they wound through passersby on the pavement until they were able to walk abreast again, deciding to set aside the topic of the ravens for a moment. "The motive for murder is most often money. However, I think we can rule that out in this case."

"Yes. The second most common reason is a family disagreement. That isn't likely either."

"Right. I continue to think Pritchard overheard something he shouldn't, given what we've been told about his propensity for eavesdropping. He was searching for the raven along the riverbank, heard something then shut off the lantern, which we can assume since it still contained fuel. He left it on the bank and returned up the stairs—"

"—where someone cut him to pieces before dragging him back down the stairs to the river and then tossed him in." Fletcher's moustache twitched. Perhaps the memory of the state of the body still upset him.

"Yes." Henry pondered the information. "Blast it, I keep returning to the poisoning of the ravens."

"What purpose would it have served if they'd been successful? Why try to stir superstition?" Fletcher asked.

"To show England is unstable." It was the only possible explanation.

The sergeant halted abruptly to stare at Henry, eyes wide in surprise. "Do you truly think that is their purpose?"

"It's only a guess. But you must admit it's possible."

"Perhaps. But an unsettling idea to consider." Fletcher started forward only to stop again. "That would tie in the news sheet we found in Pritchard's pocket."

"It would." Having Fletcher confirm his assumptions was reassuring. He might be on the right path, even if he still didn't have any true answers.

Fletcher nodded as they started forward again. "There is a logical connection between those clues. Did you learn anything of interest at the printing office?"

"Not particularly. It sounds as if the man behind the news sheet has created a few enemies, though I don't know if that's relevant to the case." He didn't add that he learned those details from a conversation with his father. "He wasn't home when I called, but I intend to try again to see if he can shed any light."

They soon arrived at T.M. Sutton. The black painted storefront was well maintained. Small gold lettering on either side of the name on the window proclaimed them a goldsmith and jeweler as well as diamond merchant. Three golden balls were in one corner, a symbol of pawnbrokers. Henry had always liked the story that the balls represented St. Nicholas, who saved three young girls by loaning them each a bag of gold so they could marry and avoid destitution. Whether it was true...perhaps it was just as apocryphal as the ravens.

The front window displayed silver vases and flatware along with jewelry of various types. Nothing of significant value that could be grabbed if the glass was smashed, but sparkly enough to catch the eye of potential customers walking by.

Henry opened the door to see business was brisk inside the shop. They were well known for their discretion and not only sold fine jewelry and wares but provided loans to those with something to pawn in exchange.

Pawnbrokers were required to follow strict rules and provided a way for the poor to obtain loans. But even kings used their services, including Edward III, who pawned items in the Middle Ages to raise money to wage war with France.

This wasn't Henry's first visit to the establishment, and he nodded at the familiar clerk who stepped forward to greet them.

"Good morning, Inspector." The clerk looked at Fletcher. "Sergeant." He glanced around to see if any customers were concerned by their presence. Talking with the police wasn't exactly reassuring to customers.

"Morning. I'm wondering if you've seen anything like this." Henry handed him the sketch.

"Lovely pieces." The clerk frowned. "Can't say that I have. Shall I show it to the other clerks?"

"I'd appreciate it."

Fletcher fidgeted while they waited, heaving a frustrated sigh when one after another of the clerks shook their heads. "Why is nothing ever easy?"

"Excellent question—one I've considered often throughout the years without an answer." Henry thanked the man and returned the sketch to his pocket. "It's a good thing we got an early start to our day. Looks like we'll be visiting a few more shops."

Seventeen

Henry and Fletcher tried two more pawnbrokers without success, then visited Lord Somerset who quickly shared his frustration that it had taken so long for a detective to call on him regarding the theft.

"My apologies, my lord," Henry said. "A murder investigation has taken most of our time the last few days. You are, of course, our twin priority."

"Hmm." The older man pursed his thin lips as if undecided whether that was an acceptable explanation.

Lord Somerset proceeded to repeat the same details the constable had noted in his report. Twelve guests had been at the dinner party, four family members and the rest longtime friends. None could've possibly stolen the jewelry, according to the lord.

"Inconceivable," he said with a shake of his head.

The box was kept in his wife's bedroom in a drawer, although it was unclear whether it had been left out after the lady selected the items she'd chosen to wear that evening.

Unfortunately Lady Somerset wasn't at home and couldn't be questioned. Lord Somerset insisted that was unnecessary, but of course, it was.

"Who do you think could've taken it?" Henry asked.

"How should I know? Isn't that your job to discover?" Lord Somerset's displeasure with the question was obvious. "Clearly someone must've entered the house and stolen the box while we were at dinner."

That theory seemed unlikely when none of the servants had seen anyone. Henry spoke with the butler and the housekeeper and neither had any ideas as to who might've taken it.

Henry and Fletcher left with the promise to return the following morning to speak with Lady Somerset...but without having learned anything new. That only worsened Henry's frustration at dealing with the case when he had a more important one to solve.

Luckily, the Somerset residence wasn't far from the street corner where the flower lady worked, who was one of Henry's contacts. The lady knew everyone and often heard gossip from sources she rarely divulged.

Instead of the person he was expecting, a young girl emerged from an alleyway holding a basket of white and pink carnations nearly as big as she was. She was definitely not the flower lady Henry was in search of.

"Flower for yer lady, sir?" the girl asked, wearing a striped frock and a black chip bonnet, both of which had seen better days.

"You might have more success if you ask those who actually have a lady accompanying them." Henry shared an amused look with Fletcher before looking back at the girl.

The girl's brow wrinkled as she stared at him, head tilted to the side as she attempted to puzzle out his meaning.

"Thank you, but no flowers for us today," Henry added when she continued to look expectantly at him. It had been a long while since he'd had anyone other than his mother for whom he'd consider buying flowers.

"Sarah, try the gents just down the way." An older lady stepped out of the alleyway, also holding a basket of flowers, though hers was piled high with roses in various shades. "These men don't have need of our flowers. Not today anyways."

"Madam." Henry dipped his head at the familiar woman, who wore a bright red shawl wrapped around her thin shoulders. Her brown wool gown matched her hair and her eyes. Whether there was a husband somewhere was something he'd never been able to determine. The lady had always been protective of her personal life. "I hope the day finds you well."

"Well enough, I suppose." Her focus shifted to the girl, watching to make certain she followed the order.

"Isn't she rather young to start in the business?" The girl couldn't have been more than five or six years of age. Certainly younger than Maeve by the look of her.

The older lady smiled but it wasn't a happy one "It's never too early to earn yer keep."

The thought was a dismal one though unfortunately true for those who lived in this neighborhood. That the impoverished and the wealthy lived so near one another never failed to amaze Henry.

"What brings you by today, Inspector?" She glanced at Fletcher but quickly dismissed him.

"I wondered if you'd heard anything about the ravenkeeper's murder."

"A death at the Tower always creates a stir, doesn't it?" Her grin was out of place for the morbid topic.

"It does. Finding who did it would as well."

"Perhaps. Rumor says he was sliced to bits. Is that true?"

Henry shared a look with Fletcher. How those sorts of details spread was a frustrating mystery when only a limited number of people were privy to the specifics of the case. Granted, yesterday's headline mentioned a slasher, but the article hadn't detailed the numerous cuts on the body. He and Fletcher had deliberately not told the people they'd questioned and asked Chief Yeoman Warder Wallace not to disclose it either.

Someone had a loose tongue.

"Is anyone claiming responsibility?" Henry asked, unwilling to confirm the rumor.

A cunning look entered the woman's expression. "What's an answer worth to ye?"

"I'd make it worth your while." Henry waited, hope building despite the voice in his head that cautioned him otherwise. That was often a criminal's first mistake; crowing over it in one of the taverns.

She glanced between the two of them. "Being as both of ye came to ask, I'd hazard a guess that it's important." She adjusted the basket she held as if to draw out the moment. "I can't say as I heard, not yet, but if I do, I'll send word."

Henry released the breath he'd been holding as disappointment washed over him. "I'd appreciate it."

"Yer a handsome one, Inspector." She smiled again. "I have hope that one of these days, ye'll be coming by to purchase some roses fer a lady. Don't disappoint me."

That seemed unlikely, but he smiled and touched the brim of his hat. "Let me know if you hear anything."

She nodded and he and Fletcher moved on.

"How did she know about the cuts?" Fletcher shook his head. "Difficult to keep secrets in this business."

"Especially when it involves murder."

Next they stopped by a fishmonger who'd also proven helpful in the past. The disadvantage of speaking with the man was the smell. Much like visiting Mr. Taylor's, it was best to breathe through one's mouth when near the open market stall.

"The topic is on everyone's lips, rumors abound, but no one seems to know the truth." The stout man with a grizzled face leaned close. "There's a wager at the Bull and Oar Tavern on the identity of the killer. I'd appreciate any hints you can provide as I have yet to place my bet."

"Do you think we'd be asking if we knew?" Fletcher frowned at the man.

"Come now, you must have an idea. I could use the extra money if I won."

"We can't help you." Henry shook his head. "Send word if you hear anything, and I'll reward you for it. Double the wager."

The man gave a curt nod, clearly disappointed.

"This isn't going particularly well." Fletcher patted his belly. "Perhaps it's time to quench our thirst and have luncheon while we ask a few questions at the Bull and Oar."

"Excellent idea," Henry agreed with a wry smile.

The Tower wasn't far, and it made sense that whoever had killed Pritchard might live in the area and frequent the tavern.

Fletcher led the way down the street and turned left at a crossroads to where the establishment had stood for decades. Business was brisk as many stopped by for a pint and a meat pie for their luncheon.

Henry pointed to a thankfully empty table near the door, and they took a seat. He studied those around them until a serving maid approached.

"What can I get for you two fine gents?" she asked with a smile and raised brow.

"Two meat pies and two pints." Fletcher returned her smile, his gaze taking in her generous bosom revealed by a low neckline that dipped even lower as she ran a damp rag over the tabletop.

"Very well." She moved to the next table, graceful in her movements as she worked her way back to the bar to place their order, gathering empty glasses and chatting with customers as she went.

"Efficiency in motion," Fletcher murmured as he watched.

"Interesting how often women are exactly that." Henry wasn't above watching her either.

"What is our plan for the afternoon?" Fletcher asked.

"I'd like you to return to the Tower in case anything interesting has arisen." Four days since the murder. Memories would start to fade. They had to collect every detail they could.

"Anyone specific I should speak with?"

"Daniels again, for one. Be sure to see how the ravens are today."

Before Fletcher could respond, the serving maid returned to deposit two pints on the table, the contents sloshing near the rim but not spilling over. She was gone before they had time to thank her.

"Who else?" Fletcher asked before taking a drink.

"Let's dig into the details of those who work in the Tower but aren't yeoman warders, such as Elliott from the Mint and Blackwell from the Armoury and any others you can find. How long have they been there? What hours do they keep? What loyalties? Any other details you think might be relevant."

"Shall I check in with Wallace as well?"

"Yes," Henry said with a nod. "I'm going to the Greystone residence again to see if Maeve can give us any details."

"Wouldn't that be helpful." Fletcher's expression made it clear he thought it unlikely.

Henry held out hope. Even if she couldn't identify the killer, a few details could help point them in the right direction. A rough age. A description of clothing, anything.

"I'd hoped Wallace might know of someone who carried that particular type of blade, but he couldn't think of anyone," Fletcher said as he stared out a nearby window. "Men with knives often like to show them off, not to mention display their skill."

"Unless they have a tendency to use it to hurt others." Henry sipped his drink as he considered the subject. "That might make them more prone to secrecy about their skill."

But Fletcher had a point. Men who enjoyed wielding knives like the suspected murder weapon practiced with them and not necessarily in private. Someone might have noticed it.

The maid quickly returned with their steaming meat pies, the scent emphasizing with a jolt in the stomach just how hungry Henry was.

Before the woman could depart, he slid a coin across the table. "We're looking for something else. Information."

"Oh?" She eyed the coin but didn't reach for it, clearly wanting to know what it would cost her.

"We understand there's a wager about who is behind the murder at the Tower."

She frowned as she looked between Henry and Fletcher. "Aren't you the police? Surely you're supposed to know who did it."

"If we knew, there wouldn't be a need for a wager, now would there?" Fletcher's exasperation was clear.

Her lips twisted as she considered, then nodded. "True enough. I'll send the owner over. He's the one keeping track of the bets." She returned to the bar, swathing a different path through the tables this time.

Henry and Fletcher started on the meat pies as they watched her speak with the barkeep who glanced in their direction and nodded but continued to fill drink orders. He arrived at their table just as they finished their meal.

"Got a question?" the brawny man asked with a lazy grin. "Or do you wish to place a wager?"

"Who do most think did it?" Henry asked.

"Wouldn't be fair if I told you, would it?"

"It would since we're not wagering." Henry tapped the coin that still sat on the table. "We'd be happy to add to the pot though."

The owner hesitated only a moment before pocketing the coin. "A few are convinced it must be the Irishman. Others think it's one of the warders."

"Who's the Irishman?" Henry asked.

"Don't know his name as he only comes around occasionally. But he carries a sticker that would make anyone think twice about crossing him."

"What does the knife look like?"

"Does that mean it's true?" He raised a bushy brow. "The victim was sliced up good, then?"

"We aren't at liberty to share any details." Henry waited to see if the owner would answer the question.

The man shrugged. "I only caught a glimpse of it once. Some sort of dagger. It's long compared to what most men might carry, which is why it caught my eye."

"How long?" Fletcher asked.

The owner shook his head. "Difficult to say from a glance. Six or seven inches, I suppose."

"What else can you tell us about him?" Henry asked.

"Tall. Near your age, I would say. Dark hair. Dresses nicely. Carries the knife in a worn leather scabbard on his hip."

"Where does he live?" Try as he might, Henry couldn't keep his voice unconcerned. *Near his age. A knife of the right length...*

"Don't know. He's a bit secretive, comes in alone most of the time. But he's here often enough that he must live or work in the area."

"You don't know where he works?"

"No. He's quiet for an Irishman. Only has a hint of a brogue."

It wasn't much to go on but more than what they had so far. After a few more questions, none of which the owner could answer, Henry and Fletcher departed.

"The Irishman might be a possibility," Henry said as they paused outside the tavern.

"Daniels has a hint of an Irish accent," Fletcher pointed out.

"True. But it seems doubtful that he secretly carries a knife like the one we're looking for."

Fletcher scowled as he studied the street. "You're right. We need to know more about the Irishman, but how?"

"Ask a few other businesses in the area on your way back to the Tower," Henry suggested. "Then ask there, too."

"Very well. Good luck with the ravenkeeper's daughter."

"Thanks. I have no doubt I'll need it."

Eighteen

"Inspector Field, madam," Fernsby announced from the doorway of the drawing room as the afternoon sun broke through the clouds.

Amelia breathed a sigh of relief. She'd hoped he would arrive earlier to try again to speak with Maeve. With each hour that passed, her nerves had drawn tighter and tighter as she considered the reasons someone had been watching the house last evening.

"Will you bring in Maeve, please?" she asked the butler.

"Of course, madam."

Knowing that Fernsby had come to the same conclusion about the stranger they'd both seen was reassuring. Otherwise, she might've blamed her imagination for his presence.

She hated to admit how many times she'd looked out the window already to see if he'd returned. Then again, just because she couldn't see anyone didn't mean he, or someone else, wasn't watching.

Maeve was in the kitchen again, assisting the cook to make biscuits. Mrs. Appleton had managed to convince her to help roll out the dough rather than merely watching. Her slow, careful movements as she pushed the rolling pin suggested she wasn't accustomed to it. Hopefully that meant the simple task occupied her attention. Amelia knew from painful experience that it was imperative to pull one's thoughts away from overwhelming grief and trauma.

Amelia rose as Inspector Field entered the room. His calm, capable demeanor helped to ease her worry. He had a soothing manner that must be an advantage in his line of work when dealing with overwrought victims or their loved ones. It had certainly helped her when Matthew died.

"Good afternoon, Inspector."

He studied her for a long moment. Long enough to make her wonder what he saw. "Mrs. Greystone. I hope the day finds you well."

"It does. And you?"

"Fine, thank you." His gaze swept the room.

"I'm certain you're anxious to speak with Maeve again. However, I wanted to advise you of an incident last evening. I...we believe there was someone watching the house."

"Oh?" His brow creased as he studied her.

She felt heat rise in her cheeks, well aware she'd told him something similar several times in the weeks following Matthew's death. Inspector Field had been patient with her concerns and had gone so far as to have a constable make extra rounds on her street. But nothing had happened.

She told him what she'd seen, hoping she was clear and succinct. "Fernsby noted the man as well," she quickly added. She had not imagined it, she reassured herself.

"Were either of you able to see him well enough to offer a description?"

She shared what little they'd been able to discern, not that it was particularly helpful. "It was dark, and he wasn't standing beneath the streetlight."

The inspector gave a single nod. "We will have someone keep watch this evening."

"Thank you." Relief trickled through her. "Do many people know Maeve is here?"

"Such things always find a way of spreading." He scowled at his statement.

Had something else become public knowledge that he would've preferred to keep to himself?

Before she could ask, Fernsby appeared in the doorway with Maeve's hand in his. He bent to look in her face and squeezed her shoulder. A hint of a smile curved her lips in response.

Amelia walked forward to offer her hand. Maeve took it even as she cast a wary glance at Inspector Field.

"Hello, Maeve." The inspector dipped his head with his greeting. The girl stared at him solemnly in return.

Amelia led her to the settee and gestured for her to sit before joining her. She leaned down to meet Maeve's gaze. "The inspector wants to ask you some more questions."

Inspector Field knelt before the girl once again. "I need your help."

Maeve worried her lower lip but watched him with narrowed eyes.

"I want to find the man who killed your father," he said slowly. "I want to bring him to justice for what he did. Your father deserves that."

The girl's face crumpled, going from somber to grief stricken in an instant. While it wasn't clear how much she comprehended of what the inspector had said, she must have understood most of it.

Watching her pain squeezed Amelia's heart, yet all she could do was place an arm around the girl in support.

Maeve slowly raised her hand and held up two fingers as her eyes filled with tears.

Inspector Field drew back in surprise as Amelia swallowed a gasp. "Two?" He reached out to touch her small fingers. "There...there were two men?"

Maeve nodded then covered her eyes as her shoulders shook.

The inspector's eyes met Amelia's, and she couldn't suppress a shiver.

It did not feel long before Henry was once again knocking on the Greystone residence that evening with a constable at his side.

As always, Fernsby promptly opened the door. How the butler managed to be nearby each time when he had numerous other duties was a mystery.

"Good evening, Inspector." Fernsby gave a slight bow.

"Fernsby." Henry nodded in return. "This is Constable Dannon. He'll be keeping an eye on things over the next few nights."

"Very good, sir." He nodded at the constable who did the same.

"If Mrs. Greystone is available, I'd like to introduce him to her as well."

"Of course. Please come in." Fernsby opened the door wider to allow them entrance.

Henry didn't miss how he glanced past them to the street, ever vigilant.

Good. They needed all the eyes they could get to ensure Maeve's safety and possibly Mrs. Greystone's as well. The last thing they needed was a missing witness—or another murder.

The butler shut the door behind them and then led the way up the stairs to the drawing room to announce them.

A fire burned in the hearth, welcome in both appearance and warmth as it warded off the chill of the damp evening. No doubt the faint drizzle would soon become heavier, making for an uncomfortable night for the constables patrolling London's streets.

"Inspector Field, madam, with Constable Dannon." Fernsby moved aside to reveal Mrs. Greystone working at her desk with a lamp at her elbow.

She blinked as if to clear her thoughts and cast a glance at the paper on the desk, clearly reluctant to halt in the middle of whatever she was doing.

Henry had already presumed Maeve was elsewhere, perhaps the kitchen again, a place she clearly enjoyed.

Her revelation earlier that two men had been involved in the murder of her father had surprised Henry. Yet it also made sense. Pritchard was an experienced soldier, so knowing he'd been overwhelmed by two opponents was logical. It also lent credence to the idea that Pritchard had overheard something and gone back up the stairs to investigate—only to be caught.

Unfortunately, Maeve had been too upset to share anything else. Her continued tears convinced Henry to take his leave and allow Mrs. Greystone to calm her.

Still, Henry considered it a breakthrough. One piece of information at a time would help lead them to the murderer. Or rather—murderers.

How much should he press Maeve? While he didn't want her memories of that night to fade, neither did he want to push her to the point where she shut down completely. That vague, distant look of hers made him worry that she might retreat to a place where they couldn't reach her.

The risk was great, either way.

He needed to be patient but not too patient. Where that line was, he had yet to determine.

Henry pulled his thoughts back to the moment and smiled at Mrs. Greystone. "Good evening. My apologies for intruding once again, but I wanted to formally introduce Constable Thomas Dannon. He'll be keeping watch along the street this evening."

The hint of surprise on her face suggested she hadn't expected him to follow through so quickly with his promise. Did she think he hadn't taken her concern seriously?

While she had said the same thing soon after her husband's death, that didn't mean he didn't believe her—then or now. For all he knew, whoever had been watching last night might have done so because of her husband rather than Maeve.

He wasn't taking any chances no matter the reason.

"It's nice to meet you, Constable." She studied Dannon. What did she see?

Dannon was an experienced officer in his early thirties. He had nearly a decade of work behind him and was fit enough to handle most trouble that came his way. Not all constables could make that claim.

"Evening, Mrs. Greystone." Dannon dipped his head respectfully, his hat tucked under his arm. "It's a pleasure." He smoothed the large, dark moustache that hid his lips.

"I'm relieved to know you'll be keeping an eye on things," she said politely.

"You can count on that. Inspector Field said the man had been across the street?"

"Yes. He left as soon as he realized we were watching him."

"That sounds rather suspicious. Did you notice anything particular about him?"

"It was too dark to determine many details, but he was of average build, I would say, and wore a bowler hat."

"That's helpful, madam."

"Do let us know if you have need of anything." She glanced at the butler, who nodded in agreement. "We're happy to provide assistance in any way."

"Thank you." Dannon glanced at Henry. "If that's all, sir, I'll start my rounds and return soon."

Henry nodded. "Very good." He waited until Fernsby and the constable departed before turning back to Mrs. Greystone. "How did Maeve fare the rest of the day?"

"She rested in her room for a time before I convinced her to rise. We did a little sketching. I hoped she might draw what happened—she has drawn pictures of the ravens and the Tower but not her father or that night."

"Excellent thinking." And clever of Mrs. Greystone to consider it. "Perhaps she might next time. Please know how much I appreciate the attempts you've made to provide a way for her to communicate."

Mrs. Greystone sighed. "I wish one of them had been more successful. I don't suppose what she shared this afternoon provided a direction to pursue?"

"Yes and no." He was still mulling it over. Two villains to search for changed the situation. "Everything we learn is helpful. Sometimes we don't realize how much until later."

She nodded. "I expect we'll see you tomorrow?"

He smiled. "Yes, if you don't mind. My apologies for the disruption this is causing you and your household."

"Not at all. My heart goes out to Maeve. I only wish there was more I could do."

"You've given her a safe haven away from the Tower, however briefly. That is more than enough." He glanced at the fire, wishing he were settled before it with a book and a whiskey. The desire surprised him; it wasn't often that he longed for the more domestic comforts in life.

He gave himself a mental shake to clear his thoughts. "Soon I will need to bring her back to the Tower to see what more she can show us. Definitely before her family arrives."

"That won't be easy for her."

"No, but we'll visit in the light of day with the hope it won't upset her overly much."

"Let me know if you'd like me to join you."

"Thank you." He had hoped she might offer. "I'm sure that would reassure Maeve." He glanced at her desk, wondering what she'd been working on so intently when they'd arrived.

She followed his gaze. "I'm preparing for an interview tomorrow with the oldest clockmaker in London."

"How interesting. It sounds as though you've had some unusual assignments."

"I have. I realized after my first one that it's more effective to prepare ahead of time, so I have a better sense of the questions to ask."

Henry nodded. "I read the one you wrote about Pritchard. Very interesting. You have a knack for revealing the unusual aspects of things."

"That's a requirement for this particular magazine," she said with a smile.

"Then apparently they've found the right person for the position."

Her smile widened, reminding him how attractive she was. Her smiles were rare, and he couldn't help but stare for a long moment, aware of his heart speeding its beat.

Clearly, it was time for him to take his leave.

"I hope you enjoy the rest of your evening." He turned to go, surprised by his regret at doing so.

"Are you officially off duty, Inspector?"

He turned. "I have one more stop to make before I return home."

"You keep long hours."

Henry shrugged. "It happens occasionally." More often than he'd like.

Other inspectors kept similar schedules, so he knew he wasn't alone in the time he spent on some cases. He didn't care to think of the hours he'd put in on her husband's murder thus far, with little to show for it.

The thought had him looking at her once again. "Please know that we continue to investigate your husband's death. It has not been forgotten by any means."

Surprise flashed across her face but was gone so quickly that he wondered if he'd imagined it. "Thank you. I appreciate that."

"Has anything surfaced that you think could be helpful?"

"No." She answered quickly, but Henry could not shake the sense of her uncertainty.

He waited to see if she added anything, but she remained silent. There was no doubt she was as anxious to solve the mystery of her husband's death as he was.

"I'll wish you a good evening then."

"Good night."

He took his leave, unsurprised to find Fernsby at the front door, waiting to let him out. "I hope you have an uneventful evening."

"As do I, sir." The older man nodded with a smile.

The lock bolted after Fernsby shut the door behind him, and Henry smiled. Mrs. Greystone had a fine guard in the butler.

Dannon had already departed on his rounds, so Henry walked along the quiet street to have a look himself. The tree-lined street with tidy gardens and wrought-iron fences was charming even in the dark. Especially with a warm glow coming from many of the windows.

He pushed away a pang of envy as an image of a family gathered together for the evening filled his mind and picked up his pace. He had a tavern or two to visit to see if anyone was familiar with an Irishman who carried a knife. He couldn't dwell on hopes he wouldn't permit himself to feel.

Nineteen

"Enjoy your outing, madam." Fernsby bowed as he opened the door for Amelia to depart into the morning air.

"Thank you." She paused to look back into the house one last time. "I'm sure all will be well." Her reluctance to leave home was nothing new, although the past few days had intensified it once again. The unsettled feeling had been especially difficult to overcome in the months following Matthew's death.

At the time, she'd put it down to the fear that whoever had killed him might come after her. While that concern had frightened her, she soon realized there was more to her disquiet. It was easier to remain home and only speak with the servants, stay busy puttering in her lab, reading, or with one of her other past times. Venturing out meant putting herself at risk. At least, that was how she felt.

Most of the time, she was pleased her parents had pressed her to find a reason to leave the house and talk to people. Doing so gave her a more balanced outlook. A healthier one. Each time she left the house without issue helped to allay her uneasiness. The magazine correspondent position was perfect for just that reason.

Of course, she occasionally visited friends as well, but even those trips made her anxious. That was when she realized it was a problem she needed to overcome. The slight panic she felt each time she was ready to depart was still a challenge to work through—especially this afternoon since she was leaving Maeve.

"We'll do our best in your absence," Fernsby reassured her. "Don't fret about the child."

Maeve was resting in her room and more than likely wouldn't even realize Amelia had left. The girl was comfortable with the servants. The chance of an intruder entering in the middle of the day just because Amelia had departed was unlikely and she knew Fernsby would lock the door behind her.

"You are reassuring as always. I won't be gone long." She'd considered delaying the interview, but that might cause her to miss her deadline at the magazine. No, the sooner she left, the sooner she could return.

The thought was enough to have her proceeding down the front steps. The clockmaker's shop on Bowling Green Way wasn't far, so she'd chosen to walk after being inside for the last several days. Exercise was good for the soul and eased her anxiety. If the weather turned or she felt she'd been gone overlong, she'd hire a hansom cab for the trip home.

Not for the first time, Amelia appreciated the freedom of being a widow. While she still brought a maid with her on occasion, it wasn't required. The choice was welcome today when she'd much rather Yvette stayed with Maeve.

She checked her reticule to make certain her notes were inside, along with a pencil, but didn't bother to review them. She was as ready as she could be and looked forward to learning more about the clockmaker.

Her gray gown was one of her better ones. She supposed she could have a few new made in lavender or violet since it would soon be a year since Matthew died, but she didn't mind the gray. The color helped to clarify her status as a widow, which in turn created a barrier of sorts from the world. She appreciated not having to rebuff a man's interest or endure disapproving looks from older ladies who noted she had no chaperone.

She purposefully took a moment to admire the neighbors' tidy gardens as she passed. It took all her resolve not to look over her shoulder, but giving in to fearful behavior was something she refused to indulge in, even if—or perhaps because—it took effort.

The uniform townhomes soon gave way to shops as she walked. She slowed to look in the windows, the lingering panic easing as she went. She brushed elbows with others, pleased when she wasn't bothered by it. The street bustled with carts, carriages, and riders, everyone intent on hurrying to their destination.

Amelia crossed the street, taking care to avoid the carriages, then paused outside the trunk maker's shop to admire a barrel-stave trunk in the window that boasted leather straps with metal rosettes embellishing them. What a fine way to travel that would be.

She turned to continue on her way when she caught sight of a young girl walking alone in the same direction a few shops ahead. Her heart caught in her throat at the girl's resemblance to Maeve, complete with her long brown braid and a doll tucked under one arm. The crowded walkway hid her from sight, and Amelia shifted to peer around the people between them.

She gasped. *Good heavens.* It was Maeve.

Amelia rushed forward only to watch in horror as a man grabbed the girl. Panic struck in full. "Maeve!"

Calling her name was futile when the girl couldn't hear, but the man's head snapped around to meet Amelia's gaze. A brown bowler hat shaded his narrowed eyes, and his mouth tightened in displeasure.

He had dark hair, was clean shaven with a pock-marked face, and must've been near her age.

Something about his beefy build along with the set of his broad shoulders and his bowler hat made her think of the man she'd glimpsed watching the house the other night, though it had been too dark to say for certain.

"Halt!" Amelia called, holding out a hand as if that would stop him. She dodged around the few people who paused to see what the problem was, heart racing, desperate to reach Maeve.

The girl fought as if her life depended on it, keeping the man from fleeing with her. Her doll fell to the ground as she flailed and uttered a wordless cry, clearly terrified by the stranger's grip.

"Release her at once!" Amelia lunged forward to grab his arm with both hands to help free Maeve. The panic she'd worked so hard to soothe flooded her body with strength.

The man shoved her with one hand and sent her stumbling back. Amelia quickly regained her balance and reached for him again. She refused to let him take her.

"Help! Someone help us!" Amelia didn't look to see if anyone considered joining the fray, her focus on her mission.

"Leave off," the man ground out and tried to shake off her grip.

"Let her go!" Amelia thrust her elbow into his side and received a grunt in response.

Maeve's terrified eyes met hers before the girl fought even harder, as if she sensed freedom was within reach. She writhed and punched and kicked. The man had his hands full just trying to hold her. People stepped around them, slowing their pace as they tried to determine what was happening.

Amelia stomped on his foot and jerked on his arm. "Release her, I say!"

"Damn and blast," the stranger muttered.

"You there," another voice called. "Cease at once."

The man looked over Amelia's shoulder at whoever had called out. His dark eyes widened in alarm. He released Maeve and ran in the opposite direction.

A shrill whistle cut through the air. "Halt!"

Amelia glanced behind her to see a uniformed constable running toward them.

"Are you all right, madam?" he asked breathlessly, one hand holding his billy club.

"Yes, we're fine." Amelia drew Maeve into her arms and squeezed her tight to reassure them both.

The girl's thin shoulders shook. So did Amelia's.

Before Amelia had finished speaking, the constable rushed after the attacker.

"Is all well?" A gentleman walking by paused to ask.

"Y-Yes. Yes, thank you," Amelia replied as she drew another breath to calm her pounding heart.

He nodded and, after hesitating, continued on his way.

Amelia eased back to look into Maeve's face, brushing a strand of hair from the girl's cheek. "Are you hurt?"

She didn't answer. Instead, she buried her face in Amelia's stomach and wrapped her arms around her waist as if she'd never let go.

Amelia returned the embrace, allowing her heart to settle before she tried again, bending low to catch the girl's gaze. "Did he hurt you?"

The girl shook her head then released Amelia long enough to retrieve her doll before hugging Amelia once more.

How the girl had managed to follow her was a mystery when the servants would've been—should've been—keeping a close eye on her. There was no point in asking Maeve. Clearly the girl was clever and determined enough to do so. Amelia need only remember that she'd followed her father out of the Tower gate in the dark of night.

Keeping an arm around the girl, she looked in the direction of where the constable had gone but could neither see him nor Maeve's attacker.

She bent down to catch Maeve's attention again. "Let's go home."

The interview with the clockmaker would have to wait.

The girl nodded and turned with Amelia in the direction of home. She winced if anyone passed by too closely, eyes still wary and dark with fright.

Amelia kept a close watch as they went, concerned the man would find a way to elude the constable and return to try to take Maeve again.

That had been no random act. Whoever had murdered the raven-keeper believed his daughter had witnessed their crime. They'd already killed once. She had to think they'd do so again if given the chance.

The realization had her tightening her grip on Maeve's hand and keeping a close watch all around them as she hailed a hansom cab.

They couldn't return home fast enough.

Twenty

"Tell me again exactly what occurred." Henry forced himself to concentrate as Mrs. Greystone repeated the story, this time in more detail.

His thoughts whirled as she spoke. He should've taken her concern that someone was watching the house more seriously—a mistake he wouldn't repeat.

"He reminded me of the man I saw on the street outside the other night. At least, his build was similar as was his hat," she added. Her hand brushed along Maeve's hair in a slow, steady motion as she spoke. "I wish I could say for certain."

The girl sat by her side and stared into the distance with the vacant look he'd come to detest. It was a dark reminder that he had yet to find her father's murderer, and the child was very much in danger until he did.

Thank goodness Mrs. Greystone had realized what was happening and managed to stop the man who'd tried to kidnap Maeve. Whoever had killed Pritchard must've realized there was a potential witness to the crime.

So their troubles were not over. Chances were they'd attempt to take Maeve again.

The event confirmed that the killers believed Maeve might identify them. But pressing her now wouldn't be wise when she needed time to recover from her fright.

After listening to Mrs. Greystone's concise report a second time, which included a detailed description of the man, Henry rose. "Might be best if you remain inside for now, you and the girl. I'll find out the name of the officer who gave chase and whether he was able to catch him. A constable will be assigned to keep watch day *and* night from this point forward."

Based on Mrs. Greystone's puckered brow, she didn't find the promise reassuring. "I still don't understand how Maeve managed to follow me. Nor does Fernsby."

Ah. Perhaps her unease was a result of her own guilt. That was something to which he could relate.

"She was resting in her room when I left," she continued. "In fact, I didn't tell her I was leaving because I didn't want her to worry. Perhaps that was a mistake." She studied the top of the girl's head.

"You are not to blame." Henry wanted to make that clear. He looked again at Maeve to make certain she wasn't looking at either of them. "Communicating with her is difficult, let alone under these circumstances. You couldn't have possibly guessed that she'd see you leave or choose to follow you."

The last thing he wanted was for Mrs. Greystone to feel guilty. She'd already done more than anyone could expect by caring for a frightened, grief-stricken girl—especially given the widow's own grief from the two losses in her life.

"Thank you, but I feel like I should have." Mrs. Greystone pressed a hand to her heart as if it still raced. "If I hadn't paused to look at a trunk in the window, she probably would've remained behind me, and I wouldn't have seen her. She would've been taken, and we'd be left wondering what happened. I don't think I'll ever forget the sight of his hands on her."

Her shudder tugged at him. If only he had the power to clear that memory from her mind.

"I'm pleased you witnessed it else we'd be searching for Maeve rather than wondering how she left." He didn't bother to say how impossible that task would be. Nor did he add that he feared the girl would've shared the same fate as her father.

That would hardly reassure the shaken woman.

Henry hesitated as he watched Mrs. Greystone, uncertain what more to say to reassure her. "I don't think I've properly expressed how grateful I am that you've kept watch over Maeve these last few days. Her staying with you has helped keep her safe." He cleared his throat. "But...but if this is becoming too difficult, I certainly understand."

Mrs. Greystone had been through more than most in the past few years. The situation couldn't be easy. Was it wrong of him to have asked for the girl to stay with her?

She glanced at Maeve, seeming torn how to answer. "I'll see it through. She seems comfortable here...or at least, she was."

"I would agree." He didn't want Mrs. Greystone to put herself or her servants in danger by keeping the girl. If only Maeve could tell them what she'd seen, and he could find who killed her father.

And that was when an idea came to mind. It was a bold one, indeed, but he wasn't certain whether it would be helpful—or acceptable—to the lady.

"What is it?" Mrs. Greystone asked as she watched him, seeming to see his mind latch onto an idea.

Why not leave it up to her to decide? "I realize this is untoward but given what happened today, I would like to spend the night here to help keep watch."

She stilled, eyes darkening with concern. "You think whoever it was will try again."

"I think it's a distinct possibility." Henry wouldn't lie to her. He'd much rather she remained on guard rather than being placated by empty reassurances. Besides, it was not in his nature to hide the truth.

She slowly nodded. "That's probably wise. I'll have the guest room readied; it won't take Mrs. Fernsby a moment."

"There's no need to go to any trouble. Chances are that I'll spend most of the night roaming the house."

"You have to sleep some time, or you won't be of use to anyone, including Maeve. The room will be ready when you need it."

"Very well. Constable Dannon has returned to watch this afternoon. Another will relieve him later. Between us, we should be able to deal with any trouble." His focus shifted to Maeve. Unable to resist, he knelt before her, unsurprised when she didn't react. Still, he gently brushed her cheek with the back of a finger, willing her to look at him.

His patience was rewarded when at last she did, her brown eyes wary as she tightened her hold on her beloved doll.

"The man who grabbed you. Was he the one who killed your father?"

The girl's face furrowed as she shook her head, then drew her knees to her chest, tucked her head down, and curled into a ball to rock back and forth.

Henry reached for her shoulder only to have her pull away as if his touch burned.

That, or her memories did.

With a sigh, he shared a look with Mrs. Greystone, noting the concern in her expression. "I don't know if that means he wasn't the killer, or he was the one accompanying the killer that night, or she doesn't want to talk about it."

"She might need a little more time before she can offer help," she suggested.

"Unfortunately, we're running out of that." He pushed to his feet, trying to hide his frustration. "For her sake and ours, I hope she can share more soon."

Mrs. Greystone nodded as she placed an arm around Maeve and pulled her close. "Once she settles down, I'll ask her again."

"Very well. I'll return this evening if that's acceptable."

"Of course. I'll have Fernsby set an extra plate for dinner."

"I'm not certain what time it will be." He was feeling more and more how much of an inconvenience his presence would be.

"Oh, that's no trouble. You can eat whenever you arrive."

"Thank you." He reached for the hat he'd left on the nearby table, his thoughts moving to what needed to be done next. "I'll see you soon then."

He hurried down the stairs only to pause when Fernsby reached for the door to let him out. "I'll be staying the next few nights to help keep watch."

The older man appeared relieved at his words. "Excellent idea, Inspector. We shall all continue to be on guard."

With that, Henry took his leave. Thank goodness the attempt to take Maeve had been unsuccessful. However, he didn't think he could depend on her to identify the killers. He needed something tangible to follow up on rather than hope.

He returned to Scotland Yard, taking a hansom cab to save time. The sooner he discovered which constable had given chase after the man the better. He might have additional information to offer at the very least. Even if the assailant wasn't one of the killers, he could lead them in the right direction.

Johnson manned the front desk as always. At Henry's question, he shuffled through several papers until he found the schedule he was looking for. "That would be Stephens. He just returned a quarter of an hour ago."

"Thank you."

Henry entered the main office and quickly found him.

The constable's look of regret after his explanation tightened Henry's chest. While not surprised the officer had little to offer, he was still disappointed.

"I wasn't able to catch the man," Stephens said. "He disappeared into the crowd or perhaps took off down an alleyway. He was nowhere to be found. When I returned to where the lady and the girl were, they'd already departed."

"Did you get a good look at him?" Henry asked.

"Good enough to provide a description. I returned to write a report in case the lady decided to file a complaint."

"The man could be connected to the ravenkeeper's murder. The girl he tried to take was the victim's daughter."

"Ah." Stephens' eyes lit with interest. "The body found near the Tower."

"Yes. Did you see his face well enough to help someone sketch it?"

"I think so."

Henry nodded. "Excellent. I'll find someone to draw it and then see if the lady has anything to add." Excitement built inside him. This was the closest thing to a lead they'd had. Showing the sketch to the yeomen warders and others at the Tower might lead to something more.

After asking a few of his fellow detectives, he had the name and address of a sketch artist who often worked with the Yard. He sent one of the constables to her house with a request that she come as quickly as possible, not wanting Stephens to forget what he'd seen.

Henry was looking through the case files on his desk when Fletcher arrived. "I was hoping to find you here. I have an update on the Somerset jewelry case."

The sergeant had spent the day interviewing the servants and visiting additional pawnshops in search of the missing jewelry as well as stopping by the Tower.

"Good. Let's find somewhere quiet." Henry glanced around then led the way to an empty interview room where they could speak without interruption.

"Did something happen with the murder investigation?" Fletcher asked as soon as Henry closed the door. "You look more tense than usual."

Henry told him what had occurred and that they would soon have a picture to help with their inquiries.

"Excellent news. This might be the break we needed," Fletcher said as he smoothed his moustache.

"I hope so. I imagine Maeve's family will arrive from the country to take her soon. Hopefully she'll be able to tell us whether this man is one of the two who killed her father."

Fletcher frowned. "Couldn't we just ask if the man who tried to take her—"

Henry shook his head before the sergeant finished the thought. "I tried that already. She shook her head but was so distraught that I'm left to wonder. She might have meant no, or she might have been telling me she didn't want to answer. I'm just not certain."

"How unfortunate. Perhaps Mrs. Greystone will have better luck after the poor girl has a chance to recover from her fright."

"I hope so." Henry shifted in his chair, aware that with every day that passed, the odds of them making an arrest lessened. "How did the interviews with the servants come along?"

"As you might expect." Fletcher shook his head with an exasperated look. "No one saw anything. A few pointed fingers at others, although it seemed to be out of spite rather than actual evidence. Most have alibis but not all."

"Any luck at the pawnbrokers?"

"None. I think we'll have to question the guests from the dinner party, even if Lord Somerset would rather we didn't."

"I'll speak with him and Lady Somerset before we do so. You know how the nobility can be about these things." He hated to be pulled away from the Pritchard case when they had a new lead but neither did he want Lord Somerset to complain to the Director that he wasn't doing his job.

Unfortunately, questioning the guests would fall to him not Fletcher, as those in Society tended to respond better to inspectors than sergeants.

If only there were two of him.

Twenty-One

"A message arrived for you, madam." Fernsby handed the envelope to Amelia in the drawing room a few hours later. "Thank you." Amelia opened it, hoping it was a reply from the clockmaker, Thomas Buggins, the owner of Thwaites & Reed. She'd penned a message to him earlier to apologize for not keeping their appointment, sharing an emergency had arisen without the particulars.

How could she expect him to believe the truth when it was such a wild, complicated tale?

To her relief, Mr. Buggins was amenable to rescheduling their appointment for the following day but was leaving town the day after for a week. If she wanted to write the article in time for her deadline, she must visit him tomorrow.

One thing was clear—she couldn't leave Maeve again. Would Inspector Field be willing to watch over her while Amelia went to the interview?

She almost smiled at the thought of him sitting with Maeve for a few hours. He had a calm demeanor, but she had no doubt that hid a man of action whose thoughts were always moving a step ahead of his feet. The image of him pacing the drawing room while Maeve watched nearly made her smile.

Now that it was clear someone wanted to harm the girl, it wasn't fair to leave the servants with such a responsibility. Nor did she want to put them in danger.

She'd half-expected one or two to hand in their notice after Matthew's death. Given that he'd been murdered, no suspect found, she'd worried they would fear for their safety. To have them all choose to stay was a blessing for which she was grateful.

She glanced at Maeve who sat in a nearby chair, a magazine open on her lap. Rather than looking at the pictures, the girl stared into the distance, making Amelia wonder where her thoughts had taken her. Was she reliving yesterday's altercation or thinking of her father?

Amelia set aside the message and rose to kneel beside her. She ran her hand over her thin shoulder and smiled when Maeve's focus shifted to her. "Shall we have tea and cake?" She made the motions of drinking and eating to help make her question clear.

Maeve blinked and for a moment, Amelia feared she wouldn't answer; that she'd retreated to her silent world and wouldn't re-emerge. But at last, she slowly nodded.

With a smile, Amelia stood and rang for Fernsby. After he departed with her request for tea, she returned to Maeve's side. She didn't want to upset her again, but Inspector Field needed to know if the man who'd grabbed her was the same one who'd killed her father. If Amelia didn't ask her, the inspector would. While he was always kind and patient with Maeve, Amelia knew the girl better and hoped she'd respond to her. If Maeve could answer this one question, it could help solve the case.

"Maeve." Amelia cupped her cheek to encourage her to meet her gaze. "Was the man who grabbed you the one who hurt your father?"

The girl's lip trembled, and worry filled Amelia. She held tight to the girl's shoulder with her other hand, hoping to lend her support and strength.

"Was he one of the same men?" She mouthed the question slowly.

Maeve shook her head and hunched her shoulders.

Amelia wasn't certain whether to be pleased or disappointed by the answer. "No?" she asked to clarify.

Again, Maeve shook her head.

Amelia wrapped her arms around the girl and held her. The thought of not one, not two, but three men involved in this situation was terrifying. What had Pritchard seen or heard that would cause such alarm? Did they truly think Maeve could recognize them or were they merely tying up loose ends?

The knowledge that Constable Dannon was outside watching the house was comforting, but he was no guarantee of safety. She was suddenly anxious for Inspector Field to arrive, though it might be several hours before he did.

When Fernsby arrived with the tea tray, Amelia stood and reached for the tray, careful to keep her back to Maeve. How much Maeve could read lips was still unclear. She didn't want the girl to know what she wanted to tell Fernsby. It would only upset her again.

Fernsby's startled look suggested he was affronted by her action, and he kept a firm hold of the tray.

She smiled in case Maeve could see her and said, "The man who grabbed her this morning was not one of the men who killed the ravenkeeper."

"Oh?" Fernsby looked at Maeve in alarm.

"A smile, if you please," Amelia cautioned him.

The butler did as she requested, though she'd never seen him reveal so many teeth.

"That is concerning," he added, the odd smile still in place.

"It is. But knowing forewarns us. Perhaps you should advise the others so we can all take extra care in the coming days."

"Indeed." Fernsby helped her set the tray on the table. "I shall share the update with Constable Dannon outside as well."

"Thank you."

The butler started to go, then paused to bend down to look into Maeve's face. "Have a cake for me, will you?" He asked her the same question each day when he served tea. Yesterday, she'd gestured for him to take one, but he refused, only to allow her to finally convince him to have one. The sweet interaction had warmed Amelia's heart.

Today Maeve barely glanced at him before looking away, not responding in any way.

That confirmed her continued distress. Amelia couldn't blame her when she was distressed as well. How could any of the household relax until Pritchard's murder had been solved and Maeve was truly safe?

Henry was more than tired by the time he arrived at the Greystone residence later that evening with a small bag in hand. His shoes pinched and his back ached from the walking he'd done while showing the sketch of the man who'd attempted to abduct Maeve to those at the Tower and anyone else he could think of, all without success.

Unfortunately, his day was far from over.

"Evening, Inspector." Constable Stephens tipped his head as Henry approached the house. The constable had relived Dannon earlier. Someone would be guarding the house day and night while Maeve was staying there.

"Stephens. Anything of interest to report?"

"No, sir. Quiet as a mouse." Stephens patted his stomach. "Nice of Mrs. Greystone to send a plate of food out for me. Makes watching easier when you know you're appreciated."

Henry smiled. Mrs. Greystone was a thoughtful person and her staff followed suit. "I'm sure it does."

His own stomach growled at the mention of food. Luncheon had been a long time ago and that had only been a bit of bread and cheese, nothing more. "Please stay alert. We don't want anything to happen to our potential witness."

"No, we don't, sir. I have a babe at home, so you can be sure I'll keep on my toes."

"Good to hear."

Before Henry could knock on the door, Fernsby opened it. "Good evening, Inspector."

"Fernsby."

Henry had stopped by earlier to have Mrs. Greystone review the sketch. She'd suggested a few minor changes and had even taken a pencil to the image to make them. The lady's numerous talents surprised him.

Maeve had been resting so he hadn't had the chance to ask her to look at the image. Mrs. Greystone had told him that Maeve confirmed the man who'd tried to take her wasn't one of her father's killers. While the news was disappointing, he was still determined to find the person in the sketch as he could lead them to the murderers.

"All is well?" he asked the butler.

"It is, sir. Your dinner is ready when you are."

"Thank you." He pressed a hand to his grumbling stomach, silently telling it to wait just a little longer.

"May I take your things?" Fernsby asked.

"Thank you." Henry handed him the bag that held a few items for his stay. "Is Mrs. Greystone available?"

"She is in the drawing room awaiting your arrival."

Henry blinked. He supposed he shouldn't be surprised that she waited for him rather than going on with her normal routine. No doubt she wanted to know if any progress had been made from showing the sketch to those at the Tower. "I'll provide her with an update before dining."

"Very well." Fernsby dipped into his usual half-bow.

Henry turned and went up the stairs to find the lady of the house in a wingback chair near the fire with a book in her lap.

"Good evening, Mrs. Greystone."

"Good evening." She must've heard his arrival as she showed no surprise at his greeting. Her gaze swept over him, making him wonder what she saw. "You look as if you could use a hot meal and some rest."

Apparently, she saw more than he'd like. "It has been a long day." He rubbed a hand over the back of his neck. "How is Maeve?"

"Better, I think. She's in the kitchen with the maid at the moment."

"I'd like to speak with her again to see if she can share anything more."

"Certainly." Mrs. Greystone set the book aside and stood. "Why don't you eat while I get her? If you don't mind, I would like to be there when you speak to her."

"Excellent idea. She clearly finds your presence reassuring."

"Perhaps between the two of us, we can coax her to somehow tell us more." She started toward the door only to look back at him. "Are you coming?"

"Yes." He must be more tired than he realized because the chair near the fire looked quite tempting. He cleared his throat as he followed her down the stairs. "Constable Stephens said all has been well here."

"So it seems, though it's difficult to relax. I confess to looking out the window more often than I should." Mrs. Greystone glanced over her shoulder at him as she spoke.

"No sight of anyone watching?"

"Not that I've seen."

"Stephens' presence should discourage whoever it was from lingering." He was careful not to make any promises. He could not prevent the risk completely.

"I hope so." She paused before the dining room door. "I'll leave you to your dinner and meet you afterward in the drawing room with Maeve."

"Thank you." He opened the door and found a place setting at the table with two silver trays with covers nearby.

Relieved not to have a servant staring as he ate, Henry sat and placed the cloth napkin on his lap and removed the cover.

His mouth watered at the generous pile of thinly sliced roast beef along with potatoes and carrots. Thick slabs of bread and pads of butter were beneath another cover.

"Here you go, sir." Fernsby came in a different door carrying another tray. With practiced ease, he set down an open bottle of wine, along with a glass and a gravy boat. "May I bring you anything else?"

Henry shook his head. "This looks wonderful. Thank you." Much better than anything he normally ate in the evenings.

Fernsby left him to eat in peace and quiet. He savored each bite certain he hadn't enjoyed such a delicious meal since he last dined with his parents. The wine was excellent, and he poured himself a half-glass more after finishing the meal, appreciating a few more minutes of quiet.

The events of the afternoon filtered through his mind. Chief Yeoman Warder Wallace had studied the sketch for a long moment but shook his head. "I wish I did if he was involved in Pritchard's murder."

They'd tried Daniels next. He didn't recognize him either, though Henry had noted a slight hesitation before he answered.

Henry still had mixed feelings about the new ravenkeeper. That he'd tossed away the possibly poisoned meat when it could've had something to do with Pritchard's murder was suspicious. His excuse for doing so seemed flimsy.

While Fletcher was more than capable of showing the sketch to those who'd known Pritchard, Henry had wanted to see the reaction of those he considered possible suspects himself, but they hadn't managed to find everyone. Fletcher would continue the process with the remaining yeoman warders come morning to see if someone could help determine the man's identity.

He couldn't risk focusing all his time on the man in the sketch. Maeve was still the only potential witness, and he hoped she could provide a few more details.

With that in mind, he started to push back from the table only to see Fernsby entering the room with another tray. "A bit of trifle for dessert, sir."

Though already full, it would take a stronger man than him to pass up trifle. The layered dessert was one of his favorites. As far as he was concerned, the sweet treat contained the best of several desserts—cake, fruit, and custard.

The butler cleared his dinner plate and set a generous portion of the trifle in front of him in a smooth motion.

"Thank you. Please extend my gratitude to the cook. The meal was delicious, and dessert looks to be so as well."

"Mrs. Appleton will be pleased to hear that."

Henry made quick work of the dessert then rose to return to the drawing room. It never failed to amaze him how much better one's outlook and energy were with a full stomach.

As Mrs. Greystone promised, she awaited him in the drawing room with Maeve at her side. The girl was sketching while Mrs. Greystone embroidered. It was a domestic scene he rarely saw and touched him in a surprising way.

Maeve stiffened at the sight of him. That was understandable, but still gave him pause. No doubt he represented the terrible events which had happened in her life.

"Thank you again for dinner," Henry said to the lady. "It was delicious."

"I'm pleased you enjoyed it." Mrs. Greystone smoothed Maeve's hair.

He appreciated the effort she made to connect with the girl and help her feel comfortable. At least one of them managed to do so.

Since his presence was only upsetting Maeve, he might as well try to talk to her now.

He knelt before her and was pleased that she watched him rather than staring across the room, even if her expression was cautious. "You said there were two men who hurt your father." He spoke slowly and held up two fingers with the hope of making himself clear.

Maeve nodded, eyes wide.

"Did you know them?"

She hesitated then shook her head. *Well, that wasn't a surprise.*

"Were they short or tall?" Any kind of description might help.

Maeve shook her head and shrugged as if she wasn't sure.

"Were they about the same height as your father?" He held a hand near the top of his own head, eager to keep questioning as she seemed ready to talk—afraid at any moment that he'd overstep. "Or me?"

She looked to the side, and he feared he'd lost her. But she appeared to be trying to remember for she looked back at him and held a hand near his nose.

"A little shorter than me," he said to confirm, relieved when she nodded.

"Were they fat or thin?" Again, he used his hands to show a large girth then a narrow one.

The girl reached for his hands and pulled them apart to more of an average size.

He glanced at Mrs. Greystone who watched closely and seemed as pleased by the progress as he was.

Henry touched his face. "Whiskers?" At Maeve's nod, he placed a finger over his upper lip. "Here?" Then again on his jaw. "Or here?"

Maeve considered the question then leaned forward to touch both areas of his face.

"Both?" Henry asked.

Again, she nodded.

"If only that didn't describe half the men in London." Mrs. Greystone sighed even as she gave an encouraging smile to Maeve.

"Indeed." But Henry refused to give up.

The girl's eyes darted about as if searching her memory. After a moment, she held up one finger then touched her upper lip and cheeks. Then she held up two fingers and rubbed in front of both ears.

"One has a beard and the other sideburns," he said, wanting to confirm her meaning.

Maeve nodded.

"Did they say anything?" He touched his mouth and moved his hands to indicate talking. At least, he hoped that was what the motion would mean to the girl.

Maeve frowned but slowly nodded.

How unfortunate that she couldn't share what it was since she hadn't heard it. Unless...

"Were they angry with your father?"

A fearful look came over her face and she edged closer to Mrs. Greystone.

"I would say that means yes," the widow whispered as she put an arm around the girl's shoulders.

He dearly wanted to know why they'd been angry and what they'd said, but even if Maeve had understood parts of the conversation, how could she share them? Then there was the trauma of that night and her young age to consider.

His best hope was if he found the killers, she'd be able to positively identify them.

"Is there anything more?" he asked, uncertain if she'd understand but gestured to his face and body. Something distinctive would truly be helpful.

She looked down at her hand, which lay in her lap. As he watched, she tightened it into a fist and then made a stabbing motion. Again and again. High and low. Left and right. Her expression grew fierce as she moved, but her eyes filled with tears.

Mrs. Greystone gasped in horror even as Henry's heart ached at what she'd witnessed. That was something no one should ever have to see, let alone a child. His determination rose. Henry would find those who'd killed her father and make them pay.

Twenty-Two

"Do you truly think this is necessary?" Amelia asked Inspector Field as she frowned at the constable standing nearby.

"Yes." The inspector's tone brooked no argument.

The time had come for her to leave for the appointment with the clockmaker, and Inspector Field had insisted a constable accompany her.

"You won't even know I'm there." Constable Stephens nodded as if to convince her.

How could having a uniformed officer accompany her be ignored by anyone, but most especially her? While she appreciated the constable's remark, she had to protest. "It's Maeve who needs protection. Not me."

"You might be in danger as well. We will not take any chances." The inspector pulled out a gold pocket watch from his waistcoat. "How long do you think you'll be?"

Clearly the subject wasn't open for discussion.

Amelia sighed. "Two hours should be adequate, I think."

"Very well. I'll remain with Maeve until your return." He glanced at the girl who sat on the settee nearby with a scowl on her face and arms folded over her chest, clearly displeased by the turn of events.

Amelia walked over to her and bent to look into her eyes. "I'll return soon. The inspector will make certain you're safe." She gestured to Inspector Field to make her point clear.

The attempt to reassure her apparently failed as the girl's unhappy expression did not change. Amelia squeezed her shoulder, still worried about leaving. She wished she could've delayed the interview without missing her deadline. She took pride in being a woman of her word, perhaps because her late husband didn't always do so.

"You'll keep a close eye on her?" Amelia asked the inspector.

He lifted a brow as if surprised by the question. "Yes."

Had she insulted him? She reached for her reticule. "I'll return as soon as possible."

"Very well."

Though it was on the tip of her tongue to remind him that Maeve might try to follow her again, she bit it back. He already knew that. Nor did she need to offer any suggestions about what the two could do in her absence. He was a grown man and surely capable of watching a young girl for an hour or two, wasn't he?

"Thank you for your assistance," she told him then gave Maeve's shoulder one last squeeze and walked down the stairs with the constable following behind her.

"We'll see you soon, madam," Fernsby said as he opened the door.

"Thank you." With another glance at Constable Stephens, she walked to the hansom cab which had arrived to take them to the clockmaker's shop.

Stephens held open the door and handed her up then closed it. At her questioning look, he said, "I'll keep watch with the driver."

She released a relieved breath. At least she wouldn't be required to make polite conversation. She had too much on her mind to do so.

When the cab rolled forward, she pulled out her notes to keep her thoughts occupied for the short ride to her destination yet couldn't help but wonder if someone was following them, after Inspector Field had put the concern in her mind. She found herself glancing out the carriage window more often than not.

Her suspicions proved to be unfounded when nearly twenty minutes later, they arrived at Thwaites & Reed.

Founded in 1740, the shop had been in Clerkenwell until a few years ago when it moved to Bowling Green Way. The sandstone building had wide windows, and clocks of all sizes and shapes were visible inside.

The sight lifted Amelia's mood as she alighted, but she also found herself looking around the bustling street for anyone who looked suspicious. After giving herself a mental shake, she opened the shop door before the constable could do so and stepped inside, determined to ignore him as much as possible.

The tick tock of a multitude of clocks greeted her, and she paused with a smile to take in the sights and sounds of the small shop. Did those who worked here grow accustomed to the relentless ticking?

"Mr. Buggins, please," she told the clerk who approached her with a wary look at the constable.

"Perhaps you'd prefer to wait outside," she suggested when the clerk turned away with a frown to fetch Mr. Buggins.

"Of course." Constable Stephens took one last look around the shop before stepping outside to stand guard by the door. She hoped his presence didn't deter any patrons.

She hadn't waited long before Mr. Buggins arrived to show her around the shop. A salt and pepper moustache, muttonchops, and wire-rimmed spectacles lent a scholarly look to his stout form. He appeared to be a pleasant enough fellow but frowned when he caught sight of the constable standing outside.

"He accompanied me," Amelia told him with a polite smile without explaining why. "What a marvelous timepiece—one of your own?"

It was clear the owner took great pride in the items they manufactured. After pointing out a few interesting clocks, many with visible mechanisms, he escorted her to his small office in the back.

Thwaites & Reed was not only the oldest clockmaker in London but claimed to be the oldest in the world.

He withdrew a worn, leather-bound book with numerous sketches and opened it carefully. "These are drawings dating back to 1610. Our specialty is turret clocks which are mounted in clock towers in churches and other public buildings. We've made nearly four thousand since the company's founding." His pride in the company's long history was evident in his smile. "One of our clocks is in the turret at the Horse Guards Parade."

"The one with two faces?" Amelia asked, having seen it several times.

"Yes. Each face is over seven feet tall."

Amelia found it fascinating that the founder's widow, Mrs. Henrietta Thwaites, had kept the business going after her husband's death with the help of her nephew and made a note to include that in her article.

Mr. Buggins didn't seem in the least offended that she'd missed their appointment the previous day. Nor did he act bothered by the fact that she was a woman. To her delight, he was an avid reader of the magazine and had read her article on the ravenkeeper.

"I always knew the ravens were at the Tower, of course," he said brightly. "But I didn't stop to think about what sort of care they require. Clever creatures, aren't they?"

"They are." Amelia hesitated. Revealing the fate of Pritchard would be unpleasant, but she didn't like the idea of Mr. Buggins learning about it elsewhere and wondering why she hadn't told him. "Unfortunately, Warder Pritchard was killed nearly a week ago."

"Oh? I'm terribly sorry to hear that."

"As was I." To Amelia's relief, he didn't ask for details, though he was clearly curious. She was surprised he didn't already know since it had been reported in several news sheets.

After more questions about his clocks, she was certain she had the information she needed and took her leave, promising to send a copy of the magazine when it was released.

With the constable in tow Amelia returned to the waiting hansom cab, her gaze once again perusing the street and the people passing by before getting in.

As they started to pull into traffic, she caught sight of a man standing along the street a short distance away who stared directly at her through the cab window. A vaguely familiar man in a bowler hat.

Her heart leapt to her throat. *It was him—the same man who had tried to take Maeve!*

She rapped on the roof of the cab in a panic. Constable Stephens hopped down to look at her through the window once the vehicle halted in the middle of the street.

"The man who tried to take Maeve is over there." She pointed to where she'd seen him—but he'd already disappeared.

Stephens looked to where she pointed. "Where?"

Before she could say anything, someone shouted as the man shoved people out of his way to depart in haste. With a muttered oath, the constable crossed the busy street to give chase.

"Shall we wait for the constable, ma'am?" the driver asked through the small door in the roof that allowed him to speak with passengers.

"Yes, please." Amelia kept her gaze on where Constable Stephens had disappeared. Shouts rent the air, but these came from behind them. Their position in the street made it nearly impossible for any other vehicles to pass by.

The driver maneuvered the cab as far to the edge of the road as he could. A few carriages and carts managed to get past them, but the other drivers made their displeasure clear.

With each minute that passed, Amelia's worry increased. Was Constable Stephens all right? Would the man she'd seen try to circle around to reach her? The thought had her heart pounding with fear even as she kept watch. In truth, she hadn't actually believed she would be in danger...until now.

"Madam, we can't wait much longer," the driver said a few minutes later through the small door. "The road is almost entirely blocked. I can take you home and return for the constable."

Amelia didn't want to leave the officer but understood the problem as the shouts and curses coming from behind them grew louder.

She looked one last time for the constable to no avail. An unsettled feeling lodged in the pit of her stomach, for her own safety or that of the constable's, she didn't know.

Remaining here, she was an easy target If Maeve's attacker returned.

"Yes," she agreed. "Perhaps that would be for the best."

Before the words had left her lips, the cab jerked forward. The traffic had now snarled into a tangled mess. They moved forward in fits and starts with the driver adding his own shouts to the mix.

Amelia's nerves stretched taut as she did her best to keep a watchful eye, telling herself her imagination was gaining the better of her. Still, various scenarios of how she could defend herself if the man opened the cab door and grabbed her ran through her mind. All she had were her reticule and her fists, not particularly helpful in a struggle. Perhaps she needed to consider a way to better protect herself from this point forward.

When the traffic finally eased and their pace increased, she breathed a sigh of relief. It was unlikely anyone could follow at this speed.

When the cab halted before her house, she alighted before the driver could assist her. "You'll return immediately for Constable Stephens?"

"I will do my best, ma'am."

"There will be a generous tip for you if you do. Thank you." She nodded and the driver was off with a flick of his reins.

Amelia glanced around, still unsettled as she walked briskly to the door where Constable Dannon nodded in greeting, only to frown.

"Where is Stephens?"

"In pursuit of the man who tried to take the girl," Amelia replied. "The hansom cab is returning for him."

Fernsby opened the door before she could say more. "How was your outing, Mrs. Greystone?" Fernsby asked, only to frown as he looked more closely at her. "Is something amiss?"

"We saw Maeve's attacker on the street as we left the clockmaker's," she said as she removed her cloak and gloves with trembling hands. *Anything could have happened. It hadn't. But it could have.*

"Dear heavens. You're unharmed?"

"Yes." Amelia pressed a hand to her heart, unsurprised to find it still beating rapidly. "Constable Stephens gave chase, and the cab driver has returned for him. Please inform me when the constable arrives." She didn't add *if* he did.

"Of course." Fernsby dipped his head. "All is well here. Inspector Field and Miss Maeve are in the drawing room."

"Thank you." She hurried up the stairs only to pause in the doorway at the sight of Inspector Field sitting beside Maeve.

The scene gave her pause as an image of Matthew sitting with Lily flew through her mind and forced a painful lump into her throat. She took a ragged breath, and the inspector quickly stood.

"What happened?" he asked urgently.

Amelia glanced at Maeve, attempting to calm her upset before the girl realized something was wrong. When the girl looked up from the magazine on her lap, Amelia forced a smile, though she knew it was stiff.

Worried Maeve might read her lips to catch the events, Amelia walked forward to press a kiss on her head then straightened. As if appreciating her gesture, the child leaned her head against Amelia. Amelia's concern eased as she kept a hand on the girl's shoulder and only then told Inspector Field what had occurred.

"Perhaps Stephens was able to catch him. He knows what he looks like." He frowned. "Perhaps I should've accompanied you after all."

"I am pleased you were here with Maeve. I couldn't bear the thought of anything happening to her."

"Nor could I." His gaze met Amelia's. "To either of you. We must take every precaution possible."

Amelia nodded. She was now convinced of that. "I will be relieved when this is over."

The flash of doubt that crossed the inspector's face gave her pause.

Her chest tightened at the reminder. She need only think of Matthew's murder to know that there was a chance it would never come to an end. The thought was a terrifying one.

Twenty-Three

An hour later, Henry was at Scotland Yard listening to Stephens' report.

"I chased him for several streets, but he must've ducked into an alleyway or the like." The constable shook his head. "I'm sorry to let you down again, sir. And the lady."

"We'll find him," Henry said despite his disappointment. "Why don't you return to the area with the sketch to see if anyone recognizes him?" Though doubtful as it seemed more likely the man had only been there to follow Mrs. Greystone, they had to try every avenue. *Someone somewhere had to know him.*

"Of course."

"Field?"

Henry looked up to see Director Reynolds standing nearby. Based on his expression, whatever he had to say wasn't positive.

Bracing himself, he followed Reynolds into his office. "Yes, sir?"

The older man sat in his chair and tapped a piece of paper on his desk. "The Home Secretary is requesting an update on the ravenkeeper's case."

The news was unwelcome, if not completely unexpected. Events at the Tower were tied closely enough to the government that anything out of the ordinary warranted attention.

Henry cleared his throat, wishing he had more progress to report. "We are continuing to search for the man who tried to take the ravenkeeper's daughter with the help of the sketch. He made another appearance this afternoon when Mrs. Greystone stepped out for an errand. Constable Stephens pursued him without success, but he is returning to the scene with the sketch to question onlookers."

"No one at the Tower recognized him from the drawing?"

"Not thus far, no. Fletcher is continuing to question the warders and others nearby about the man's identity."

Reynolds stared across his office, clearly trying to think of what additional action could be taken.

Henry waited to see if the Director suggested anything he'd overlooked. That was one of the advantages of keeping Reynolds abreast of the investigation each day. While Henry would've preferred to have already solved the murder on his own, he hadn't. That didn't bode well for his reputation at Scotland Yard since others already thought he'd only been promoted through the ranks because of his father and grandfather.

He shoved aside the thoughts. No purpose could be served in worrying over such things. His focus needed to remain on the current moment and the next step.

"Still nothing from the daughter?" Reynolds asked heavily.

"We know that there were two men of average height and build with facial hair who murdered her father and that the man who tried to take her was not one of them. She mimicked the stabbing so clearly saw it."

"We need more from her. Something substantial to help us find them."

The anger that speared through Henry took him by surprise. Why didn't the Director look into Maeve's ravaged brown eyes and press her for more? The child had been through more than *anyone* should have to endure, let alone a girl her age.

Instead, he cleared his throat of emotion and reached for logic. "Maeve's age and her inability to communicate, not to mention her distress over what she witnessed, make it difficult for her to share much of anything. However, I am continuing to work with her as is Mrs. Greystone. One of the advantages of me helping to guard the house at night is it gives me more time with Maeve."

"True. Perhaps she'll share more if she begins to trust you."

Henry nodded. "We are working on the other clues we have, with the exception of the poisoned meat. There's nothing unique about it. Anyone could purchase meat and cut it up. The arsenic used is readily available from numerous places as well."

"Unfortunate but also true," Reynolds agreed. He picked up a small stack of already tidy papers and tapped the edge of them on the desk to straighten them, a sure sign that he was pondering suggestions to offer.

Henry took a deep breath. *There was one last lead.* "Another issue of *Justice*, the news sheet I found in the victim's pocket, was released today. I intend to pick one up to see if it offers any insight."

Reynolds leaned forward with his elbows on the desk, his fingers steepled and his brow furrowed. "I can't say that I care for that clue. It would be concerning if the murder was politically motivated."

"The Home Secretary won't like it if it is." Henry knew that to be true. "I still find it curious that someone tried to poison the ravens twice. Perhaps it's nothing more than because the creatures are a pest to some, but the motive might also be to stir the public regarding the legend."

"Playing with superstitions can certainly do so. Especially those connected to the Crown as well as England."

"The fact that the victim was badly cut is already known on the street." That worried Henry. "When enough people realize someone who likes to kill in such a manner has not yet been caught, we could have a problem."

"Good thing 'ravenkeeper' isn't an especially popular position or we'd already have riots on the streets."

Henry suppressed a shudder at the thought. He'd been tasked with trying to keep the peace in two riots in the past. They were not to be taken lightly.

Reynolds leaned back in his chair, his displeasure obvious. "I speak with the Home Secretary at four o'clock. If something helpful arises before then, let me know with all speed."

"Yes, sir." Henry turned to go.

"Field?"

Henry looked back, his stomach tightening at the hard tone. He'd heard it before, when Matthew Greystone's murder continued to remain unsolved. "Sir?"

"Don't muck the investigation. We need to solve this without mistakes."

"Yes, sir." Frustration rose to the surface and churned in his stomach. He hadn't made any mistakes with Greystone, but neither had he found who'd killed him.

But he wasn't done with either case yet.

With another glance at his desk, which had several more files stacked on it, he strode out the door. Nothing was more pressing than Pritchard's case now that the Home Secretary was inquiring about it.

He headed toward the Tower, stopping at one of the numerous news stands along the way.

The abolition of the stamp tax nearly three decades previously that was paid to the government and passed on to readers, had increased the number of publications, and it often felt like a thousand different news sheets moved across England with the help of the railway.

He waited in a short queue at the stand, pleased to see a small stack of the one he wanted. A glance at the headlines of the other papers didn't cause any alarm. Only one mentioned the murder on the front page.

After paying a threepence for it and taking the free copy of *Justice*, he stepped out of the way to scan the headlines. The first one demanded the Monarchy cease efforts abroad and instead, spend their time and money fixing the problems at home. The other articles seemed to be much the same.

"*Justice*?" A lad holding a stack of news sheets under his arm approached. "Justice for who?" He guffawed at his joke. "Sure ye don't want one of these, mister?" The boy tapped the one he was trying to sell. "Much more interestin'."

"These are the only ones I need today." Henry eyed the lad. "Any exciting news of late?"

"Like what?"

"The grisly kind people seem to find so intriguing." He didn't want to mention the ravenkeeper but was curious if people on the street were talking about it.

The boy grinned, showing uneven teeth. "I heard a few days ago about a murder. The man was sliced up real good."

"Oh?" Henry lifted a brow, hoping he'd share more. Or rather, hoping he didn't as that would mean he hadn't heard much.

"He kept the ravens at the Tower." The boy leaned closer as if to share a secret. "No one knows who killed him though."

"How unfortunate."

"Whoever did it is still out there." He shook his head. "Can't count on the police to catch him. They're all worthless."

"Not all of them." But Henry didn't bother trying to change the boy's mind.

Public opinion of the Metropolitan Police had been a concern since its beginning. Viewed initially as little more than spies intent on removing the basic freedom of people, it had taken time for them to be seen as helpful. Those who found themselves the victim of a crime were quick enough to ask for police assistance, but that signified little. Opinion had plummeted when several detectives were convicted of accepting bribes several years ago. The department had since been reorganized with significant changes made. Henry liked to think the public's view was now swinging in the opposite direction, but it was difficult to say.

Henry glanced at the *Justice* headlines as he walked. From what little he could see, this edition was similar to the last one, promoting the socialist reforms and the party that supported them.

He put it in his pocket to read later and was soon waved through the gate at the Tower. The gray of the day had eased with faint sunshine that cast a deceivingly warm glow over the grounds. The air was still crisp enough to make him grateful for his wool coat. Luckily, it didn't take long for him to locate Fletcher.

"Sorry to say I have yet to find anyone here who recognizes the man in our sketch." The sergeant shook his head, clearly frustrated with the lack of progress.

Henry shared his updates, including news that the Home Secretary himself had requested an update on the case.

Fletcher groaned, looking anything but pleased. "As if we aren't doing all we can to find the murderer."

"Quite." Henry glanced around the grounds. "I'm going to have another visit with Daniels."

"I haven't seen him since yesterday when we spoke with him."

"Perhaps he's remembered something by now."

Based on Fletcher's expression, he was doubtful. So was Henry, but something about the man sat wrong. That alone made it worth speaking to him.

After agreeing to meet in an hour or so, Henry walked to the area where the ravens normally could be found and caught sight of the yeoman warder standing near a grassy area where the ravens were feeding.

"Good afternoon," he called to him with a casual tone. "No tours today?"

Daniels watched his approach with a wary look, his body stiff. Clearly the man didn't like him either. "I had several earlier."

"Any other trouble with the ravens?" Henry studied the black birds as they walked along the grass, pecking and fluttering. They always looked larger than he expected.

"No more poisoned meat, if that's what you're asking." Daniels glared for a moment before returning his attention to his charges. "Figured you'd be in search of whoever killed Pritchard rather than pestering me."

"We continue to pursue all avenues." How Henry hated the empty answer. He'd given it far too many times in the course of his career.

"Hmm." Daniels scowled. "Some are saying as how we can't feel safe in our beds at night until the killer is caught."

Considering the Tower gate was locked tight every night, and it was unlikely that one of the warders committed the murder, Henry didn't see how that could be true.

But he understood the man's point. "We're doing all we can to find the guilty party." He didn't mention that two were involved as that would only stir trouble. He'd much rather the warders continued to cooperate with the investigation.

Daniels looked past Henry's shoulder, eyes narrowed. "If you ask me, I still think Mr. Elliott is up to something."

Henry followed his gaze to see the Mint manager standing on the opposite side of the lawn, watching the ravens. While he found the man's apparent fascination with the birds odd, that didn't mean he wanted them, or their keeper, dead. But perhaps it was time to have another conversation with him to see if anything else came to light.

"I've spoken with him several times, but it won't hurt to do so again. Good day." Henry nodded to Daniels and strode toward Mr. Elliott.

Was Daniels truly suspicious of Mr. Elliott or was he trying to cast suspicion away from himself? Henry hadn't eliminated either man completely from his list of suspects. There was almost no one he could eliminate. Neither had a solid alibi, even if they didn't have an apparent motive to kill Pritchard.

"Inspector Field." Mr. Elliott dipped his head in a polite greeting. "Allow me to guess. Yeoman Warder Daniels directed your attention to me."

Henry smiled. No purpose would be served in hiding the truth. "I do believe he wonders why you're so often watching the ravens."

"Pritchard had the same question. I told him that I find them interesting. Watching them helps me sort through my thoughts."

"Oh? Is something troubling you?" Henry didn't expect him to reveal anything meaningful, but one could learn much from what a suspect didn't say as well as from how they reacted to questions.

"I'm a manager at the Royal Mint. I am always troubled."

"A position of great responsibility, I'm sure." Henry waited to see if he'd say more.

"Yes, well." Mr. Elliott met his gaze. "Let us hope that we won't be forced to call the police for what's bothering me at the moment."

"Illegal activity of some sort?" Henry asked.

"A suspicious one, for now. We shall see if anything comes of it."

"I'm happy to assist if I can."

Mr. Elliott nodded. "Thank you. I'll keep your offer in mind. Forgive me if I say that I hope I don't need you."

"As do I." But perhaps not for the same reason Mr. Elliott did. The number of files stacked on his desk was like a nagging headache that refused to ease. "The offer stands." Henry paused a moment before changing the subject. "Have you noted any questionable activity around the ravens? There was an attempt to poison them a couple of days ago."

Elliott's look of surprise and concern appeared genuine. He looked at the ravens as if to make certain they were well. "I can't say that I have. Surely Daniels doesn't think I had anything to do with that?"

"We're asking everyone who frequents the grounds whether they noted anything and are requesting them to remain on alert."

"Sergeant Fletcher came by my office yesterday and showed me a sketch, but I didn't recognize the person. Then he proceeded to ask me the same questions I've already answered." His frown suggested he hadn't much cared for that. "I thought it ridiculous for him to waste both of our time when a killer might be walking among us."

"We often question potential witnesses numerous times. The Metropolitan Police are nothing if not thorough." If only being so could guarantee a crime would be solved. Henry shifted his shoulders, frustrated by the lack of progress. "Please do keep us apprised of anything unusual you see."

Mr. Elliott pressed his lips tight, clearly unappreciative of the request, but he nodded all the same.

Henry intended to watch Mr. Elliott in case Daniels was right. Besides, he didn't care for either of them. How could it be that his list of suspects wasn't narrowing after six days on the case?

Twenty-Four

A melia heard the front door open from where she sat in the drawing room before dinner. Fernsby's quiet greeting and Inspector Field's response echoed through the house. The inspector had departed that morning prior to her coming down for breakfast, so she hadn't seen him yet that day.

While he was earlier than he'd been the previous night, his day had still been a long one. The hours he kept were enough to make her weary just thinking about them. Yet she knew firsthand that time was of the essence when he was working on a pressing case, especially one that involved murder.

How unfortunate that his efforts hadn't proven fruitful with Matthew's death.

If asked, she would be the first to attest that Inspector Field had done everything in his power to find her husband's murderer. Though she felt disloyal to even think it, part of her felt if anyone was to blame for the unsolved case, it was Matthew. He'd been involved in something unsavory, based on the secrets he'd kept.

Would she ever know what happened to him and why?

She shook off the question and smiled as the inspector entered the drawing room. "Good evening, Inspector."

"And to you, Mrs. Greystone." He looked alert though shadows marked his eyes. As always, he wore a brown wool suit; his hair, neatly brushed to one side, still needed a trim. His gaze swept the room.

Amelia knew that look. "She's in the kitchen but will join us for dinner." Did he ever think of anything other than work?

"Good. Fernsby mentioned the meal would be served soon. I hope you didn't delay it on my behalf."

"Not at all." She glanced at the clock on the mantle which showed it was just before seven o'clock. "We normally eat around this hour."

He gave a single nod, his expression watchful as it so often was. He always seemed to be on duty, regardless of what was happening around him. Then again, his arrival was hardly a social call.

She would hazard a guess that he didn't have much of a life outside of work, considering the hours he kept.

"Thank you for including Maeve." He took a few more steps into the room but seemed uncertain what to do next. "I'd like to spend more time with her to see if she can provide any additional details."

"I thought that might be your preference." Amelia rose and gestured toward the sideboard which held two crystal decanters, one of sherry and one of a whiskey her father liked. "May I offer you something to drink before dinner?"

It was odd for her to have a guest for dinner unless her parents visited, and the inspector's company was...pleasant, she realized much to her surprise. Perhaps that was because she was coming to know him outside Matthew's case. Talking about her husband's murder always made her uncomfortable. She couldn't help but feel she should somehow be doing more to help solve it.

He drew a slow breath as if attempting to relax. "That would be enjoyable. Thank you."

She walked over to pour a finger of whiskey for him and a sherry for her. "Did anything of interest arise today?"

She couldn't resist asking, though she assumed he would've told her if there was.

"Nothing especially helpful." He took the drink and a seat after she gestured toward a chair near the fire.

The day had been crisp, and he was surely chilled if he'd been out of doors for long.

"I'd hoped someone might identify the man in the sketch." She waited to see if he'd provide any details.

"We've shown it to nearly everyone at the Tower with no success."

"Interesting." She sipped her drink as she stared into the glowing coals of the fire, her thoughts turning over the information. "Do you think that suggests Pritchard's killer doesn't work there?"

"What makes you believe that?" he asked, his expression curious.

"From what I learned during my interview with Pritchard, it is a close-knit community. Logic suggests that any friends or associates, or any frequent visitors of those who work in the Tower would be known to them."

"I agree." He took another sip of his drink. "I wonder if Pritchard's tendency to listen to the conversations of others might have played a part in his death."

"When I interviewed him, he mentioned that when he tended the ravens, people often didn't see him."

"Almost as if he were invisible, like a part of the Tower's structure rather than a guard," Inspector Field mused.

"I'm sure that was true. The ravens are a distraction," she said lightly.

"They are fascinating to watch, especially the more one learns about them and their intelligence. I tend to think Pritchard didn't deliberately set out to listen to conversations. It just happened."

Something came to the back of Amelia's mind, but she couldn't quite put her finger on it.

"What is it?" Inspector Field asked.

Pleased when the memory came to her, she said slowly, "He told me that...some of his time in the military was spent gathering intelligence. I suppose old habits are difficult to break."

"How interesting. No one else mentioned that. Thank you for telling me about it." The man nodded in approval, a hint of respect glinting in his brown eyes.

She was pleased to help. One of the reasons she enjoyed her work in the lab was because she liked to solve puzzles, and a mystery was just that. "I just wish I knew something from my conversations with him that would provide a proper clue."

"That is the challenge with clues. You never know which ones will prove helpful until you pursue them."

Amelia smiled. "May I ask what made you chose to be a detective, Inspector Field?"

"Please, call me Henry. I always feel as if my father or grandfather are nearby when I hear Inspector Field."

"Very well. Please do the same." It was pleasant to be on a first-name basis, given how long they'd known one another.

"Thank you, Amelia." He said her name carefully as if trying it on for size.

She stiffened with surprise as awareness trickled through her. Her reaction to him saying her given name made her realize that until now, she'd only thought of him as Inspector Field, not a man. It was quite disconcerting to think of him differently.

"As to your question," he continued, drawing her from her thoughts, "from a young age, I was interested in my grandfather's and father's work. For as long as I can remember, in fact. I enjoy helping people and seeing justice served."

"Those are admirable reasons."

"Solving a case can be immensely satisfying." He held her gaze, a look of regret clouding his face. "Needless to say, not being able to bring one to a conclusion is...upsetting."

Amelia nodded, presuming he spoke of Matthew. "I'm certain it's like a sliver in one's thumb, always nagging at your thoughts."

"That's an apt description, though more like a knot in the head rather than merely a sliver."

Her sympathies grew at the realization of how much it bothered him. "I wish I had additional information to offer about what happened to Matthew as well."

"You've been more than helpful. As you know, I don't believe your husband was killed in a random act. Yet if we can't determine any suspects or a motive, the case is difficult to solve."

She twisted her lips to the side as she stared into the fire, stomach tightening. "I tend to think he angered someone. As I've mentioned before, we had grown apart before he died. He was clearly involved with people I had never met, possibly doing activities he knew I wouldn't approve of."

"Based on his behavior?" Henry asked. When she hesitated, he added, "I know we've spoken of this before, but it never hurts to go over it again with the hope that something new surfaces. If you can bear it, that is. There is no expectation."

Amelia smothered a sigh. Apparently, a pleasant evening wasn't to be after all. The memories were still painful but less so as time passed. If she were honest with herself, some of the pain was caused by her own guilt for not being a better wife. If she hadn't been so distraught after Lily died, perhaps he wouldn't have been killed.

She pushed aside that troubling thought and drew a deep breath. "He had become secretive and stayed out late far more than he'd ever done before. When I asked what kept him, he'd only smile and shake his head, insisting it was work." She sighed. "I should've pressed him about it. In all honesty, after Lily died, it was hard to care about anything."

"That's understandable. Your thoughts were elsewhere."

So was her heart. Matthew had become a familiar stranger rather than her husband. But she didn't say that.

"His work as an importer and exporter of goods provided a nice living, though some months were better than others." She met Henry's gaze. "Yet he accumulated more wealth than I could've guessed. The amount in the bank was twice what he'd earned in the past decade. What could he have been doing to make that much in a year or two?"

"Perhaps there was a particular item he sold that was more lucrative than anticipated."

She shook her head. "I don't know what that would've been—and if it was, why wouldn't he have mentioned it to me? Nor did he note anything of the sort in the ledger he kept. You saw that for yourself."

"He might not have recorded it. Could he have been trying to avoid paying taxes on the sale?"

"I suppose. You'll remember I found money in his desk, too. Strange, for a man who rarely kept more than a few pounds in his wallet."

"That's not uncommon in general. People often keep significant amounts in their homes for one reason or another. Could he have meant to take it to the bank?"

"Hmm. He'd never done that before, to my knowledge. I worried for some time that someone would come looking for it." She frowned as she thought over the dark days following his death. "I still think someone was watching the house after he died."

Henry nodded. "That must have made it even more alarming when you realized it was happening again with Maeve."

She hesitated, wondering if she should give voice to her worry before at last deciding no harm could come from it. "I worried whether the instances in the past were real or imagined. Sometimes my nerves get the better of me. But Fernsby saw the same man I did a few days ago. I am not imagining things."

"You are not. You have every right to be concerned in both cases. We should listen to our instincts more often."

Before she could say anything further, Fernsby appeared in the doorway. "Dinner is served."

"Thank you, Fernsby. We'll be down directly." Amelia was relieved by the butler's timing, otherwise the discussion might've continued. While she would like to help solve both mysteries, no doubt Henry was weary of talking about them.

Henry finished the last of his drink and stood, returning the glass to the sideboard. Amelia did the same before leading the way down to the dining room.

"I could grow accustomed to having such fine dinners every evening if this one is anything like the last," Henry said in a light tone.

Amelia smiled and relaxed at the change in topic. "I would guess that Mrs. Appleton is doing her best to impress you. Do you normally dine at home in the evening?"

"My landlady serves dinner, but often I arrive too late, so I stop at a pub on the way home for a quick bite."

She couldn't imagine such a life. "I suppose I enjoy being home. That was something Matthew never seemed to understand." She gave herself a mental shake. She'd been grateful for the change in the conversation and here she was returning it to her late husband.

"Was he gone much?"

"Not overnight. But he left early in the morning and often returned late. Especially after...after Lily died."

She pressed her lips tight, not wanting to talk about her daughter or her death. That was something from which she would never recover. Time may have eased her loss from a sharp stab to a dull ache, but it still hurt terribly.

"I suppose we all cope with grief in different ways." The gentle understanding in Henry's tone was comforting as they walked along the corridor.

She could only nod as she opened the dining room door, uncertain whether she could get anything past the sudden lump in her throat.

The sight of Maeve waiting for them at the table gave her a start. Just for a moment, Amelia saw Lily sitting there. Then she blinked and Maeve came into focus. Pressing her hand to her heart did nothing to ease the ache.

That was the hard part of grief—it swept over you when you least expected it and threatened to take you under.

After a steadying breath, she continued forward, noting how Maeve's brown eyes widened in alarm at the sight of Henry entering the dining room.

"Inspector Field is joining us for dinner," she told the girl after touching her shoulder then moving to her regular seat at the end of the table where Henry waited to pull out her chair.

Maeve didn't respond but watched carefully as Henry took a seat across the table from her.

"Good evening, Maeve." Henry dipped his head in greeting.

When Maeve's gaze swung to her, Amelia lifted a brow in expectation. The girl seemed to understand what Amelia wanted as she looked at Henry and nodded to acknowledge his greeting.

Surely it was good for Maeve to be expected to act properly, despite her grief. Having boundaries and rules had helped Lily feel safe and secure. Amelia hoped that was the case for Maeve.

After smiling in approval, Amelia took her napkin and placed it on her lap, noting that Maeve watched and followed suit.

She wasn't certain what Henry expected of the girl. Trying to gain her trust without truly being able to converse and interact with her was a challenge. Amelia didn't know if Maeve would've trusted her if they hadn't already been acquainted through her father and the lab experiments they'd done. If not for that, Maeve wouldn't have arrived on her doorstep.

Yet as Fernsby served a dinner of roasted lamb, it seemed that Henry didn't expect anything of her. He made polite conversation with Amelia and smiled often at Maeve.

It was impossible to tell how much of the talk Maeve understood. Most of the time, her attention remained on her plate, but every so often, she watched them both for a few minutes.

She ate well, if not with great enthusiasm, especially when it came to the cooked carrots. They weren't one of Amelia's favorites either, but she ate them, too.

As the carrots slowly disappeared, Henry shared an amusing story about his grandfather, who'd also been a chief inspector.

"You met Charles Dickens?" Amelia asked with astonishment.

"On numerous occasions. He and my grandfather were friends for many years until their deaths. In fact, Dickens wrote an essay about my grandfather, and some think he served as inspiration for Inspector Bucket in *Bleak House*."

"Truly?" That made Amelia want to read the book again. "How fascinating. I enjoy his books very much."

"He was a talented man. His interest in social causes made a difference for many and convinced those with the means to create change to do so."

Henry stared past her, clearly immersed in memories. "Rumors abounded that Dickens wasn't the only one to base a character on my grandfather. His blithe assurance and compelling presence made him a fascinating character, even to me. People not only listened to him but trusted him."

"I can't imagine the places Mr. Dickens visited with your grandfather." She realized her error as soon as she spoke. "How silly of me. You have surely visited those same places. From Seven Dials to Devil's Acre to Bethnal Green."

"Yes, I have." His expression tightened, suggesting what he'd witnessed was unfit for dinner conversation, and said nothing more.

In Amelia's opinion, his reaction spoke of his character. If someone in his position became accustomed to the terrible conditions the less fortunate endured, they would no longer be useful. One needed empathy to aid those in troubling circumstances. Otherwise it would be easy to turn away and abandon them to their fates.

That was one area of her life Amelia wanted to change. She intended to take a more active interest in the ills that plagued London. Perhaps once Pritchard's murder had been solved and Maeve was reunited with family, she could find a way to do so. She'd been too caught up in her own trials to reach out a hand to help others. Perhaps she could write an article or two for the magazine that focused on charitable issues, though the editor had assigned her topics thus far.

But if she put the proper light on a problem and suggested it, he might be willing to allow her to write about it.

"That was delicious." Henry returned his silverware to his now clean plate. "Thank you again."

Maeve's focus shifted from her own clean plate to the door Fernsby used with anticipation, making Amelia chuckle. "Dessert is Maeve's favorite course."

"Who can blame her?" Henry asked. "The trifle last evening was wonderful."

Maeve straightened as the door opened and Fernsby returned to clear their plates.

"Maeve is anticipating the final course," Amelia told the butler.

"I shall return directly with it," the butler said with a nod of approval as he took the girl's clean plate.

True to his word, only a few minutes had passed before he returned with another tray.

"What has Cook made for us this evening?" Amelia asked.

"A French apple tart with cream, madam."

Her guest's audible sigh of appreciation had Amelia laughing. "You are in for a treat, Henry."

Maeve couldn't see what was on the tray the butler held until he set a plate before Amelia. The girl licked her lips as Fernsby served her next, waiting impatiently for him to serve Henry before picking up her fork.

"Our Maeve has a sweet tooth," Amelia remarked as she watched the girl dig into the dessert. After the first two forkfuls, she slowed her pace and savored each bite.

"Nothing wrong with that." Henry lifted a fork of the tart toward Maeve to show his agreement.

Maeve caught the gesture and returned it.

The smile on both their faces warmed Amelia's heart. Gentle moments like this made her wonder if the future would work itself out. That living without additional heartache was possible.

She hoped Pritchard's murder would soon be solved even...if she was no longer sure Matthew's ever would be.

Twenty-Five

The sight of Fletcher's solemn expression in the crisp morning air as he waited outside the Tower gate was enough to make Henry's stomach tighten. Clearly, the sergeant had bad news to share.

Henry supposed the last two nights of calm and quiet at Amelia's had lulled him into thinking the case was progressing and would soon be solved. Perhaps the limited sleep he'd gotten the past two nights was affecting his thinking because based on Fletcher's face, matters had worsened.

"What is it?" Henry asked rather than offering his customary greeting.

"Another body has been found, sir."

His stomach dropped. "Another—where?"

"Same place." His moustache twitched, another indication of his upset. "Same method."

Dismay and disbelief swept over him. "Stab wounds?"

"Yes. Unfortunately, we're both familiar with the victim."

"Who?"

"Thomas Elliott. The Mint manager."

"Damn." The murder of a suspect shook Henry to the core. Not only was it concerning to have another crime on their hands, but it also confirmed that his suspicion of the man had been misplaced. Having a second victim connected to the Tower tripled the concern. Reynolds was not going to like this. The Home Secretary was not going to like it. "Where is the body?"

Fletcher tipped his head, and they set off, skirting the Tower grounds, and moving toward the river.

Henry tried to process the news and what it meant as they walked, but the news made him feel off balance, making it difficult to think. A second murder committed in a similar fashion would gain the attention of the public and caused an entirely different set of challenges.

"Who found him?" Henry had to focus on the routine questions that came with an investigation and hope the answers revealed a path to follow.

"A fisherman passing by on his boat saw a body washed on the shore and reported it after he docked."

Once again, Constable Stephens stood guard at the top of the stairs that led to the river. "Morning, sir."

"Stephens. You might as well join us," Henry advised.

"Yes, sir." He straightened and tugged on the hem of his jacket as if to brace himself, and then followed Henry down the stairs.

The body lay on its side, facing the river. Water lapped gently at the shore less than a foot away from an outstretched arm.

Henry studied the scene from the foot of the stairs before slowly walking forward. No footsteps were visible on the ground. The man's clothes were wet as was his hair. Whether Mr. Elliott had been tossed in the river or left on shore would need to be determined by the postmortem.

"Once again, they made no effort to make certain the body remained in the water," Fletcher remarked, obviously puzzled by the choice.

"No, they didn't." Clearly, the sergeant believed the two who'd murdered Pritchard had also killed Mr. Elliott. Henry tended to agree.

Bold. And arrogant, as if they didn't fear they'd be caught. That might become their downfall.

The back of the black wool coat had several cuts. Henry walked around to the front to see the familiar face now pale, the eyes staring lifelessly toward the opposite shore.

"Poor bastard." Fletcher shook his head. "No one deserves to die like that."

"No, they don't." Guilt speared through Henry. *If he'd been able to identify the murderers, Mr. Elliott wouldn't be dead.*

Dwelling on such thoughts wouldn't get him anywhere. He blinked, shifting his focus to the body. He was determined to do everything in his power to bring the killers to justice. That meant sifting through the situation for clues.

A glance at the constable showed that he remained on the bottom step, staring at the body. At least he didn't seem to have the urge to retch again, even if he looked uncomfortable.

Henry checked the shoes and found scuff marks on the heels. "He was likely dragged along a pavement at some point." Henry carefully pushed the man's shoulder to roll him onto his back.

The slices across the front of his clothing were numerous, some going through the coat, waistcoat, shirt, and into the flesh beneath. Once again, the worst cut was the slash across his neck nearly from ear to ear.

A muffled groan from the constable suggested that he could see the damage from where he stood. Henry glanced up to see Stephens staring across the river, struggling to regain his composure.

Fletcher squatted near the body. "The skin on his knuckles isn't torn like Pritchard's was. Nor are his nails." He glanced at Henry. "He must not have put up much of a fight."

"He wasn't a trained soldier like the ravenkeeper, and they may have caught him by surprise, especially now we know there's two of them."

Henry lifted the coat to better see the injuries. "The pattern of the wounds looks similar to Pritchard's."

"They do," Fletcher agreed. "A mix of angles just like the raven-keeper's."

"The postmortem will tell us for certain if it's the same weapon." He didn't bother to count the wounds this time.

Once again, the questions were who and why. Mr. Elliott had seemed to be a nosy sort based on how often he'd inquired about the murder investigation. Not dissimilar to Pritchard. But he'd also mentioned a problem at the Mint that might require police assistance.

Were the two situations connected?

Henry checked the man's pockets, finding a watch, some change, a penknife, and a small wooden disc about the size of a shilling. Henry studied the odd disc, turning it over to find a large J carved into it. "Interesting."

"Humph. Not especially helpful." Fletcher scowled. "You'd think victims would have the decency to leave us a helpful clue."

Henry appreciated his attempt at levity even if they were staring at a dead body. Somehow it helped provide objectivity and allowed them to focus on their job rather than the brutality of the crime.

Henry wrapped the items in a handkerchief then finished his examination of the scene as quickly as possible since, once again, the tide would soon rise to wash away any evidence—and possibly the body if they let it.

"Was he simply at the wrong place at the wrong time?" Fletcher asked as they prepared to carry Mr. Elliott up the stairs.

"Or inserting himself into something he shouldn't. Hard to say. We'll ask around to see if he mentioned suspicions about anyone specific."

"I would hope he would've already told one of us, given how often we've been at the Tower of late," Fletcher grumbled.

"You would think so." *Had the man decided to do some investigating of his own, only to stumble upon the killers?* "He mentioned a troubling matter at the Mint yesterday when I spoke with him," Henry added. "Now I wish I had pressed him harder for details."

He shook his head then gestured for Stephens to join them to help carry the body. This wasn't the time for regrets. Those would have to wait until the middle of the night, along with the rest of his doubt and dark thoughts.

"He didn't say anything to me about it," Fletcher said as he reached for the man's shoulders.

"Perhaps our killers are associated with the Tower in some manner," Henry said as he lifted Mr. Elliott's leg and Stephens picked up the other while keeping his eyes averted from the body. "Mr. Elliott didn't truly work there but had business in the vicinity."

Fletcher nodded and started toward the stairs. "Seems too much of a coincidence that both victims have a tie of some sort to the place."

"We'll speak with Chief Warder Wallace first to see if he has any personal details about Mr. Elliott before we venture to the Mint. Hopefully the surgeon will be able to examine the body quickly."

"Reynolds isn't going to be happy about this, is he?" Fletcher asked, his tone shadowed with dismay.

"No." That issue wasn't his concern at the moment. He needed to focus on solving the murders.

"Looks like we have an onlooker."

Henry followed Fletcher's gaze to see a tall, slender, well-dressed man with black hair wearing a bowler hat watching them from nearly thirty yards away near the Tower wall.

To Henry's surprise, rather than moving along once he realized he'd been seen, the stranger continued to observe them. Unsettled by his presence, Henry directed the men where to place the body then started toward the man, only to watch him turn and stride away.

"That was odd," Fletcher said when Henry returned.

"Very." The man was out of sight, leaving Henry to wonder.

The next few hours were filled with activity. The body was taken to Mr. Taylor's, Henry and Fletcher spoke with Wallace, and then the pair of them went to the Royal Mint.

The stunned disbelief of the man who greeted them was something Henry didn't think he'd ever become accustomed to. Nor did he want to. The day he stopped caring was the day he would find another line of work.

An assistant manager worked daily with Mr. Elliott but wasn't there. The man they spoke to promised to send him to the Tower upon his return where Henry intended to go next. Speaking with a few others who'd worked with Mr. Elliott gained them little. The victim had high expectations of the staff, kept to himself, and none had known him well. After looking through Mr. Elliott's small office, gathering his home address and the name of a cousin who lived in London and was thought to be the next of kin, Henry and Fletcher sent Stephens to find the cousin then returned to the Tower.

The operations of the Mint at the Tower were limited and involved only a handful of employees. They seemed reluctant to share much about the man, but Henry wasn't sure if that was out of respect for the dead or because they simply hadn't known him well.

Fletcher and Henry expanded their questioning to the yeoman warders next. Only a few had spoken with him at length. Potential clues were few and far between.

Henry was headed in search of Daniels when he heard his name called.

"Inspector Field." Wallace waved from across the grounds and approached with another man at his side. "This is James Ball, who works at the Mint with Mr. Elliott." Wallace frowned as he looked between the two men. "Or rather, worked," he corrected himself.

Mr. Ball, a younger gentleman in a brown tweed suit with a slim build and a hooked nose, looked quite distraught and continually shook his head. "I just can't believe it. Who would want to kill Mr. Elliott?"

Henry took his notebook out again and flipped to a fresh page. "How long did you know him?"

"Less than a year. I began working at the Mint last November as the assistant manager."

"Had Mr. Elliott seemed upset or worried of late?" Henry asked.

"He was very concerned about Warder Pritchard's death, as we all are. It was the subject of the majority of our recent conversations."

"Did he say anything out of the ordinary yesterday?"

Mr. Ball thought for a long moment before shaking his head again. "We have both been busy and didn't converse overmuch. I can't think of anything in particular. Just business as usual."

That was odd, given what Mr. Elliott had told Henry. Perhaps he hadn't wanted to worry Mr. Ball. Or Mr. Ball was part of the reason for his concern.

"When did you last see him?"

"Just before closing at six o'clock yesterday at the new building. As I'm sure you know, he often made several trips between the old Mint that's located here and the new one."

"Did he mention his plans for the evening?"

"I don't think so." He shook his head again, his distress obvious. "Though I'm so shocked that it's difficult to remember. He lived alone and normally dined at home, I believe. He had a quiet life. I didn't know him well."

"Is this familiar?" Henry asked, showing him the wooden token.

Mr. Ball made no move to take it for a closer look. "No. Nothing to do with the Mint."

Henry returned it to his pocket. "If you remember anything that could be helpful, let us know." Fletcher joined them, and Henry excused himself after making the introduction, leaving the sergeant to speak with him further.

He tucked his notebook back in his pocket and, with quick strides, made his way to the South Lawn where Daniels should be. He wanted to see his reaction to the news if he hadn't already heard.

Daniels' scowl suggested he was less than pleased to see Henry approaching. The ravens fluttered around the area, some on the grass and others on the nearby bench with one eyeing the trash bin.

"Away from there," Daniels said, with a wave of his hand at the curious raven, sending the bird fluttering away with a protesting croak.

"Daniels," Henry said as he paused before the warder.

"What's happened?" His expression tightened. "Is Maeve well?"

"She is." Henry appreciated his concern for the girl. "Unfortunately, there's been another murder."

Daniel's eyes went wide. "Good God. Who this time?"

"Mr. Elliott." Henry waited a moment for the news to sink in, watching his expression closely. If his shock was an act, he was good at pretending.

The warder shook his head in disbelief. "I *knew* he was up to no good. He took more interest in Pritchard's death than most."

"Why does that mean he was up to no good?" Henry asked. He didn't retrieve his notebook; he didn't want Daniels to think he was being questioned. He just wanted him to talk.

"Anytime someone puts their nose into things that don't concern them, it isn't good." Daniels' brow lifted as if daring him to argue. "Wouldn't you agree?"

"Not necessarily," Henry countered. "It's only natural that he was curious since he knew Pritchard."

Daniels didn't look convinced. "What happened to him?"

There was no point in hiding the basic facts. "He was killed in the same manner."

The warder huffed out a breath. "What a terrible way to go."

"It is." Henry watched the ravens, careful to look away when one appeared to look back at him before returning his attention to Daniels. "Do you know if anyone took issue with Mr. Elliott?"

Daniels paused as if to give the question serious consideration. "I wouldn't say he was well liked. He was fussy and could be difficult when things didn't go his way. He offered his opinion on matters that didn't concern him."

Henry wished he had known more of this before the man's death. But then, the questions one needed to know never presented themselves until it was too late. "Did you overhear complaints about him?"

"Not any more than myself that I recall." He reached into his pocket and withdrew a handful of peanuts to scatter across the grass. Two of the ravens immediately investigated, but the rest ignored the gesture. "They prefer meat, but they've already had their share of that this morning."

"Mr. Elliott mentioned yesterday how much he liked to watch the ravens." Henry found himself doing the same again. The iridescent feathers with their pearl-like sheen changed colors as they moved from pink to purple to almost white then back to the deepest black. The sheen made them look as if they were coated in crude oil.

"I asked him if he didn't have something better to do with his time. It makes me nervous when people watch the ravens like that." The warder lifted one shoulder in a shrug. "Perhaps he was harmless after all."

"When was the last time you saw Mr. Elliott?" Henry asked.

Daniels glared at Henry. "Why? Am I under suspicion?"

"We've had two murders that involve the Tower and those within it. Everyone is under suspicion."

"I hardly think the yeoman warders, including myself, could be involved. We are here to protect the Tower and all within it. It is our sworn duty—and you insult me, along with the rest of the warders, by suggesting otherwise."

"I mean no offense," Henry said without heat, reassured by the man's anger. "I'm sure you can appreciate that I am only doing my job. All that matters is finding who murdered these two men."

Daniels shifted his feet as if trying to adjust his attitude. "I suppose. But you need to hurry. Another murder." He shook his head. "Nothing good can come from this."

"On that we agree." Henry nodded. "Let me know if you think of anything else that might be helpful."

He sighed as he walked away, thoughts churning. The new raven-keeper was a grumpy sort but seemed unlikely to have anything to do with the murders. Mr. Elliott had been viciously eliminated from Henry's short list of suspects.

He had to hope the postmortem would provide something helpful because he was running low on leads.

Twenty-Six

"We have another victim, eh, Inspector?" Mr. Taylor asked when Henry entered Mr. Taylor's office that afternoon.

"Unfortunately." Henry wondered if his tone reflected his frustration and the dimming hope that he'd solve the two murders.

Mr. Elliott's cousin had been distressed at the news but confessed he only saw him during holidays or rare family gatherings. They hadn't been in touch for months. He didn't recognize the token, nor had the few yeomen warders he'd shown it to. Mr. Elliott's office and apartment hadn't provided any clues either. It merely added to the mystery.

As seemed to be the case with Pritchard, no one had seen anything. At least, no one who could point them in the direction of the guilty, he amended, as his thoughts went to Maeve.

Mr. Taylor returned his attention to the naked body on the table before him. From the looks of it, the doctor had already made significant inroads on the autopsy. The body cavity was spread open, and several metal dishes waited on a nearby table.

Henry had stopped to speak with Mr. Taylor before reporting in at Scotland Yard. Reynolds would want to know what the postmortem revealed, and so did he.

The same attendant as before stood to one side of the doctor. He nodded at Henry then returned to his notes.

"Definitely the same killer," Mr. Taylor said. "And more than likely, the same murder weapon."

"I thought as much."

Mr. Taylor gestured to the pale skin of the abdomen with its many cuts. "The one to the midsection here between the lower ribs was likely the fatal one." He used his scalpel to point to the narrow slit. "Based on the inflammation and bruising around it, the victim was still alive. It struck the liver and did significant damage."

"The rest were simply for the killer's entertainment?" The notion had him swallowing back regret that he hadn't prevented the man's death, his stomach burning in response.

"That's one way to put it. As I mentioned with the last victim, the murderer apparently finds some pleasure in the act, or he wouldn't slice with such abandon."

"It didn't appear as if Mr. Elliott put up much of a fight."

"No." Taylor set down the scalpel to lift the victim's right hand and examine it. "Other than a raised hand, most likely in an effort to protect himself, there aren't any defensive wounds."

Henry could see a cut on the edge of Mr. Elliott's palm from where he stood. "He didn't seem the type to box or the like, so perhaps he didn't know how."

"What was his occupation?"

"Manager at the Royal Mint."

"Another victim connected to the Tower." Mr. Taylor's brow furrowed as he held Henry's gaze, a hint of sympathy in his eyes. "Truly unfortunate."

"Indeed." Henry looked again at Mr. Elliott's lifeless form. Dignity was stolen from those who failed to die peacefully in their sleep. Instead, they were studied, examined, and measured until all their secrets were revealed, including what they ate for their last meal.

But not always who killed them.

Henry hoped that when he died, he passed away in his sleep and drifted peacefully from this life to the next, whatever that might be. He'd found it difficult to hold onto religious beliefs, given his occupation. Witnessing the horrors people did to one another caused him to question how a higher power could allow such atrocities to occur.

What made the job difficult was also the reason it was important. It mattered, therefore, he mattered. While he couldn't claim this occupation was in his blood given his adoption, it had seeped into his bones, and he couldn't imagine doing anything else.

But on days like this, he wished he were better at it.

He pulled his thoughts back to Mr. Elliott's demise. His purpose was to find a killer, not ponder religious ideologies.

"Time of death?" he asked.

"The water casts the exact hour into question as before but let us say between ten o'clock and midnight." Mr. Taylor tilted his head to the side as he studied the man's face. "More likely ten, I think. I'll know better after I take a look at the contents of his stomach."

Discovering what had kept Mr. Elliott out at that hour would be helpful. Whether that was possible remained to be seen, since the man had lived alone.

"I'd be interested to know if he'd been drinking." That might help to know where he'd been.

"I will have a look at his stomach and be sure to mention the contents in my report."

"Any estimate on when that will be complete?"

"Another hour or two." His gaze met Henry's again. "I'm certain you're in a hurry for it."

"I am. Thank you."

Henry departed for Scotland Yard only to slow his pace as the hair on the back of his neck prickled with unease. He had the distinct feeling he was being watched. *Interesting*.

He kept a steady stride for several paces then quickly turned to study the area behind him. Few others were on the street, none seeming to pay him any mind.

So, whoever followed him was taking care not to be seen. Were they merely wondering what he intended to do next, or did they hope for an opportunity to harm him and slow the investigation?

After another glance around, he continued on his way. He needed to warn Fletcher to take care, though it would take a brave man to attack the sergeant given his size and expertise.

The unsettled feeling continued, and he halted before entering Scotland Yard to peruse the area. At the very least, he wanted whoever was watching to realize he knew they were there.

One thing was certain—the case was building. Henry could feel it. The guilty were growing bolder. That was when they often made mistakes.

He entered the building, nodded at Johnson who was at his usual post, then walked directly to Reynolds' office and knocked on his open door.

"Field." Reynolds sharp gaze swept over Henry as he nodded. "I've been expecting you. What do you have so far?"

Henry pulled out his notebook to make certain he didn't leave out any details. "The victim was a Mr. Thomas Elliott, age forty-three, manager of the Royal Mint for the past two years. He was found near the same location as the ravenkeeper, reported by a fisherman, and appears to have been murdered in the same manner as Pritchard. We should have the postmortem report in a few hours, but Mr. Taylor believes the same killer used the same weapon."

"Damn." Reynolds heaved a sigh. "The Home Secretary won't like this."

"When word spreads that another person from the Tower was murdered, the public won't either."

"Indeed. I suppose a reporter will soon catch wind of it. We should prepare for that outcome."

Henry nodded. An outcry might arise since the police hadn't yet found the guilty party. It took surprisingly little to cause a riot, and they were ugly. He needed to catch the killers as soon as possible.

"Any additional leads?" Reynolds asked.

"We're narrowing down when Mr. Elliott was last seen and where. He lived alone, which makes the information difficult to gather. It's clear someone associated with the Tower is involved. Fletcher is continuing to question everyone there." Henry didn't mention that he thought he was being followed. That was irrelevant until he caught whoever was doing it.

"Nothing more from the daughter?"

"No. I'm escorting her to the Tower this afternoon to see if she recognizes the killers." He hated to potentially upset Maeve, but a second murder meant he had to move quickly. Before there was a third.

"Good." Reynolds frowned as he studied Henry. "I'm surprised you haven't already tried that."

His protectiveness of the little girl warred with duty, something that had been a struggle from the start of this case. "Her wellbeing remains a concern given what she's already been through. Besides, the calmer she is, the more information I'll gain." He didn't want to push her to the point where she remained completely unresponsive.

"Understandable, I suppose. But she'll remain in danger until the killers are caught."

Henry dreaded putting Maeve into what could be a difficult situation, but he didn't see any way around it. He pulled his watch from his pocket. "There should be enough time yet this afternoon to take her."

"Let us hope something comes of it."

"Yes, sir." With a nod, Henry departed.

He stepped outside, searching the area to see if anyone lingered nearby. His instincts told him they were gone. Still, he took a hansom cab to Amelia's to make it more difficult for anyone to follow him.

He hoped she'd be willing to accompany them to the Tower. Maeve would feel more comfortable with Amelia at her side, and so would he.

He chose not to wonder at the reason why.

Twenty-Seven

"Now?" Amelia stared at Henry in surprise. Though he'd mentioned he wanted to take Maeve to the Tower, the request seemed sudden and unexpected, as was his arrival in the middle of the afternoon.

Yet a closer look at his grim expression suggested there was more to the timing of his request. She glanced at Maeve, who'd paused in her drawing to look between them as if sensing tension in the air.

Henry looked at the girl, too. After managing a smile for her, he returned his attention to Amelia and tipped his head toward the doorway of the drawing room.

Amelia placed a hand on Maeve's shoulder, gestured for the girl to wait, then followed Henry out. There was definitely something wrong. "What's happened?"

"There's been another murder."

She gasped, a chill running along her skin. "Who?"

"The manager of the Royal Mint. I don't think Maeve knew him. Certainly not well as he only spent a portion of his time at the Tower."

Nor did Amelia. Still, the news of another murder involving someone at the Tower was frightening. Terrifying, in fact. "You think it's the same killers."

While only a guess, Henry's upset was visible in the set of his shoulders and the shadow of concern in his eyes. That made it an easy assumption. "Yes."

She pressed a hand to her heart, but its rapid beat didn't slow. "Oh, dear."

"Quite." The single word spoken in his deep voice said so much more.

Clearly, the investigation had gone from pressing to urgent. It was also clear that Henry still didn't have answers, if he wanted to take Maeve to the Tower.

"I see."

Exposing Maeve to what could be a frightening situation went against everything Amelia wanted for the girl. Her protective instincts as a mother demanded she refuse—especially since a second murder had occurred. Someone had already attempted to take the girl. Walking her around the Tower to see if she might recognize her father's killers seemed far too dangerous.

"Time is of the essence," Henry added, his fingers tightening on the brim of the hat he held, clearly ready to depart.

That subtle sign of tension had her looking closer at his expression, noting the tightness around his mouth, a reminder of his concern.

Her reluctance must've shown, for he said, "I won't leave her side. She'll also see some familiar faces that might bring her comfort." His brow furrowed, suggesting he was aware of how the visit would more likely affect Maeve.

Amelia pressed her lips together to prevent a denial from escaping. It didn't matter what she wanted. Whoever had killed Maeve's father had killed again. Who was to say there wouldn't be a third victim?

"Your presence would surely bring her comfort if you're still inclined to join us." He released a quiet breath. "It's been nearly a week since Pritchard's death. Her family could arrive any day, our opportunity gone."

Amelia nodded, realizing she didn't have a choice. "Allow me to get our things." She returned to the drawing room to look at Maeve, who put down her pencil and watched them both, eyes wide with worry.

"Do we try to tell her?" she asked.

"Perhaps in the cab. The driver is waiting."

"Very well." Amelia didn't bother to pull the bell. Instead, she left the room to go first to the attic to fetch Maeve's cloak before stopping in her own room for her own things.

She glanced at the contents of her reticule. *What did one require to possibly identify a murderer?* She shook her head at the thought, shut the reticule, and hurried from the room. Now that she was committed to the task, she wanted it over and done.

After advising Fernsby of the outing and bidding the constable on duty goodbye, they were soon in the hansom cab with Maeve's stiff form between them, her doll clutched in her arms.

Amelia rubbed the girl's shoulder and shared a worried look with Henry. Then she leaned forward to catch Maeve's eye. "We're going to the Tower. Perhaps you can see your friends."

Maeve showed no reaction, leaving Amelia to wonder whether she'd understood. The girl unexpectantly glanced at Henry, who offered a small smile and a single nod.

As if somehow reassured, Maeve relaxed slightly and stared out the window.

Traffic was busy, but it took less than twenty minutes for them to arrive at the Tower where they alighted. The yeoman warder at the gate waved Henry through then caught sight of Maeve.

The man's bushy gray whiskers lined his jaw, making his expression difficult to see, but his blue eyes twinkled in delight beneath the brim of his hat as he squatted down. "Miss Maeve." He offered her his gloved hand. "How good to see you."

She took it, still holding her doll while a hint of a smile curved her lips.

"Come for a visit, have ye?" he asked.

She nodded.

"Everyone inside will be pleased to see you and Miss Molly." He reached out a gloved finger to gently touch the doll she held.

Guilt settled heavily on Amelia. She hadn't known the doll's name until now. She hadn't even thought to ask Maeve what it was. How terrible of her. Was it any wonder the child had shared so little when Amelia hadn't inquired about such a basic detail?

The warder straightened and nodded at Henry and Amelia. "Hope she enjoys her visit."

Amelia smothered a curse. If the visit was successful, Maeve wouldn't enjoy it at all. Yet she couldn't blame Henry for wanting to try this approach. The second death surely placed additional pressure on him to find the killers.

She wasn't certain whether to hope Maeve recognized whoever it was or not. She didn't want the girl upset, but she wanted this over for the benefit of them all. Living in a state of fear was no way to live.

Some of Amelia's mixed emotions must've shown on her face, for Henry's gaze held on her for a long moment. "Ready?"

"Yes." She tightened her grip on Maeve's hand and nodded, managing a smile when the girl looked up at her.

Maeve's wary expression suggested she hadn't fully succeeded in masking her concern. Or perhaps Maeve was simply nervous to return to the Tower when it would be a stark reminder of the loss of her father.

Before Amelia could think of a way to reassure her, they were walking through the gate and onto the grounds where Henry paused and glanced around.

"What do you propose?" Amelia asked.

Henry looked down at Maeve, his brow furrowed. "I wonder if she would like to stop by her home. Would it provide any closure, do you think, or only upset her?"

Amelia had no idea. Her understanding of what might be going through Maeve's mind was limited, clouded by sympathy for the girl mingled with the grief of her own losses. "We...we could walk past and see if she seems inclined to go inside."

"Excellent idea. We'll see if anyone in particular catches her attention as we go."

Amelia appreciated that he didn't come directly out and say 'recognize the murderers' even though she knew that's what he meant. Somehow the distinction made their outing less frightening.

They made their way toward the casements where the warders lived but paused by Chief Yeomen Warder Wallace's office.

"Maeve." He gently touched her shoulder in greeting and smiled. "Good to see you, lass."

She looked at him but didn't show any reaction to his words.

"Is her apartment open?" Henry asked. "We thought she might want to stop in."

"I'll come along to unlock it. We haven't cleared it out as of yet. Thought we'd wait to do that with Pritchard's relatives when they arrive. They might want to take some of the items with them."

"That makes sense," Henry said. "We're not certain if Maeve wants to go in, but I'm relieved it won't be empty if she does."

"I live nearby. My daughter and wife will be pleased to see her." They started forward, but Wallace kept his gaze on the girl, sympathy etching his face. "Poor lass. I hope her future brightens once she moves away from London and is with family."

Amelia ached at the thought of the difficulties ahead of Maeve. The changes Wallace mentioned wouldn't eliminate her sadness but perhaps they'd help to ease it. She just hoped what they were about to do wouldn't worsen her grief.

Keeping an eye on Maeve, Amelia studied the people they passed. Was one of them the murderer? Did they wish Maeve harm? Many ignored the girl, but a few greeted her warmly. They passed several warders, tourists viewing the grounds, and others who seemed to have business there but wore no uniform.

They reached the Chief Warder's home, and he stepped inside to alert his wife and daughter that Maeve was with him. She made it clear she didn't want to go inside, so the two came out to greet her.

The other little girl tightly hugged her, a gesture which Maeve returned half-heartedly while holding her doll. The moment made Amelia wonder if she'd already released her grip on her previous life in an effort to distance herself from further pain.

Mrs. Wallace had difficulty controlling her emotions. The tears streaming down the portly woman's face which she swiped with her apron had Maeve easing back. Amelia couldn't blame the woman when her own heart ached for Maeve as well. It was nice to see how much Mrs. Wallace cared.

The woman gave Maeve a final hug and managed a watery smile. "Goodbye, dear. We'll see you again soon."

When she released her, Maeve turned to stare a few doors down at her own home, ignoring those around her.

Amelia bent to look her in the eye. "Do you want to go in?" She gestured to Maeve then pointed to her home to make herself clear.

The girl considered the idea for a moment then slowly nodded and took Amelia's offered hand.

"Very well then." Wallace cleared his throat as if he, too, were overcome with emotion. Then he stepped forward to unlock the door, his wife and daughter moving back but watching closely.

Amelia shared a concerned look with Henry, trying to hold back her own tears as they neared the door to the only home Maeve had ever known. He appeared equally worried.

Of course, Maeve had already been inside since her father's death. Chances were she'd return again when her family arrived. But the moment still brought a lump to Amelia's throat as she tried to imagine what Maeve might be feeling.

"Inspector Field," a voice called from a short distance away.

Amelia wrenched her gaze from Maeve to see a well-dressed gentleman a few years older than her approach.

"Good afternoon, Mr. Blackwell," Henry said.

The stranger nodded at him and then Wallace but barely glanced at Amelia and Maeve. "Any news on the most recent crime?" His tone was impatient, his lips pressed together as if he was prepared to disapprove of Henry's response, whatever it might be.

"We're in the process of investigating it," Henry replied, his expression unreadable.

Mr. Blackwell shook his head, clearly unsatisfied. "Surely the police have clues to pursue rather than wasting time touring the casements." He gestured toward Maeve's door, and the girl tightened her grip on Amelia's hand, easing closer. "Aren't there more interesting areas that might actually lead to the murderer?"

Whether Mr. Blackwell's obvious frustration or his movement made Maeve nervous, Amelia did not know.

"Every possible avenue is being pursued." Henry's tone was calm, but his eyes narrowed, suggesting he didn't appreciate the implication that he wasn't doing his job.

Did Mr. Blackwell not realize how rude he was being or that he was upsetting Maeve?

"I find that difficult to believe," the man continued. "Don't you realize how concerning it is to know a killer is in our midst?" His gaze shifted to Wallace as if even the Chief Warder wasn't above suspicion.

"It is concerning." Wallace stepped closer, eyes glinting with anger. "For *all* of us. Especially those of us who live here." He glanced over his shoulder at his wife and daughter. "If you haven't noticed, the police have been here every day."

Mr. Blackwell's focus switched to Henry. "For all the good it has done. Obviously, they need to look elsewhere." With a nod at Wallace, he turned on his heel and strode away.

"Pay him no mind, Inspector Field." Wallace shook his head, his gaze still on Mr. Blackwell as he crossed the Tower grounds. "He must be having a bad day."

Henry nodded, his expression revealing little, but Amelia knew him well enough to see his upset over the confrontation. She couldn't imagine the pressure he felt to solve the murders, especially with comments like that being thrown at him.

"Who is he?" she asked.

"He's in charge of the Armoury," Wallace advised as he turned to Pritchard's door with a key in hand. "Let's let Maeve have a look. Perhaps there's something inside she'd like to take with her. Remind her of home."

The feel of Maeve pressing against her side had Amelia looking down, shocked to realize the girl was trembling. With a gasp, she bent down to comfort her. The girl's tear-filled eyes met hers. "What is it?"

Was she upset to enter her home or had Mr. Blackwell's presence frightened her?

Twenty-Eight

S mothering an oath, Henry glared over his shoulder to where Blackwell was still visible across the grounds. Had the man frightened Maeve or was her distress caused by worry over returning to her home?

Henry shared a worried look with Amelia, then squatted before Maeve, wondering how best to find out. "Do you want to go inside?" He gestured to the door.

After a moment of hesitation, she nodded, sniffing as her upset eased. Yet she glanced over her shoulder to where Blackwell disappeared inside a building.

Henry raised a brow at Amelia, unable to decide what the problem was, but she seemed to be as confused as he was.

"Maeve." He gently held her shoulder to regain her attention. "Do you know him?" He pointed to where Blackwell had gone.

Her little brow puckered for a moment as if she was considering his question but undecided how to answer. At last, she looked at him and shrugged.

"Was he one of the men who hurt your father?"

Maeve switched her focus to where the man had gone with a frown.

That was no answer. Henry blew out a breath he hadn't realized he'd held and straightened, frustration simmering.

"As I said, don't pay Mr. Blackwell any mind," Wallace said quietly. "He hasn't been the same since he lost his son last June." He shook his head. "In the Victoria Hall calamity in Sunderland."

"How terrible." The horror in Amelia's face matched how Henry felt.

"The traveling magic show that performed at Victoria Hall?" Amelia asked.

Wallace nodded. "Which ended in tragedy when over a thousand children rushed into a narrow stairway for a gift being offered near the stage. Mr. Blackwell's only child, five years of age, among them."

One hundred and eighty-three, ages three to fourteen, were crushed and trampled to death. Henry shook his head, the details something he would never forget. A public outcry had arisen over the disaster.

"While I'm pleased legislation was quickly passed to require emergency exits at such venues to help prevent a similar recurrence," Amelia began, "it doesn't bring back those who were lost or repair the hole left from the death of a loved one gone too soon."

Wallace grimaced. "I'm certain not a moment goes by that he doesn't think of the lad and that terrible day."

"Such a tragedy," Amelia murmured.

So was the death of her own daughter, Henry wanted to add but kept the thought to himself. Losing a child would be a blow no matter what the cause.

Blackwell's behavior seemed out of character compared to the other times Henry had spoken with him. Perhaps he was having a difficult day, as Wallace had suggested. It wouldn't be the first time Henry had borne the brunt of someone's foul mood. Nor would it be the last.

Still, it wouldn't be the worst idea to look deeper into Blackwell's background, something he hadn't yet done.

"Here we go." Wallace rattled the keys then made quick work of unlocking the door and held it open.

Maeve released Amelia's hand to walk forward and stand in the doorway, peering inside.

Did she hope by some miracle her father might be in there?

The thought tugged at Henry. While he tried not to become emotionally involved with victims or their families, Maeve made that difficult. The somber girl and her perilous circumstances touched him.

He waited patiently as she took one step inside then halted again and looked around. Amelia gripped her hands together as if to keep herself from following to offer comfort and support. She had already done more than her share to aid the girl. Henry made a mental note to thank her again when he had the chance.

Maeve walked farther in, focus shifting from a faded chintz-covered chair to the kitchen table to a painting on the wall. She clutched her doll even tighter then walked briskly to the stairs.

Amelia looked in surprise at Henry, who was as confused as she was by the girl's behavior. The woman followed her up the stairs and Henry did as well, his curiosity caught.

Maeve went directly to her room, pulled open the drawer of a narrow dresser, and withdrew a red ribbon. She set her doll on the bed, smoothed its yarn hair, and then carefully tied the ribbon around it.

Then she turned to look at them both before leading the way out of her room and out of the house.

Wallace waited by the door. "What was she after?"

"A ribbon for her doll's hair," Amelia answered with a sniff, clearly touched by the girl's behavior.

He nodded. "Sometimes it's the simple things that bring comfort, eh?"

"Apparently so."

He locked the door behind them. "I'll let you continue on your mission. I have other matters to attend to."

"Thank you," Henry said.

"Do let me know if anything comes of this."

"Of course." He didn't bother to say that the Chief Warder would know as soon as he did, since news seemed to travel quickly around the Tower.

Maeve took Amelia's hand and looked expectantly at Henry.

With a smile at the girl, Henry led the way in the direction of the South Lawn where the ravens usually were. He watched Maeve as they passed several yeomen warders along with tourists, but she paid them no mind.

Soon Daniels came into view, kneeling on the grass as he attempted to coax one of his charges to come closer.

Again, Henry observed Maeve who watched the ravens but ignored the yeoman warder. They drew nearer and, once again, Maeve released Amelia's hand to walk forward.

As if recognizing her, one of the ravens hopped close. Another, the one Daniels had been trying to lure forward, stretched its wings and lifted into the air to glide along the ground before landing directly before Maeve.

Daniels stood, his lips twisted into a scowl. "They seem to remember her. At least, Bartram and Ava do." He didn't look especially happy about it.

Henry walked nearer to Maeve to see her reaction to their greeting. A hint of a smile appeared as if she were pleased they had come to her.

"Bartram," Henry repeated. "Isn't he the one that was missing at the time of Pritchard's death?"

"Yes. He was Pritchard's favorite. Him and Ava."

"They're a couple, correct?" Amelia asked. "He told me they mate for life."

"That's right," Daniels said with a nod.

The ravens bobbed before Maeve, making their croaking sounds, so different than the songbirds Henry preferred. But he would admit to a growing respect for the creatures even if their intelligence made him slightly uncomfortable.

If only they could tell him who had killed Pritchard.

Maeve squatted down then rose back up again, seeming to imitate the ravens' motions. The birds croaked in approval. At least, that was how Henry interpreted their sounds.

Maeve's genuine smile was a welcome relief after her earlier tears.

"How is she faring?" Daniels asked after joining them.

"As well as can be expected," Amelia answered after Henry looked at her to answer. "Some days are better than others, but it will take time."

"Of course." Daniels bent down to look at Maeve and smiled. "Good to see you, Maeve."

The girl's brow puckered as she studied him before nodding to acknowledge his greeting. Her lack of reaction to the warder helped confirm that it was unlikely he'd been involved in her father's murder.

Henry waited as Maeve watched the ravens a few more minutes before catching Amelia's attention. "We should continue on."

"Yes." She reached for Maeve's hand, gentle as always in her inter-actions with the girl. "Let us walk some more," she told Maeve when she had her attention.

The girl came along easily enough, and Henry bid Daniels goodbye.

"Which way now?" Amelia asked.

They crossed the lawn, passed Traitor's Gate, moving toward the stairs that led to the Armoury. They passed groups of tourists guided by warders whose booming voices echoed against the stone walls as they told the history of the Tower.

"I can't imagine giving tours every day," Amelia said to Henry as they paused to allow a group to pass.

"It takes a special soldier to be charismatic enough to hold people's attention as well as one respectful of history to act as a guide." Henry certainly wouldn't want the job.

"They're wonderful storytellers." Amelia sighed. "Even Warder Pritchard, though a rather gruff man, could share bits of history with flair."

Intriguing. It was difficult for Henry to imagine the type of person Pritchard had been when his only reference was viewing his corpse, along with the details of his life during the investigation.

Maeve glanced at some of the warders they passed. A few ignored her, seemingly caught up in the stories they shared with the crowd. Others waved at Maeve and smiled if they caught her eye.

She didn't act fearful of any of them.

They were leaving the Armoury when a man strode out the door. He carried a cane, though he didn't seem to need it, his fine wool suit nicely tailored. With no more than a glance in their direction, he swung the slim black staff then flicked it into the air and caught it, never breaking his stride.

Maeve halted, eyes wide as she watched the man. Then her brow furrowed, and her shoulders hunched. Henry shared a look with Amelia, uncertain what to make of it.

She didn't seem to know either.

Henry bent low to meet the girl's gaze. "Are you well?"

Still she watched the man but at last she nodded.

"Do you know him?" he asked.

Rather than answer, she shifted to move slightly behind Amelia, almost as if she didn't want the man to see her...or she didn't want to see the man.

Henry straightened to hurry to catch up with him. "Excuse me, sir."

The man slowed to a stop and turned to look Henry over from head to toe. "Yes?"

"Inspector Henry Field of Scotland Yard. May I have your name?"

"What business is it of yours?" His Irish accent caught Henry's notice, speeding his heartbeat. *Irish.*

"We're investigating a murder that took place on the Tower grounds."

The man almost smirked. "Which one?"

"Both." Henry didn't appreciate the man's attitude.

He was tall and slender with black hair, blue eyes, and long sideburns. Henry found his confident demeanor irritating rather than admirable.

"Good to know Scotland Yard is working hard to keep London safe."

"Your name, sir?" Henry repeated.

"Aidan Sloane."

"What is your business at the Tower?"

"Visiting."

"Who?" Henry planted both feet to make it clear he was prepared to stand there the rest of the afternoon asking questions. Short answers would only lengthen the interview and delay the man's departure.

Sloane heaved a beleaguered sigh and glanced around the grounds, clearly displeased. As he turned, Henry noted a faint dark spot marked his jaw. Whether it was a faint bruise or a bit of dirt was difficult to say. "I have a friend who works at the Armoury."

"And that would be?" Henry retrieved his notebook and pencil to jot down his answers.

"Michael Blackwell." The man raised a gloved hand to adjust his bowler hat.

"How often do you visit him?"

The man blinked at him, disbelief at the question in his eyes. "Allow me to check my calendar and get back to you."

Henry waited for a real answer, not appreciating his sarcasm.

Mr. Sloane sighed. "Once or twice a week, I suppose."

"Where were you on the night of October fifteenth?"

"I'm sure I don't know. At home, I suppose."

Henry continued questioning him and noted his address as well as his place of work, a bank that wasn't far.

Though tempted to ask more questions about the Armoury manager, Henry held off. Sloane might choose to tell his friend. Henry would prefer to have the opportunity to make inquiries about Blackwell without him knowing, for the time being.

Aware of Amelia and Maeve waiting a short distance away, Henry ended his questions. "I appreciate your time, sir. I will be in touch if I have additional questions."

The man nodded, the twist of his lips suggesting he was displeased. He looked vaguely familiar to Henry. Perhaps he'd seen him on the Tower grounds before.

"Anything of interest?" Amelia asked as they watched Sloane walk away.

"I don't know yet. Did Maeve have any further reaction to him?"

"She continued to stare at him from my side." Amelia shook her head. "I'm not sure what to make of it."

Henry bent to catch Maeve's attention. "Do you know him?" He pointed at Sloane who was about to round the corner of a building.

She didn't answer, continuing to watch the man, a wary look on her face.

Henry sighed, wishing Maeve could speak. If she could, he'd have solved the case by now.

Twenty-Nine

"Maeve did not seem to like either of those men we came upon," Amelia murmured as the hansom cab started toward her home.

"No." Henry glanced down at the girl between them, clearly exhausted from the outing from the way she leaned into Amelia's side. "But I would hesitate to say for certain whether they were involved in her father's murder."

"Their general descriptions are correct, from what little she shared with us. And it is intriguing that they know one another."

"Indeed." That particular fact struck Henry as a suspicious coincidence. "I intend to look into both of them."

"While I can't say I had a good first impression of Mr. Blackwell, it's impossible not to feel sorry for him." Amelia briefly looked at Henry, perhaps wondering if he felt the same.

"Truly terrible circumstances." He shook his head. Experiences like that could change people.

He glanced at Amelia, whose attention had returned to the passing scenery, wondering how much her own losses had changed her. While she had every reason to be bitter and withdrawn after the difficult hand life had dealt her, he was pleased she was not.

The cab slowed to a stop, and Henry exited, nodding to Constable Stephens who nodded in return. Reassured, he assisted Maeve and

Amelia to the pavement, taking care to make certain Maeve still had her doll and the red ribbon that bound its hair. He was pleased it brought her comfort when so little else could.

"I do believe some tea is in order," Amelia said, starting toward the front steps only to pause when he didn't follow. "Are you not coming?"

"I have a few things to see to first."

"It will be dark soon," she argued with a frown at the horizon.

"Yes," he agreed as he followed her gaze toward the softening light of day. "I will return later, of course."

Amelia gave a resigned sigh but smiled as she reached for Maeve's hand. "I don't envy the hours you keep. Do take care, Henry."

"Of course." He watched them enter the house, and then returned to the cab before he was tempted to follow them inside where a cheerily burning fire, pleasant company, tea, and biscuits awaited.

Such comforts were not for him when he had a murder case to solve.

He ordered the driver to take him to St. Thomas', then sent the cab off to find a new fare. Visiting the homes of Blackwell and Sloane had to wait until the morning when they had left for work. With luck, Mr. Taylor would have finalized his report by now.

"The contents of his stomach suggested his final meal was taken at a pub," Mr. Taylor said as he handed Henry the report.

"Oh?"

"Not sure how helpful that is given the number of pubs in London." Mr. Taylor offered a sympathetic look.

"It's a place to start." Henry thanked the doctor and took his leave, scanning the contents of the report as he walked in the direction of the Tower.

The murder weapon and the technique were the same as Pritchard's.

Little else detailed in the report caught his notice. He carefully folded the paper and tucked it into his pocket, considering his options.

Chances were that Mr. Elliott had been killed on his way home from a pub if Mr. Taylor was right. Given the location of his body, it was logical to think he might have dined at one not far from the Tower, but there were many in the area. Perhaps for once, luck would be on his side, and he'd visit the right one.

With a sigh, he entered the Red Lion. It was a popular place well known for its simple but tasty fare. Pausing inside the door, Henry allowed his eyes time to adjust to the dim interior. The scent of spilled beer and fried food lingered in the air. The place was busy, though the workday hadn't yet ended for most.

Unwilling to waste time, Henry approached the bartender who nodded. "What will you have?"

"Actually, I have two questions," he began hoping to make clear that the sooner he had answers, the sooner he would depart.

"What might those be?"

"Do you know this man?" Henry pulled out the sketch of Maeve's attacker.

The tall, beefy man leaned forward to study it before shaking his head. "Can't say that I do."

"What of this?" Henry handed him the wooden token he'd found in Elliott's pocket, still uncertain if it had any importance.

The bartender's brow furrowed as he turned the disc over. "Nope."

"Thank you." Henry slid a coin across the bar then took his leave.

Just three streets over stood the Rose and Thistle. It had a similar atmosphere with more tables for seating. The bartender polished glasses as he surveyed his customers, slowly turning to greet Henry.

"What's your pleasure?" he asked, setting aside the glass and towel.

"Some information." Henry pulled out the sketch first and handed it to him. "Do you recognize this man?"

He barely glanced at it before shaking his head.

"Are you sure?" Henry asked, lifting it to encourage him to take a better look.

The man heaved an exasperated sigh and looked again. "No."

Frustrated, Henry felt his patience slipping. "And this?" He handed him the wooden disc.

He hesitated as he turned it over before handing it back to Henry. "Try the Crown on Parsons Street."

"Thank you." Henry paid him for his help, though part of him wondered if the man had provided the pub name just to hasten Henry's departure.

Henry had been to the Crown a few times. As he walked the four hundred yards to where it stood on a corner, he wondered how many pubs he'd be able to visit at this pace. He couldn't deny the lure of a delicious meal awaiting him at Amelia's home...but Maeve was also there, and spending a few hours visiting pubs was a small price to pay if it brought him closer to her father's killers.

Gathering his resolve, he grabbed the large brass handle and opened the heavy wooden door of The Crown. The scent of meat pies wafted in the air. Over a dozen patrons were already seated on the worn leather benches, enjoying a pint, a meal, and conversation. A pair of large, gilt-framed mirrors hung behind the empty bar, casting his own reflection back at him as he drew closer.

A pock-faced man with a scraggly beard strode from the back and nodded in greeting as he tossed a white towel over his shoulder. "Have a seat wherever you like."

"I am only here to ask a couple of questions."

He looked Henry over from head to toe. "Police?"

"Yes. Scotland Yard."

His lips twisted as if he was debating how to respond.

Henry waited, hoping his expression made it clear he wasn't leaving until he had asked his questions.

The man glanced over his shoulder to see if any of his customers had noted Henry's entrance before returning his attention to Henry. "What is it?" he asked gruffly in a low voice.

This time Henry held out the token first, since that was what had prompted the previous bartender to suggest The Crown.

The bartender frowned, making no move to take it. "You're late."

"I'm sorry?"

"The meeting was the night before last."

Energy pulsed inside Henry. *Finally.* "What meeting would that be?"

The man shrugged. "Some sort of social party. The political type." He tipped his head toward the rear of the pub. "They use the room at the back, but you need one of those to be allowed in."

"Can you tell me the name of the organization?" Henry asked, though he suspected he already knew what it was.

"The Democratic Federation, I think."

J for Justice. Just like the name of the news sheet. "Do they meet here often?"

"Every week of late. Probably a dozen or so of them. Maybe more."

Henry pulled the sketch from his pocket again. "Is this man familiar?"

The bartender studied it. "Looks like the one who watches the door. He checks to make certain everyone has a token before he lets them in. Goes by the name Samuel, though I don't know if that's his given name or surname."

"Where can I find him?"

He shook his head. "Here next week for the meeting. Otherwise, I couldn't say."

"Do you know the names of those who run the meetings?"

"No, Samuel's the only one I've spoken with, and that's never amounted to much. The meetings last a couple of hours. Sometimes more. Sometimes less."

Henry leaned close, keeping his voice low. "One of the men who attended was murdered soon after he left last evening. Anything more you can tell me, anything at all, could help find the killers."

The bartender tightened his lips and shook his head. "Murder, you say? They're a secretive bunch and take their politics seriously. I think they're planning something. I don't know anything more. Come back next week for the meeting." He glanced at the wooden disc still held out. "Bring that token with you."

Henry nodded. Unfortunately, he couldn't wait that long for answers.

Thirty

"What else do you have for me?" Director Reynolds set aside the postmortem report and folded his arms over his chest, a sure sign that unless Henry told him the case was solved, he wouldn't be pleased. "We must act quickly before matters worsen."

Henry clenched his jaw to keep from protesting. He *had* been taking action since Pritchard's body was discovered. He was doing everything possible, including keeping Reynolds up to date.

He'd intended to leave the report on Reynolds' desk after he'd finished at the Crown so he could get an early start in the morning. Unfortunately he'd found the Director still at his desk, despite the late hour.

Henry tamped down his frustration. *This wasn't about him. It was only about the case.* "We took Pritchard's daughter to the Tower this afternoon to see if she might recognize one or both of the killers."

"And?"

"She reacted negatively to two men, though—"

"*Reacted*? That's hardly confirmation of guilt."

Henry's frustration resurged. "As I've mentioned before, communicating with her is a challenge. Her upset, subtle as it was, warrants further investigation into both suspects."

"Do either have a possible motive?"

Henry considered the question carefully. "The first, Michael Blackwell, works at the Armoury. That could easily mean he is familiar with weapons." He paused, still uncertain how the next bit fit in. "His only son was killed in the Victoria Hall incident."

"Hmm." Reynolds stared across the room as he pondered the information. "I don't see a particular tie to the ravenkeeper. Who else?"

"The second man is Adrian Sloane, who happens to be friends with Blackwell. He works at a bank located near the Tower. He is Irish, and there was mention that our knife-wielder might have an Irish accent. However, other than an unhelpful attitude, I'm unaware of a motivation as of yet." Henry cleared his throat. "A wooden token marked with a J was in the second victim's pocket." He handed it to the Director. "It provides entrance into weekly meetings held at the Crown on Parsons Street by the Democratic Federation, the political party behind the news sheet Pritchard had on his person. The man who attempted to kidnap Maeve guards the door at those meetings."

"Interesting." Reynolds handed back the disc. "What are your next steps?"

"In addition to looking deeper into Blackwell and Sloane, as well as trying to locate Samuel with our sketch, I'm also calling on Hyndman, the man behind the publication, to learn more about the meetings."

"At least you have had some progress." Reynolds glanced at the report again. "But we need more. I'm assigning another inspector to the case to see if we can come up with something more substantial, preferably an arrest. Possibilities aren't enough."

Henry stiffened. The news was a slap in the face. "But—"

"Inspector Perdy will be assisting you. He is older and has more experience, which should help placate the Home Secretary."

Perdy? That was more than a slap. "Sir, with all due respect—"

The Director raised a hand. "The matter is decided. Update Perdy as soon as possible. Now, if he's still here."

Henry would've preferred anyone over Perdy. He didn't like anything about the man, nor did he respect him. His abrasive manner grated on everyone, including potential witnesses. How would that benefit the case—how would he treat Maeve?

Another look at the Director's expression confirmed that arguing would be pointless.

"Very well." Henry turned to leave, wondering how he was going to bear the next few days, let alone accomplish all he wanted to.

"Field?"

Henry looked back, doing his best to mask his anger.

"Solve the damn case."

"Yes, sir." As had often been the case of late, the order was less than helpful.

To his relief, Perdy was nowhere in sight. No doubt he was already at the pub, telling everyone who would listen that his assistance was needed to find the Tower killer.

Blast it. Heaviness sat on Henry's chest. He hoped his father didn't hear the news. He hated to guess what he'd think of it.

Doubt settled over Henry as he left the Yard and strode down the street, ignoring the hansom cabs waiting nearby. He needed to walk off some of his upset before he returned to Amelia's. The lady had an uncanny knack for sensing moods, proven not only with Maeve but with him as well.

Moments like this made him question whether he'd chosen the right profession. Whether he had any talent for solving crimes or if those he'd solved had only been by luck.

In his youth, he'd wanted nothing more than to follow in his father and grandfather's footsteps. He'd listened to every story they'd told, often numerous times. As he'd grown older, he'd read everything he could about investigation techniques and even snuck case files from his father's study.

Learning he wasn't a Field by birth had put a nick in his plan and confidence. Still, he'd pursued his passion and thought he was good at it...until the Matthew Greystone case. Hitting a dead end with it had changed the nick to a notch.

Having Perdy assigned to work with him increased it to a crevasse. He knew beyond a doubt that his fellow inspector wouldn't add anything to the case. The man's sole purpose would be to make Henry look a fool. If Henry weren't careful, he'd succeed.

He drew a deep breath, then another, but that didn't help to ease the tension in his body or the doubt circling his thoughts.

While a visit with his father to talk over the case might prove helpful, it would also be unwise. Someone might discover it. He had to solve this on his own and quickly. That was the only way to save his reputation as an inspector and honor Warder Pritchard and Mr. Elliott.

With a muttered oath, he reined in his dour thoughts and the threat of hopelessness they brought. Those wouldn't aid him now. Logic and reasoning were what he needed.

He would pursue the leads he'd listed for Reynolds. Come morning, he would see what more he could discover about Blackwell as well as visit the publication office. He'd have Fletcher look into Sloane. As for Perdy, perhaps he'd ask him to speak with the yeoman warders again. *That should keep him out of my way.*

With a plan in place and less frustration simmering inside him, he hailed a hansom cab to Amelia's. Keeping her and Maeve safe remained a top priority.

"Good evening, Field," Constable Dannon said from his post at the Greystone residence.

"Dannon. Anything of interest to report?" Henry asked as he studied the quiet street.

"Not as of yet." He followed Henry's gaze. "But you may count on me to stay alert through the night."

"I expect nothing less." Henry knocked on the door, which was immediately opened by Fernsby.

"Good evening, Inspector." The butler shut the door behind him and bolted it. "You've arrived just in time for dinner."

That was a surprise, given it was an hour later than when dinner had been served the previous evening. "How fortuitous."

Fernsby smiled as he took Henry's hat and coat. "Mrs. Greystone is in the drawing room."

Henry climbed the stairs, surprised by the pleasurable anticipation filling him at the thought of spending another evening with Amelia. He'd have to cut it short though, as he wanted to review his notes on the case. It was vital he had a solid plan for the next two days.

Amelia sat at her desk near the window in the drawing room, writing.

Henry paused in the doorway to admire her. As always, her dark hair was drawn up into a twist high on the back of her head, revealing the feminine lines of her face. The lamplight cast a golden glow on her features. She truly was an attractive woman, even if it wasn't his place to notice such things.

"Good evening," he said, hating to interrupt her thoughts. It was rather awkward not to have Fernsby announce him, as he had done so often in the past. He couldn't imagine simply walking into the room and having a seat or helping himself to a drink from the crystal decanters on the sideboard.

Yet the idea was unexpectedly appealing.

"Henry." She put down her pen with a welcoming smile. "How nice to have you here again." She rose but capped her inkwell before coming forward. "May I offer you a drink before dinner?"

"Thank you. I appreciate that."

"Please have a seat." She gestured toward one of the wingback chairs near the fire. "You must be tired after such a long day."

Henry slowly walked toward the chair and the inviting fire that took the chill from the room but didn't sit. *Times such as this were dangerous.* It would be easy to become accustomed to them: to have someone waiting for him who inquired about his day and showed interest in his answer, someone to share the burdens and celebrate the victories.

That wasn't his purpose here, and he couldn't allow himself to forget it.

He cleared his throat and prevented his thoughts from wandering. "How is Maeve?" Better that he focused on the case than Amelia and her warm hospitality.

She poured them both a drink, herself a sherry and him a whiskey, and brought them over. After she sank gracefully into a chair and he followed suit, she said, "She remained a little out of sorts after our return. Whether that was due to visiting her home or encountering Mr. Blackwell or Mr. Sloane, I wish I knew."

"As do I." At last, Henry permitted himself to have a sip. The whiskey was smooth and obviously of excellent quality. He wondered if it was left from her husband, though the thought lessened his pleasure of the moment.

"She'll join us for dinner, but she's tired and will most likely retire early."

"Good." Only too late did he realize his reply could be taken the wrong way. "I mean good that she's joining us for dinner. I continue to hope that the more time I spend with her, the more comfortable she will be around me."

"Of course." Amelia sipped as she watched the fire. "The more I think about it, the more convinced I am that both men upset her."

"I have to think the same. We'll know more about both of them soon." He would make sure of it.

"Do you think the tragedy that befell Mr. Blackwell could be related to the case?"

Henry relaxed as he thought over the possibility once again. "I don't know, but it's certainly something to consider."

"I've been thinking about it all afternoon, trying to put myself in his shoes."

Henry's admiration for her increased, and his curiosity rose. "And?"

"I'd be so angry at such a senseless tragedy. One that could've been avoided." She shook her head. "But who would he be angry at? The organizers of the event, I'm sure. And whoever manages Victoria Hall, as well. They're miles away."

Henry waited for her to continue, not wanting to interrupt her train of thought. Her opinion was helpful to hear and aided him to sort out his own thoughts.

"I think he might be angry at the government, too," she continued. "After all, they were quick enough to pass legislation to prevent a similar occurrence. If only changes had been in place beforehand."

"You might be right." He hadn't considered the possibility. "The hall's name connects it to the government even more."

Amelia gasped. "How true. I didn't think of that." She tapped a finger against her lips as she worked through it. "But even if he were angry with the government, how could that be connected to Pritchard?"

"Therein lies the question." If they weren't about to be called to dinner, he would've been tempted to pull out his notebook to review the few notes he had on Blackwell.

"He worked in the proximity of Pritchard and obviously knew him, but what else?" Amelia asked, her eyes narrowing.

Henry hesitated. While many people liked to think of themselves as detectives, he was surprised Amelia had put so much effort into making a connection.

"I'm sorry." She offered a wry smile. "You would probably rather discuss anything except the case. Or perhaps you can't talk about it at all. My apologies." She waved her hand in the air as if to dismiss her question.

"Not at all. It's helpful to hear your ideas. I welcome them. And if there's something I can't divulge, I'll say." He leaned forward to say more when Fernsby came to announce dinner.

As they rose and set aside their glasses, Henry added, "I would like to continue the conversation after dinner. If you're interested in doing so, that is."

"I would enjoy that very much." Her smile added to the warmth the whiskey had left in its wake.

Thirty-One

I t had been a long time since she'd enjoyed herself, Amelia thought as they walked to the dining room. She'd attended two dinner parties in the last two months, and while they'd had entertaining moments, those were often overshadowed by uncomfortable ones.

Dinner parties often involved couples, and she wasn't part of one anymore. People either expressed a morbid curiosity about her husband's murder or avoided the topic, neither of which she appreciated.

With Henry, she didn't have to explain any of that as he was intimately aware of the particulars. Any silence was the companionable sort, rather than awkward.

The meal passed quickly. Both she and Henry interacted with Maeve...or tried to. At times, she only looked at them blankly, and it was nearly impossible to determine whether she understood what they said. She nodded or shook her head, but trying to frame every question into one that required a yes or no answer was a challenge.

Henry raised the topic of Mr. Blackwell first, describing him with a combination of gestures and words. Yes, Maeve had seen him before. Yes, her father had known him.

But when Henry had asked if he'd hurt her father, Maeve only frowned and shifted her attention to her plate. Amelia tried as well, followed by a question about Mr. Sloane, with little success. Frustrating, yes, but having Henry to share it with eased that considerably.

Maeve picked at her food and Amelia knew the conversation was to blame. Discussing the murder of someone you loved certainly curtailed one's appetite. She studied the girl, noting her neatly combed hair and wary brown eyes. Maeve was thin but Amelia didn't think she'd lost much weight in the last week and had the staff to thank for that.

Henry seemed to understand a change in the conversation was due and by the time dessert was served, he shifted to lighter topics. He made an excited face for Maeve's benefit when Fernsby placed a slice of cake before him and managed to earn a small smile from the girl.

When the usually so serious man placed a dot of frosting on his nose and tried to do the same to Maeve, the smile turned as close to laughter as Amelia had seen. The moment touched her. Henry Field was a good man.

Maeve departed with Fernsby to the kitchen when he cleared the dessert plates while Amelia and Henry returned to the drawing room. They settled into their previous chairs, and Amelia waited with bated breath to see if they could return to their discussion about the case.

"I wonder—" Henry said just as Amelia started to speak.

"What of—" Amelia halted. "Please go ahead."

"Not at all. Ladies first."

"I was going to ask about the possible motive, but perhaps you'd prefer to speak of other topics rather than the case."

Henry smiled and stretched his feet out before him, crossing them at the ankles. "I intended to ask if you minded if we continued our conversation. Your insights are most helpful."

Amelia was pleased he thought so. "I should very much like to. Motive?" she repeated with a raised brow.

"Money is often the motivation in murder cases." Henry frowned. Was he thinking of Matthew?

Was that what he thought her husband's killer wanted? She need only think of the extra funds in their account or the money she'd found in his desk to think that could be the reason.

"But money as a motive is unlikely in this situation," Henry continued. "Pritchard had sufficient income to live comfortably, nothing more. No promise of inheritance or the like. He doesn't appear to have been a gambler or have been in debt to anyone."

Amelia nodded. It matched the little she knew of the ravenkeeper.

"Another common motive is a family dispute of some sort. Again, that's unlikely here as he had little family. His wife was an only child and died some time ago. His family lives in the country a fair distance from London. It's doubtful they saw each other on a regular basis."

"That sounds logical." How intriguing to be privy to his thoughts.

"My best guess is that he overheard something he wasn't supposed to. He was in the wrong place and came upon his killers while searching for the missing raven."

"What could they have been doing so late at night?"

"Excellent question." Henry nodded in approval. "What are the normal reasons people are out at that hour? Drinking, gambling, visiting unsavory places." He paused. "Or plotting something unsavory."

"Something they didn't want anyone to overhear."

"Possibly."

"So why were they near the Tower?" Amelia asked, her thoughts racing to answer the question.

"What do you think?"

"Because...because they were familiar with it. They knew they were unlikely to be interrupted or overheard."

"More than likely."

Satisfaction flooded Amelia. She was proceeding down the right path. "What might they have been plotting?"

"Considering they met so late at night, it makes one wonder."

"Something truly terrible," Amelia suggested, only to frown. "But why rise from your bed to meet an acquaintance? That seems terribly inconvenient."

Henry smiled as if pleased by the question. "They might have been on their way home from the pub or a meeting of some sort."

"A meeting of like-minded people." She considered that for a long moment. It sounded possible. "Which would make their plan even more concerning. If that's true, how would the tainted meat given to the ravens fit into this?"

Henry held her gaze but remained silent as if wanting her to come to her own conclusion.

"The ravens...the ravens are a symbol of the strength of the Crown. Of the strength of our government, our monarchy, and the country itself, at least to those superstitious enough to believe in the legend. If one or two of them died, some members of the public might see that as a sign."

Henry nodded. "It makes a certain sort of sense."

Amelia sat back in her chair and heaved a sigh. "Mr. Elliott might've learned something he wasn't supposed to, as well."

"Yes."

"My goodness. What a complicated tangle." Amelia couldn't help a shiver at what might be at stake. "Apparently whoever is behind this isn't as careful with their conversations as they should be. Whatever they're plotting must have high stakes. They might very well feel pressed to kill again."

"Or to clean up any loose ends that could lead to their arrest."

"Maeve." She didn't need Henry to confirm that. "Perhaps it's good that her relatives haven't arrived yet. I worry whether they'll be able to keep her safe."

"They will be here soon, I'm sure. I'll certainly warn them to take care." He shook his head and rubbed a hand over his eyes, obviously weary. "If only she could tell us more."

Amelia could see he wasn't telling her everything he knew about the case. Just as she worked up the courage to ask if he'd come upon any other clues, Henry shifted to the edge of his chair.

"I've taken up far too much of your evening."

She smothered a sigh but took his subtle hint. "I enjoyed our conversation. But I'm sure you're tired as am I." She rose and bid him good night.

Not quite ready to retire while her thoughts still raced, she went upstairs to look in on Maeve. She knocked quietly on the maid's door and peeked her head into the room.

Yvette sat up in bed doing some mending with a candle casting a warm glow.

"Is all well?" she whispered when Yvette rose to speak with her.

Maeve was tucked in the narrow bed, eyes closed, her doll with the ribbon still in its hair clutched to her chest.

"It took her some time to fall asleep, but otherwise, yes."

After Henry's remark about loose ends, Amelia's nerves were on edge even more. "We mustn't let our guard down. Please continue to take care."

"Of course, ma'am." The maid's lips tightened as determination gleamed in her eyes. "I will watch over her."

"Thank you. I appreciate it more than I can say."

"I feel sorry for the girl." The maid shook her head. "May I help you prepare for bed?"

"No need. I'm not tired yet, so I think I'll putter in the lab for a while," Amelia said, knowing she'd need to be quiet so as not to disturb the household.

"Very well. Let me know if you change your mind."

Amelia nodded. "Good night."

She asked more of her staff than she should, what with first Matthew's murder and now Pritchard's. While she paid them well, she wasn't certain it was enough compared to the risks they could face.

She entered the lab across the hall and turned up the gaslights, appreciating the sense of calm that overcame her. The tidy space with so much potential never failed to bring her pleasure in an otherwise chaotic world.

Out of habit, she reached for her apron from the peg near the door only to drop her hand. She didn't intend to work. She couldn't stay up long; she needed to keep her wits about her in the coming days. At least, for as long as Maeve was with her.

Perhaps she could devise another experiment the girl could assist her with come morning. Maeve seemed to enjoy them, and it would take both of their minds off the murder for a time.

She walked to the wardrobe to review the contents, hoping an idea would spark. As she pondered the possibilities of adding a bit of copper to nitric acid, a faint sound caught her notice.

A thump.

Her breath caught and she strained to listen. If not for the quiet of the house this late at night, she might not have heard it.

Was the sound disturbing only because she'd spent the entire evening—much of the day for that matter—thinking of the murder case?

The feeling of unease that crawled along her skin protested otherwise.

She rushed to the window which overlooked the street, but a glance outside revealed little. Still uncertain what she'd heard, she returned to the maid's room and opened the door.

"Did you hear that, too?" Yvette asked as she sat upright, eyes wide with alarm.

"Yes. I'll see what it was—stay with Maeve."

Amelia hurried down the stairs, still trying to place what the noise could've been, certain it had come from the front of the house. As she reached the next landing, Henry was well ahead of her, descending to the entrance hall.

Relief filled her at the sight of him. From his tense form, he'd heard the sound, too.

The gaslights had been turned down, though one remained, casting a faint glow over the hall. Fernsby and the rest of the staff had retired for the night. A glance at the door showed it was locked. But her unease didn't lessen.

Henry placed an ear to the door to listen, then motioned for her to wait as he quietly unlocked it.

Amelia glanced about, realizing that if anything occurred, she'd need to protect Maeve. She reached for a candlestick holder on the entry table, plucked out the tapers, and set them aside. The holder was tall, its heavy base making it a potential weapon if necessary. Stepping to the foot of the stairs she held the iron candlestick out before her, ready to strike if necessary.

Approval lit Henry's eyes. Only then did he slowly open the front door. Amelia peered around him, heart racing. The darkness made it impossible to see anything at first—but that didn't stop her from realizing something was terribly wrong.

Constable Dannon. He was slumped over in his chair, and she didn't think sleep was the reason.

Thirty-Two

A larm coursed through Henry at the sight of Constable Dannon tipped sideways in his chair. While he could only make out the man's silhouette in the darkness, his awkward position increased Henry's worry.

With a quick glance around to make certain whoever had struck the constable wasn't nearby, Henry checked for a pulse, relieved to feel a steady beat. "Dannon?"

No response. Any potential threat needed to be eliminated before he could see to the man.

Henry glanced behind him to see Amelia watching from the doorway. "Lock the door and bolt it. Pull a chair across if you can and keep a hold of that candlestick. Wake Fernsby. I'm going to circle the house."

Her gaze swung to the constable, her concern clear.

"He should be all right," he whispered.

Though her reluctance was obvious, Amelia did as he requested. Henry waited until he heard the click of the lock then eased down the front steps, listening closely.

He walked a few paces to look down the stairs to the kitchen entrance but saw nothing amiss, so shifted directions to make his way through the garden.

The situation made him uneasy. *Why had someone gone to the effort of knocking out Dannon but not then attempt entry through either door?*

The thought had him moving as quickly as possible through the dark garden, checking for an open window or a sign of an intruder as he went. He wanted to view the rear of the house to make certain no one was attempting to scale up it and into the room where Maeve slept.

After navigating around tall hedges, he made it to the rear and scanned the house for anything amiss. The night was dark but the moon cast a faint glow, along with light coming from a few windows.

Nothing moved.

He waited a moment, listening intently. With concern for Dannon growing, he started back only to pause at a faint noise that sounded out of place. Had it come from the front of the house?

Henry ran, pushing past hedges and jumping over flower beds, heart pounding in his chest as worry for Amelia and Maeve took hold.

He rounded the front of the house—to see Fernsby assisting Dannon to sit up. Henry muttered a curse. *They should've kept the door locked.*

He slowed, wondering if the constable's movements could have been what he'd heard.

"Did—" Before he could finish, a muffled scream from inside the house caused his heart to leap.

Henry ran up the stairs and raced inside. The entrance hall was empty. Voices came from the lower level, drawing him toward the back stairs. "Amelia? Amelia!"

"Here!" Her voice came from below and he rushed down the stairs, senses on alert.

He raced into the kitchen to see the cook sitting in a chair, hand pressed to her chest, being comforted by Mrs. Fernsby and Amelia.

"What happened?" Henry asked as he looked between them.

"I heard a noise from my room and came into the kitchen to see a man in here—a man! Scared the life out of me." Mrs. Appleton's cheeks were pale, and her breathing labored, clearly still upset. "Though I think my scream scared him as well."

Mrs. Fernsby patted the cook on the shoulder. "I was coming to the kitchen for some water when I heard her cry out. The man took one look at the pair of us and fled." The housekeeper pointed to the service door which now stood slightly ajar.

"Maeve?" Henry asked Amelia urgently.

"Yvette is with her—I'll go check on them."

Henry didn't wait to hear more but rushed out of the door and up the stairs to the street level. Fernsby and Dannon must've gone inside as the front door was closed. Nothing moved.

He would find his man. Henry ran in the darkest direction with the hope the intruder would've done the same. He slowed his pace to search the shadows and listen for any movement. The hairs on the back of his neck prickled, and he tensed as he looked around. "Show yourself," he demanded.

Only silence met his order. Certain someone was watching, he began a methodical search around fence posts, gates, and hedges. But the darkness was on the intruder's side. He could've been three feet away, and Henry might not see him.

He continued, anger and frustration rising. He wanted to find whoever was hiding with every fiber of his being. After a quarter of an hour, hope started to fade. He wasn't even certain where else to look.

Yet the uneasy feeling of being watched persisted. As long as it did, he would keep looking. On a hunch, he straightened. "Samuel, I know you're here."

Suddenly a dark form rushed out of the shadows to shove him. Caught off guard, Henry sprawled backward, landing on his shoulder before his head struck the pavement. A sharp pain made it difficult to think. Difficult to see. He blinked to clear the haze and forced himself upright.

His attacker hadn't waited but was racing down the street.

Henry scrambled to his feet, his balance unsteady. As best he could, he ran after the man, each step making it clear what had been bruised in the fall.

It quickly became evident it was too late. The intruder had too much of a head start and had disappeared from sight. Unwilling to risk leaving the house unguarded, Henry turned back toward Amelia's, touching his forehead gingerly. He was bleeding.

"Inspector?" Dannon called then walked quickly toward him. "Any luck?"

"No. Though I'm certain it was the man from the sketch. Samuel."

"I'm sorry, sir," Dannon began, one hand holding the back of his head, hat gone. "I don't know what happened. One minute I was keeping watch and the next I woke with a pounding head."

Henry sighed. Such a shame the constable hadn't seen anything before he'd been struck. "Let us go inside and take a look at your injury."

Henry shared what little he knew as they returned to the house. He didn't mention his own injuries though his head ached, and his shoulder throbbed. The slight blood on his forehead had swiftly been wiped away. Such injuries were occasionally part of the job. He'd endured them before. The aches would ease in a day or two.

He bit back an oath at the thought of what Reynolds would have to say about all this. The Director would feel justified in having assigned another inspector to work with Henry. Though he knew beyond a doubt Perdy wouldn't have done any better this evening, it brought no comfort.

If only he'd caught the man.

Fernsby waited at the door to let them in, locking and bolting it behind them. "The others are still in the kitchen," the butler advised as he led the way. "Maeve is sleeping like a lamb with the maid watching over her."

The news released some of Henry's tension. At least the intruder hadn't managed to take the girl.

Amelia, the cook, and Mrs. Fernsby were seated around the large wooden table next to the kitchen.

At the mistress' questioning look, Henry shook his head. "We should have a look at Dannon's head," he said, gesturing toward the constable.

The housekeeper tsked and instructed her husband to bring a lamp to the table before gesturing for Dannon to have a seat. "Let us see the damage."

The man's head boasted a nasty gash. Mrs. Appleton fetched a basin of water and a rag to clean it while Amelia studied Henry.

"Did you see anyone?" she asked from where they stood watching.

He nodded only to quickly stop, his head spinning. "I was searching the shadows for him down the street and must've neared his hiding spot. He shoved me backwards and took off. By the time I gained my feet and gave pursuit, he'd disappeared."

Amelia frowned, her gaze looking him over. "Were you hurt?"

His chest tightened at the concern in her tone. "Mostly my pride."

She lifted a brow. "Apparently, your head as well."

Only too late did he realize he'd inadvertently touched his head where he'd hit the pavement. "It's nothing serious."

"Let us have a look all the same." She pointed to a chair. When he hesitated, she added, "The sooner you allow me to check it, the sooner we can try to get some rest."

With a sigh, Henry sat as instructed and bent his head forward as she examined his head.

The feel of her fingers combing through his hair caused tingles to shiver along his skin. He did his best to ignore it and held still while she gently cleaned the area.

"It doesn't seem to be bleeding, but it's quite swollen." She had Mrs. Fernsby take a look to make certain she agreed while Amelia studied him. "Are you hurt anywhere else?"

"Only bruised." Henry was relieved there was no mention of stitches as he had an aversion to needles.

Dannon cleared his throat. "Thank you for tending my head," he told the housekeeper. "I'll return to my post."

"Not with a welt that size on your head." Mrs. Fernsby glared at Henry. "Surely you don't expect an injured man to remain on the job, do you?"

"She's right. You should go home, Dannon," Henry said. "I'll have someone replace you for the next couple of days."

The constable grumbled but finally agreed, assuring them he was feeling well enough to make his way home. But Amelia had Fernsby find him a cab and paid for it, insisting it was the least she could do since the constable had been injured on her front step.

Once Dannon departed, Henry helped Fernsby to temporarily repair the servant's entrance door and make certain it was secure for the night.

It seemed clear that the intruder had knocked the constable unconscious then pried open the servant's door, breaking the lock only to be caught by the cook, followed closely by the housekeeper.

"That was a bit of a scare, eh, inspector?" Fernsby said after he tested the door one more time.

"It was. I just wish we could've caught him."

"I am grateful young Maeve is still with us. That is what's truly important. Besides, I have no doubt you will catch him soon, sir." The older man held his gaze for a moment. "I have complete faith in you."

Henry nodded his thanks, touched the butler felt that way. It helped to ease a little of the frustration of the evening.

After they'd checked to make sure the other doors and windows were locked tight and Fernsby retired for the night, Henry carried a chair from the drawing room to the entrance hall and settled into it.

There was always a chance whoever had attempted to break in would return. *Would other people lower their guard, assume that the worst was over?* If he did, Henry would be ready. From here, he could hear most of the rest of the house fairly well.

He'd been on patrol enough nights over the years to function on little to no sleep. It wasn't ideal when he needed his wits about him come the morning, when he'd have Perdy to deal with, but he wasn't willing to allow anything to happen to his only witness—or the people who guarded her.

Thirty-Three

When Amelia rose the next morning Henry was already gone, the door to his room ajar, the bed neatly made. Though not surprised, she was still disappointed not to have the chance to speak with him before he left. The bump on his head must be painful and made her wonder what other parts of him were sore.

Though he was obviously fit, that didn't mean he was infallible. Hopefully Constable Dannon was recovering as well.

She shivered at the thought of what might've happened to Maeve if neither Henry nor Dannon had been there last night. Amelia needed to increase her vigilance to help ensure the girl stayed safe.

Sounds from the kitchen below confirmed she wasn't the only one awake, despite the early hour. She had already looked in on Maeve, who still slept peacefully with Yvette watching over her. For once, the girl was at an advantage, not having to hear all the ruckus the previous night.

Amelia started downstairs to make certain Mrs. Appleton wasn't the worse for wear after her fright, but the sight of a chair near the front door gave her pause. She turned in surprise to see Henry striding down the corridor toward her.

"My apologies," he said, his brown eyes warm and the hint of a smile on his lips. "I didn't mean to startle you."

"I thought you'd already left for the day when I saw your bedroom door open." She looked back at the chair as realization dawned. "You...didn't sleep in your room, did you?"

"I thought it best to make certain whoever tried to break in did not make another attempt. Fernsby and I made certain no one could come through the service entrance, and I wanted to make sure they didn't try the front instead."

"My goodness." His consideration touched her. It had been a long time since there had been a man in the house to watch over her. "How will you ever function today when you've had so little sleep?"

He shook his head, the hint of a smile on his lips. "It's of no concern. As my grandfather used to tell me, I can sleep when I'm dead."

Amelia frowned. That was a terrible thing to encourage when proper rest was so important. "How's your head, and the rest of your bruises?"

Henry touched the bump and shrugged. "Still sore but not as much as Dannon's must be. Mrs. Appleton was kind enough to provide coffee and breakfast, so I'll be departing as soon as a fresh constable arrives to watch over things."

"Very well. Is there anything I can do to help?"

"Continue to keep an eye on Maeve." He paused, his brow puckering. "I only caught a glimpse of the intruder in the dark, but I think it's the same man who tried to take her before. Our visit to the Tower yesterday might've stirred concern again."

Amelia nodded. "That crossed my mind as well."

"If we are correct, it confirms my intent to look deeper into the background of the two men who upset her yesterday."

"I hope you find something helpful."

"As do I." Henry turned to go, only to look back. "Please, take care. If you leave the house, have someone accompany you." He paused, his expression taut with concern. "As you were with us yesterday, there's a chance they might try to harm you."

"I suppose that's true." Amelia's heartbeat sped at the thought. "I don't believe any of us need to venture out for anything, so you may set your mind at ease." She didn't want Henry worrying about them when he needed to focus on the case.

"That would be a relief. Thank you."

The sound of footsteps on the front steps followed by a quiet knock at the door prevented them from saying anything further.

"That will be the constable. I will see you this evening." He reached for his hat, wincing slightly as he put it on his head.

"Take care, Henry."

"And you, as well." Then with a dip of his head, he departed.

Amelia studied the constable through the open door so she'd be able to recognize him, then locked it, deciding formal introductions could wait until later. At least until after breakfast.

She went down to the kitchen, the sight of the service door wedged shut enough to make her shudder. The sooner they had it repaired with a sturdier lock in place, the better. She'd better ask Fernsby to send for someone to take care of it.

"Good morning, Mrs. Appleton." She studied the cook, pleased to see color in her cheeks. Then again, that could be from all her activities. A floured area on the worktable suggested she'd already made bread. Several bowls sat on the counter, and a pot steamed on the stove. The room smelled delicious.

"Mrs. Greystone. I hope you slept well." The cook paused to wipe her hands on the large white apron that was still spotless, despite how busy she'd evidently been.

"I did." Knowing Henry was in the house had made that possible. "And you?"

The cook glanced at the damaged door. "Well enough. Though I will admit that every little noise sent my heart leaping."

"Only to be expected. I'm beyond relieved that nothing worse happened. We'll have someone repair the door as quickly as possible. A new, stronger lock is clearly in order."

The tightness she hadn't realized was in Mrs. Appleton's face eased, and the stout woman nodded in relief. "I appreciate that. I'm certain it's secure now, but it makes receiving our deliveries difficult. Is Maeve still sleeping?"

"Yes, though I expect she'll wake any minute."

"Would you like your breakfast now, ma'am?"

"I'll wait and have it with Maeve." After what had happened, Amelia intended to watch over her as much as possible. "I'll work in the lab and keep an eye on her door until she wakes."

She returned upstairs and opened the door of her attic lab but before she could don her apron, the door to Maeve's room opened. "Ah, good morning, ladies."

"Good morning, ma'am." Yvette smiled, as did Maeve, who still rubbed sleep from her eyes. "Shall I remain with Maeve?" The maid seemed anxious to start on her duties.

"I will watch over her."

With a quick curtsy followed by a smile at the girl, Yvette continued downstairs.

Maeve had already changed into a dress, but her hair was in disarray.

An ache filled Amelia's chest as she smoothed the girl's soft, brown strands then motioned braiding it. Maeve nodded and returned to her room to sit on the bed while Amelia saw to her hair. The moment reminded Amelia of Lily so much that she had to draw a slow breath to ease the ache in her chest.

Not a day passed that she didn't miss her daughter. There was a fine balance between remembering Lily and dwelling on her absence and some days, that balance was impossible to find.

After Maeve's hair was brushed and neatly braided, Amelia motioned eating and again the girl nodded. Amelia offered her hand, pleased when the girl took it, and they walked downstairs together to eat in the kitchen. The warm, bustling space was more welcoming than the dining room and the child seemed comfortable there.

Maeve frowned at the sight of the boarded door. Amelia wasn't quite sure how to try to explain it. Telling the truth wasn't possible, and anything else seemed difficult to communicate.

Yvette noticed Maeve staring at the door. She came forward to point at the door then put her fists together as if breaking a stick. "Broken."

Maeve nodded. The simpleness of the maid's explanation made Amelia flush. How easy it was to overthink these things.

"Would you like her to stay in the kitchen, ma'am?" Yvette asked after they'd finished eating.

"I'll keep her with me for a few hours." Amelia put out her hand for Maeve to take.

On the way upstairs, Fernsby confirmed that he had sent for someone to repair the door and fortify the lock as quickly as possible. Then she and Maeve went up to her attic lab and put on their aprons.

The light of interest in Maeve's face confirmed Amelia had chosen a good way to spend the morning. She walked to the wardrobe and opened the doors to see what ideas came to mind. Certain that Maeve would enjoy this one, Amelia retrieved a brown glass bottle of hydrogen peroxide and another of potassium iodide. The result would be similar to one they'd done previously, but hopefully it would still bring a smile to the girl's face.

Maeve pulled her stool over to the counter and watched in anticipation as Amelia set out the items, along with a large glass beaker, onto a large metal tray. Measuring the hydrogen peroxide into the beaker, Amelia added a few drops of red dye, then carefully scooped a small amount of the potassium iodide powder into a spoon.

"Be very careful," she told Maeve as she handed her the spoon.

The powder had several uses, including as a cure for syphilis, lead poisoning, and some skin ailments. But in this case, the result of the two compounds with the addition of the red coloring would surely please Maeve.

Amelia mimicked putting the powder into the beaker and watched closely as Maeve did so. Almost immediately, the liquid in the beaker turned into a bright red foam, overflowing the container, and oozing onto the tray beneath.

Maeve's mouth dropped open in amazement, her eyes wide as she stared then looked at Amelia, as if uncertain whether that was supposed to happen.

When Amelia grinned and nodded, Maeve's attention returned to the beaker, her surprise turning into delight as it continued to overflow. Her broad smile made Amelia pleased she'd thought of the combination.

Much like she'd done last time, Maeve held out a finger and raised a brow, clearly wanting to touch it. Amelia nodded.

The girl's silent laughter as she touched the tiny bubbles brought to mind her father and all the moments he would miss with Maeve.

Life could be terribly unfair.

Amelia did her best to push aside the sadness that gripped her at the thought of him.

She had Maeve help her conduct a couple of other simple experiments, but the girl's favorite was clearly the foam.

Before she knew it, the time for luncheon had come. After tidying up the lab, they made their way to the kitchen. Maeve looked at the food Yvette served them with interest, clearly hungry after the busy morning.

Perhaps Henry had discovered something of interest in the investigation. Amelia certainly hoped so.

"I'll need to speak with the girl, as well," Perdy informed Henry when they stopped at a pub for luncheon.

Henry stared in disbelief.

The other inspector had been a condescending idiot thus far. He'd insisted on Henry accompanying him as he interviewed the yeoman warders at the Tower, stating he needed to start on the case from the ground up.

The questioning look Wallace had sent Henry when Perdy forced him to recount what he'd already told Henry and Fletcher several times made the situation even more frustrating.

But with Reynolds' order to work closely with Perdy still ringing in his ears, Henry had no choice.

His plan to investigate Blackwell had been dismissed by Perdy, who'd said his involvement seemed unlikely. Henry would have to wait to speak with Blackwell and Hyndman, the publisher, once he was free of Perdy. Fletcher was spending the morning on the stolen jewelry case. While Henry hoped he'd make progress on it, solving the murders was far more pressing.

Perdy had taken every opportunity to mention that Henry's father and grandfather's influence had to be the only reason for Henry's quick rise to inspector, that Henry had clearly fumbled this case, though he refused to say how.

The jabs at Henry's abilities added to the doubt already swirling through his mind. The entire morning had been not only frustrating but also a complete waste of time.

"As I have mentioned, the girl is deaf and mute," Henry said, trying to hold back his anger. "I've already told you what she was able to share with me."

Perdy set his hat to the side, his irritation obvious. The man was nearly as tall as Henry but must surely outweigh him by two stones. He'd huffed and puffed as they made their way around the Tower grounds, making Henry even more impatient with their slow progress.

Perdy waited until they placed their order before leaning back in his chair, arms folded over his chest. He leveled Henry a displeased look. "I don't appreciate you questioning every step I take."

Henry bit back a sharp retort. The clock was ticking on the case. Another victim might be discovered. Maeve's family might arrive to take her away. The guilty party might decide to proceed with whatever plan Pritchard had overheard.

When he didn't respond, Perdy continued, "Reynolds assigned me to the case for a reason. I would think you'd welcome my guidance given the lack of results you've had thus far."

"I appreciate your assistance and have cooperated." Henry held tight to his annoyance. "However, I think it's more important to move forward rather than cover previous ground. As for the girl, she is still traumatized by her father's death and the events following it. My hope is that as she begins to feel safe again, she might remember something else. She's coming to know me better and that should help. She does not know you."

"Nonsense. She's seven years of age, not three. I'll call on her this afternoon and see what I can discover." As Henry started to argue, Perdy held up a beefy hand. "No need for you to accompany me. Your attitude is clearly not helping the witnesses, given how little we learned this morning."

Henry bit back an oath. Anger wouldn't help to solve the case. He would have to send a message to Amelia to warn her of the visit and apologize for the inconvenience, not to mention the upset it would surely cause Maeve.

At least having Perdy elsewhere would allow Henry time to dig into Blackwell's background. Perhaps he'd even have time to stop by Hyndman's home again to see what he could learn about the meetings held at the Crown and who organized them.

They ate their meat pies in silence, washing them down with a pint of beer. Henry ate quickly, anxious to move forward with his plans. He already had Blackwell's home address. More than likely, the man was at work. Perhaps his wife or a neighbor would answer a few questions.

Meal over, he excused himself and stepped outside to search for a lad to deliver a message. He found one lingering nearby and quickly scribbled a message to have delivered to Amelia, hoping desperately that Perdy didn't upset Maeve. Whether the man would prove as annoying to Amelia as he was to Henry would be interesting to hear.

He returned inside where Perdy was conversing with a serving maid. Henry waited impatiently for him to finish then stood and tossed money on the table. "Would you prefer to meet at the Yard later or will you return to the Tower?"

"The Yard will do." Perdy stood and carefully counted out payment for his own meal. If the man did everything as slowly as Henry had observed him thus far that day, how did he handle the workload of an inspector? "Reynolds will want an update."

Henry could only hope he'd have new information to share with the Director by then.

The two men parted ways, and Henry took a hansom cab to Blackwell's residence to save time. The Armoury manager lived in an apartment not far from the Tower that seemed appropriate for what Henry guessed his wages might be. The redbrick building was tidy with a narrow box hedge lining the walkway.

He rang the bell for apartment five and waited to no avail. Hoping the apartment across the hall might have someone at home, he tried that bell next.

A young maid answered the door, wearing a white apron and cap. "Yes?"

"I was looking for Mr. Blackwell next door, but he doesn't seem to be home."

She glanced at the door across the hall. "He'd be at work for the day, sir."

"I see. Do you know where he works?" It was often better to pretend he knew nothing to see what information the person provided.

"In the Armoury at the Tower," she said with some enthusiasm.

"Impressive."

"He works long hours, that's for certain." She nervously glanced over her shoulder as if worried she'd be reprimanded by her employer, but Henry wasn't willing to let her go yet.

"Do you know how long he's lived here?"

The maid was helpful, sharing that he'd moved into the apartment three years ago with his wife and young boy. She said all the residents in the building had been torn up about the lad's death. Mrs. Blackwell had taken to staying with her mother in the country for weeks at a time since then, a detail Henry found interesting since Blackwell had stated his wife and servants could vouch for his whereabouts the night of Pritchard's murder. The maid's employer had apparently mentioned that it might be better if the Blackwells moved so the memories wouldn't be so painful.

Henry had wondered that about Amelia, whether the memories in her home from both her daughter and husband were comforting or painful. No doubt it was a combination of both.

"Mr. Blackwell has some...interesting ideas," the maid whispered, looking over her shoulder again.

"How do you mean?"

"He says no one should have to work more than forty-eight hours a week. That education should be free for everyone." She smothered a giggle with her hand. "Can you imagine such things? England for all, he says. Not just for the upper crust." She shook her head, clearly amused by his beliefs.

Before he could ask additional questions, an older woman who appeared to be another servant in charge of the maid arrived. "Meg, you should be at your duties."

"Yes, ma'am." The maid bobbed her head and departed, leaving Henry with the older woman.

"My apologies for disturbing the household," Henry began with a polite smile. "I was hoping to speak with Mr. Blackwell, but the maid advised he isn't home."

"Why would he be in the middle of the day?" The presumed housekeeper's narrowed eyes viewed him with suspicion.

"You're right, of course. I understand he works rather long hours. Do you have any idea what time in the evening I might catch him home?"

Her lips twisted as if she debated whether to answer. "He might finish work soon after six o'clock but often departs two or three evenings a week."

"Oh?" Henry waited, hoping she'd explain.

"He attends meetings of some sort those nights, though I tend to think they're not related to his job."

"What makes you think that?" His heart beat faster.

"He often has a friend with him. I'm sure he's lonely with his wife gone. The two men don't look like they're going out for a night on the town even if Mr. Blackwell returns late."

Well, this was worth a try... "Is his friend a Mr. Sloane, perhaps?"

"I don't know his name. It's no business of mine."

"Of course." Henry nodded. "Is he a tall, slender man of about the same age with black hair?"

She frowned as if deciding whether to speak. "Yes. I suppose you could say that."

"It sounds as though I'll have a difficult time finding Mr. Blackwell at home. I don't suppose you know where they go in the evenings."

"I have better things to do with my time than spy on the neighbor, sir. I think you've asked enough questions, and I have work to do."

"Thank you for your time." Henry dipped his head in thanks and took his leave.

He was beginning to feel more confident that he was on the right track and wondered if Blackwell and Sloane were attending the Democratic Federation meetings. Had they encountered Elliott there?

He gave the waiting hansom cab driver Hyndman's address. With luck, the man would be home, and Henry could question him then stop by the bank where Sloane had claimed to be employed before he was due to meet Perdy. But only if he was quick.

Something had to break through soon. If not, someone would need to be blamed to appease the Home Secretary, and that person wouldn't be Director Reynolds. He could too easily imagine his father's look of disappointment when fingers were pointed at him.

The concern had him rapping on the roof of the cab to ask the driver to hurry. There wasn't a moment to waste.

Thirty-Four

"What—did—you—see?" Inspector Perdy asked in an overly loud voice as he sat with Maeve at the kitchen table.

Amelia held back her impatience, trying not to glare at the man for the way he was treating Maeve. Thank goodness Henry had sent a note to warn her about the inspector. He and Henry were nothing alike. Dealing with Perdy made her appreciate Henry all the more.

"Speaking louder won't help," Amelia said. "She's deaf, not hard of hearing. Surely Hen—Inspector Field told you that?"

It was obvious from Inspector Perdy's comments thus far that he thought Henry incompetent. The inspector seemed certain that if he asked Maeve a few simple questions, he would solve the murder.

"Oh." Inspector Perdy frowned. "Right."

"You might have more success asking short yes or no questions as she can't answer much else."

What the inspector didn't seem to realize was that he was insulting Amelia, too. How could he think that she hadn't done everything possible to discover what Maeve had seen?

Maeve was quite displeased to be sitting at the table with the strange man. She kept looking at Amelia as if wishing she'd send him away so she would be left in peace.

Amelia thought the girl had understood her explanation that he was a policeman who worked with Henry, but it was difficult to know for certain.

"Did you see someone you know?" The inspector asked more quietly, but the way he exaggerated his lip movements as he spoke had the child frowning in confusion.

"You'll have to try again, sir," Amelia said when Maeve didn't respond. "She didn't understand. If you speak naturally but slowly, it might help."

She had thought it best to conduct this interview in the kitchen where Maeve was more comfortable, but she was beginning to think that wasn't making any difference. The girl wasn't impressed by Inspector Perdy. Neither was Amelia.

The man huffed a breath, simmering with frustration.

Mrs. Appleton, who'd been working on dinner preparations, slammed a pot onto the counter. "Oh, beg your pardon," she said when the inspector turned to glare. When he returned his attention to Maeve, the cook shared a meaningful look with Amelia, obviously as annoyed by the man and his behavior as Amelia was.

Inspector Perdy pushed back his chair and addressed Amelia. "I do believe it would be helpful if you and your...staff stepped out of the room and allowed me to question the witness in private. The two of you are making her uncomfortable."

Amelia stiffened in outrage, tempted to refuse. This was her house! To be ordered out of her own kitchen was unbelievable.

Then again, the sooner Perdy realized Maeve couldn't provide the information he wanted, the sooner he'd leave. "If you insist. She is a little girl, not simply a witness. I hope you can remember that."

Inspector Perdy nodded, though his displeasure was obvious.

Amelia bent to look Maeve in the eye. "I'll be back."

Maeve's frown only deepened, and she folded her arms over her chest, her doll tucked under one arm, making her feelings clear. At least, they were clear to Amelia.

With a frustrated sigh, Amelia led Mrs. Appleton out of the kitchen and up the stairs.

"My apologies, ma'am, but th-that man makes me s-so angry," the cook sputtered.

"I couldn't agree more."

"I wanted to slam my pot alongside his head rather than the work-top."

"Understandable." The image almost made Amelia smile.

"Thank goodness he wasn't assigned to the case from the start. Imagine! Inspector Field is obviously not only a better detective but a better man."

Amelia agreed with that sentiment as well. "The sooner Inspector Perdy asks his questions and leaves, the better."

Mrs. Fernsby descended the stairs with a pile of folded linens in her arms. "What is it?" she asked, looking from Amelia to the cook.

"Inspector Perdy requested privacy to speak with Maeve," Amelia explained.

"As if you and Inspector Field haven't tried everything possible to find out what the girl saw?" Mrs. Fernsby shook her head. "How ridiculous. He'll only upset poor Maeve all over again."

"I'm afraid he already has." Amelia glanced at her pin watch. "We'll give him a quarter of an hour but no more. He has until two o'clock before I join them."

"I haven't checked the herbs we had growing last summer for some time," Mrs. Appleton announced. "I'll be in the garden until the man leaves."

Mrs. Fernsby leaned close to Amelia. "Should we listen at the bottom of the stairs?"

Though tempted, Amelia shook her head. "We'll allow him his request for privacy." She opened the door of the study, needing something to occupy herself. "I'll sort through some papers until he's done."

"Very well." The housekeeper glanced at the pile in her arms. "I'll refold these until he finishes." She paused. "I nearly forgot. Fernsby advised that the locksmith will be here to fix the door and replace the lock at four o'clock."

"Thank you. I'll be pleased to have it taken care of before nightfall."

A quarter of an hour had never passed so slowly. Amelia must've looked at the clock a dozen times before she determined it was time to check on Maeve. Worry for the girl made it impossible to concentrate on anything else.

Before she reached the corridor, however, Inspector Perdy came up the stairs, his expression disgruntled. "It's impossible to communicate with that child. She won't look at you and when she finally does, she only glares in response to questions."

"It is certainly a challenge," Amelia said with as much politeness as she could muster. "As again, I am sure Inspector Field has mentioned. Were you able to discover anything further?"

"She confirmed that there were two men who attacked her father but that's all."

"How odd. I do believe she provided Inspector Field with a basic description of them." The chance to make it clear that Henry had accomplished more than Perdy was irresistible.

"Hmm. He mentioned that, however those weren't detailed enough to be helpful." The man tugged on the bottom of his jacket. "I will be going now." He started toward the front door only to turn back. "By the way, the repairman came to fix the service door. He's working on it now."

"Oh? He wasn't expected for another two hours." Amelia frowned, well aware no one had entered through the front door. The other one was blocked shut. "How did he get in?"

"I removed the brace holding it shut for him."

While it was possible the repairman had arrived earlier than expected, unease trickled down Amelia's spine. Not bothering to say anything to the inspector, she hurried down the stairs and into the kitchen only to come to a halt.

Maeve's chair at the table held only her doll, the ribbon fallen to the floor...and the service door stood open.

No one was in sight.

Amelia's unease turned to terror. "Maeve!"

"You let the man in?" Henry stared at Perdy in disbelief as they stood in Amelia's entrance hall. Though he already knew the answer, he couldn't comprehend it.

Amelia, her staff, Constable Stephens, and Perdy had all been searching the neighborhood for Maeve while a messenger had been sent for Henry. Thank goodness he and Fletcher had just returned to the Yard, or he wouldn't yet know about the disaster that had ensued.

"How was I to know he wasn't who he said he was?" Perdy's defensiveness didn't come as a surprise, but it wasn't helpful.

Henry had brought a half dozen others with him, including Fletcher, to join the search, but he feared whoever took Maeve had already fled the area.

"Tell me exactly what happened." Henry did his best to mask his anger as he glared at the older man.

"I was speaking with the girl, who was less than cooperative I might add—"

Henry clenched his hand as the urge to punch him took hold. "You already mentioned that. Continue with your story."

Perdy scowled, clearly not pleased to have his telling of events called a 'story'. "I'd nearly concluded my questioning when a knock sounded at the service door. When I looked out the window, the man held up tools. I removed the wedge blocking the door shut to allow him to repair it."

"Then what happened?"

"He started on the work, and I went upstairs to speak with Mrs. Greystone."

"And left Maeve, our only witness, alone. With a stranger. In the middle of a murder investigation." Henry drew a breath, hoping to hold on to what little patience he had. *None of that mattered at the moment. Only finding Maeve.* "What did he look like?"

Perdy cleared his throat, his expression turning sheepish. "A tall fellow. About your age. Thin with black hair and long sideburns. He wore a leather work apron and carried a box of tools. I had every reason to believe him to be a repairman. I don't know how the constable didn't see him."

The description loosely matched Sloane's, which was interesting after he had learned the man hadn't shown up at the bank for work that morning. Hyndman hadn't been home, so he'd left an urgent message and continued on to the bank before returning to the Yard.

But what if Henry was wrong and neither Sloane nor Blackwell were involved in the murders or with taking Maeve? It might have been

Samuel, the man they had the sketch of. Or worse, someone else they hadn't come across yet.

His every mistake could cost Maeve her life.

"Henry?"

He turned to see Amelia hurrying up the front steps toward him, hope lighting her face. He shook his head, hating the way her expression fell.

"What else can we do?" she asked, not bothering to so much as look at Perdy. The way her focus held on Henry with such confidence despite her distress warmed him.

And settled his doubt.

He had to follow his gut. That meant pursuing Blackwell and Sloane.

"Wait here and keep watch," he ordered. "As resourceful as Maeve is, there's always the chance she'll escape whoever took her and try to return." He couldn't resist giving Amelia a little hope.

She pressed her lips together, clearly trying to contain her emotions as she nodded. "You'll keep me apprised?"

Her worry and fear matched his own. He couldn't bear the thought of anything happening to Maeve either.

"Of course." He strode out the door.

"Field, where are you going?" Perdy whined as he followed him down the steps. "I-I insist you tell me what you have planned."

Henry paused as he reached the waiting hansom cab. He didn't want Perdy to bother Amelia any further, but he sure in hell wasn't taking the man with him. "Wait for me at the Yard."

"But I'm supposed to be with you," the other inspector protested. "What will I tell Reynolds?"

"The truth. That your mistake resulted in the abduction of our only witness." Henry hopped into the cab, leaving Perdy sputtering.

Henry asked the driver to go slowly until Henry located one of the constables searching along the street and ordered him to the Tower to see if Blackwell was at the Armoury. If he was, the constable was to send word to the Yard and then follow Blackwell's every move while doing his best to stay out of sight.

Next, he advised one of the other constables to give orders for the others to question everyone in the area who might have seen Sloane with Maeve, from neighbors to cab drivers to shop owners. A man transporting an unhappy girl had to draw some attention.

He came upon Fletcher searching not far from there and had the driver halt, gesturing for Fletcher to join him.

"Anything?" Henry asked, though he already knew the answer from the frustration on the sergeant's face.

"Nothing. It's as if they vanished." He settled onto the seat across from Henry. "How can no one have seen anything in the middle of the day?"

Henry didn't answer, not wanting to think of how Sloane had managed that. It didn't bode well for Maeve.

"What's our plan?" Fletcher asked.

"Pay a visit to Sloane's house. The description Perdy gave of the repairman could be him. Perhaps Samuel's failure last night made Sloane decide he had to take care of the matter himself."

"You don't think he would've taken Maeve to his home." Fletcher's doubt was clear.

"Unlikely, but it gives us a starting point. His neighbors might know something."

Fletcher opened the small door in the cab and told the driver Sloane's address on Trenary Lane. He sighed, his voice quiet as he said, "I keep thinking of Maeve and how frightened she must be."

Henry only nodded. He was doing his best not to dwell on such things for fear he wouldn't be able to think clearly.

Silence filled the cab as they rounded a corner.

"If Sloane has her, where would he take her?" Henry asked, unable to cease his thoughts.

Fletcher briefly closed his eyes. "Somewhere private to kill her. He wouldn't hold onto her for long"

Henry's heart twisted even as he shook his head. "We can't think like that. Will any place do? A nearby alleyway? Where?"

"He would know we would soon be in pursuit. The girl's absence wouldn't go unnoticed for long."

"Which means he'd want to put some distance between us and them. Walking with a struggling child would quickly draw notice. He must've caught a cab."

"A few of the drivers would certainly look the other way if they were paid well."

"Blackwell strikes me as the one in charge if the two of them are involved in some plot," Henry said, thinking out loud. "Sloane couldn't take her to Blackwell if he's at the Tower. Nor would Blackwell want the girl at his apartment—but it seems reasonable to think Sloane would consult with him before taking action. That might give us the time we need to find them."

He didn't add his hope that killing a child in such a cold-hearted fashion would surely be more difficult than Sloane anticipated. That he'd want Blackwell's approval, at the very least, to complete the task.

"I suppose that's logical."

"I can only think to check his apartment and go from there."

Fletcher held Henry's gaze. "This time, there's no doubt Maeve would be able to identify him. He can't let her go."

"That's all the more reason we need to find them before he acts."

They soon arrived at the three-story apartment building. The sergeant hopped out and studied the upper windows of the soot-coated sandstone. "You said Sloane lives on the second floor?"

Henry nodded and strode inside with Fletcher behind him, quickly climbed the stairs, and knocked on Sloane's apartment, but as expected, there wasn't an answer.

Fletcher tried the door across the hall. No one was home there either.

"Let us see if there's someone on the first floor who manages the building." Henry led the way back downstairs and knocked on the apartment nearest the door.

"He's the quiet sort. Keeps to himself." The landlady looked between Henry and Fletcher with narrowed eyes. "What's he done?"

"We just have a few questions for him," Henry said. "Do you know where he might be?"

"At work."

"He didn't go in today."

The woman frowned. "It did seem like he left later than normal this morning. He isn't home often. Tends to stay out late, though I don't think it's for because he's working." She glanced up and down the hall as if to make sure no one would hear her. "The man has some wild ideas. He has political aspirations, but I wouldn't want him in the government," she whispered. "And heaven forbid if you mention the Queen."

"Why is that?" Henry asked swiftly.

"He was the worse for drink one night and went on and on about how Her Highness was to blame for the death of his family in the potato famine. Said Her Majesty didn't lift a finger to help when so many were starving."

Henry shared a pointed look with Fletcher before looking back at the woman. "Interesting, though thirty years is a long time to hold a grudge. Do you happen to know if he carries a knife?"

She gave a mock shudder. "He does. Always flipping the thing in his hand as if he can't wait to use it. Watching him sends shivers down my spine."

Henry nodded, certain more than ever that they had their man. Now they need only find him before he struck again.

Thirty-Five

Amelia watched Inspector Perdy leave, hoping she never had to see the pompous...*man* again. He wasn't worth swearing over.

"Surely there's something more we can do, madam." Fernsby stood at her side, clutching his hands.

Only now did she see how the butler was aging. Seeing him so distraught had her swallowing against the lump in her throat.

"We shall keep hope," Amelia advised but feared her tone sounded less than confident. "And pray Maeve will be returned to us."

Fernsby held her gaze as if waiting for more, but she didn't have anything to add. She never should've left Maeve with Inspector Perdy. Why hadn't she insisted on staying with her rather than abandoning the girl?

She was as much to blame as the inspector.

But such thoughts served no purpose and certainly wouldn't bring back Maeve.

Her throat ached from calling her name and her shoes pinched from rushing through the streets searching for the girl. She was drained inside and out. Yet she could only think about how Maeve must feel—scared and alone once again.

Indulging her worry wouldn't aid the situation either.

She drew a shuddering breath, uncertain how she could manage the coming hours. "I am going to keep looking," she advised Fernsby as she reached for her cloak.

"But madam—"

Amelia started toward the door, not wanting to hear the reasons she shouldn't go. Henry had told her to wait, but she was certain he'd said that to keep her safe.

How could she worry about her own safety when Maeve was in such terrible danger? Was she even still alive?

There could be no doubt that whoever had taken her wanted to eliminate her as a potential witness.

She wiped the corner of her eye as a tear escaped. "Have no worry. I'll return before dark."

Fernsby reached around her to open the door, his dedication to duty taking precedence over his wishes. "You should request one of the constables accompany you."

The door swung open, and Amelia stilled in surprise unable to believe her eyes at who was stomping up the front steps. "Maeve?"

The girl had never looked so fierce as she did now. A scowl twisted her lips under her lowered brow, strands of hair had loosened from her braid, and dirt smudged her cheeks. Her clothes were filthy, and one shoe was missing, leaving her stockinged foot with a hole in the toe on full display.

Amelia had never seen such a wonderful sight.

She rushed to take the girl into her arms and hold her tight, squeezing so hard Maeve wriggled in protest.

At last, Amelia drew back to smooth a hand along the girl's cheek, noting how her lower lip trembled and her chest heaved. "What happened?"

When Maeve didn't answer, she rephrased her question to help her understand it. "How? How did you escape?"

Maeve showed her teeth, her nose wrinkled, almost as if she were growling.

Amelia frowned in confusion...until her mouth dropped open in astonishment. "You bit him?"

Maeve nodded and clamped her teeth together to demonstrate.

Fernsby reached to pat the girl on the back, clearly impressed. "Well done, Miss Maeve."

Amelia laughed as she hugged her again, tears filling her eyes, so great was her relief. "Well done, indeed." She caught the girl's attention. "I'm proud of you."

Maeve smiled.

Yet Amelia's happiness dimmed as worry returned. "Did he hurt you?" She glanced over her more closely.

The girl held up her wrist as her brow puckered.

Amelia's heart twisted. She knelt beside Maeve, taking her slim arm for a closer look. The angry redness suggested her captor had gripped it tightly for a length of time, and Amelia could easily imagine her trying to free herself.

Then Maeve pulled up the hem of her dress and pointed to her shin where a lump was visible beneath her stocking.

"Oh, you poor dear." Amelia placed a gentle hand on the bump. "Where else?"

Maeve shook her head.

It was unbelievable to think she'd escaped with only a few bumps and bruises. Amelia hugged her again, this time more gently, still trying to take in the fact that Maeve had returned.

She had so many questions but knew there were few Maeve could answer. Where had he taken her? What had he intended? How could they find him so he couldn't do this again?

Amelia leaned back to look into the girl's face once again. It was important to try to identify him. *He mustn't be allowed to stay free.* "Where did you bite him?"

At Maeve's frown Amelia tried again, showing her own teeth to get her point across. "His hand?" She pointed to her own. "His arm?" She touched hers.

Maeve pointed to the side of Amelia's hand, and then made a stomping motion with her stockinged foot on top of Amelia's.

Fernsby chuckled. "She is one determined child, madam. No wonder she lost her shoe."

"We must send word to Inspector Field."

"Of course. I'll send a message to Scotland Yard."

Amelia nodded, anxious to share the good news. His relief would be as great as hers. "While we wait, perhaps a bath is in order."

"Excellent idea, madam. I'll alert Mrs. Fernsby. The rest of the staff will be thrilled to hear the news as well." He smiled again at Maeve then hurried to the back of the house.

Amelia looked at Maeve again, hardly able to believe she'd returned. "I'm sorry. I shouldn't have left you alone with Inspector Perdy. Thank goodness you managed to gain your freedom."

She knew the girl didn't understand all she was saying, but she had to apologize. She'd gained a second chance to care for the little girl, however brief that might be, and wanted to express both her sorrow and her gratitude.

From this point forward, she wouldn't let the girl out of her sight.

She bit her lip, wondering what more the girl could tell her. "Maeve, who? Who took you?"

Maeve's eyes darted back and forth. *Was she trying to find a way to tell her?*

"Was it the man from the Tower? The one who was angry?" She made an expression and mimicked the sweeping gesture Mr. Blackwell had made that seemed to trigger Maeve's reaction.

The girl shook her head.

"Was it the other man? The one with the sideburns?" She touched her face indicate those, trying to think of how else to describe him. "He had a cane." She made the motion of walking with one.

Maeve nodded.

"Mr. Sloane." Amelia breathed slowly. "He's the one who took you."

She had to tell Henry.

"This traffic is ridiculous," Henry said as he glanced at the window where a combination of carts, riders, carriages, and the like had tangled to a halt. Impatience boiled inside him as the cab stopped yet again. He shifted to the edge of the seat to stare out the window, trying to see the problem.

"The Queen is arriving from Windsor by train this afternoon," Fletcher said, adjusting to a more comfortable position on the seat. "A crowd is gathering to greet her at Paddington Station, I'd imagine."

"Hmm." Henry blew out a breath. "Unfortunate timing."

They weren't far from the train station on their way back to the Yard. Henry hoped to hear where Blackwell was from the constable he'd assigned to the task. It would be even better if there was a message with good news about Maeve, though he had little hope of that.

But something niggled in his mind.

"The Queen..." Henry's thoughts churned as an idea came to mind. Snippets from the past few days ran through his thoughts.

The man from the Crown saying they were planning something big.

The Socialist meetings, a philosophy that eschewed monarchy itself.

Chief Yeoman Warder Wallace sharing the tragedy that had taken Blackwell's son.

The maid at Blackwell's neighbor's home, who'd mentioned the man's idea that England needed to change to make it fair for all, not just the upper class.

Sloane's landlady mentioning the man's anger with the Queen.

The attempt to kill the ravens and stir the legend.

"Damn." A terrible fear took hold.

"What is it?" Fletcher asked quickly.

"They're going to try to assassinate the Queen." Henry whispered the words. Saying them louder would be wrong when they were too incredulous to believe.

Fletcher straightened as he glared at Henry. "What? Why?"

"Think of what we've learned." Henry repeated the reasons he'd come to his conclusion, hoping Fletcher would tell him he was wrong.

"Dear Lord." The sergeant shook his head, his expression one of disbelief followed quickly by worry. "You may be right. It all fits."

"We have to find out—and we won't sitting here." Henry threw open the cab door and quickly paid the driver. They were close enough to the train station, and it would be quicker to walk given the traffic.

But Henry hadn't counted on the thickness of the crowd who'd gathered along the route the Queen would take to travel from the train station to Buckingham Palace. People lined the street with the hope of seeing Her Majesty, or even better, being the recipient of a royal wave.

His heart pounded as he carved a path through the people as close to a run as he could manage. A glance showed Fletcher directly behind him, the look of panic on the man's face raising Henry's.

At last they neared the station. Henry scanned the crowd, desperately searching for sight of Blackwell or Sloane. The task felt impossible with so many people.

"Go to the train and see if Her Majesty has disembarked—tell her guard to beware, there may be an assailant in the crowd. Search around for the two. I'll look near where the royal carriage will turn onto the street."

Despite the chill of the day, the Queen would ride in an open carriage to wave at the crowd as she always did. That made her an easier target.

Henry was well aware of previous attempts on Her Majesty's life. The memory made his blood run cold as he continued the search.

He paused to look all around, fearing this was an impossible task. Entire families were waiting, both young and old and in between. If Blackwell and Sloane were here, they could be waiting anywhere along the nearly three-mile route.

Their best hope was to find the royal carriage and convince those who guarded Her Royal Highness to take a different route.

Henry hurried as fast as he dared, glancing about for Blackwell or Sloane as he went. At last, the royal carriage came into view, and he hoped Fletcher had warned the guards.

Though Henry worried he might be wrong, and this was all for naught, a voice deep inside—one that he wasn't always comfortable trusting—suggested he wasn't.

He continued toward the carriage which was some thirty feet away and just pulling forward when movement out of the corner of his eye caught his notice: Blackwell, pushing to the front of the crowd lining the street, glancing around nervously with one hand tucked inside his jacket.

Damn.

Henry rushed toward the man even as he searched for Sloane. Was the man elsewhere with Maeve? He had difficulty believing he wouldn't have accompanied Blackwell to help ensure their plot went as planned.

The murmur of the crowd rose near the train, suggesting the Queen had stepped out. The sound caught Blackwell's notice, and he twisted around, turning his back to Henry.

Perfect. He didn't want to risk harm to any innocent bystanders. If he could disarm the man peacefully, all the better.

"Hold, Blackwell." Henry reached for the man's upper arm with its hand still inside his jacket. "You don't want to do this."

Blackwell stared at Henry in disbelief. "Inspector Field?" He tugged at his arm. "I'm sure I don't know what you mean. Release me."

"Come to *wave* to the Queen?" Henry asked, tightening his hold.

Blackwell forced a smile even as his gaze darted around. "Why, yes. I am."

"Remove your hand slowly," Henry ordered. "You're coming with me."

"Your timing is unfortunate, Inspector." Blackwell shook his head, recovering from his surprise, his eyes glittering with a strange intensity. "You have no right to detain me."

"I'm placing you under arrest for the murder of Aberforth Pritchard and Thomas Elliott." Though he only had circumstantial evidence at this point, Henry had to hope he could quickly put the missing pieces together.

"No." Blackwell shoved Henry and attempted to pull away.

But Henry was ready for such a move and held tight to his arm even as the man's pistol clattered to the cobblestones.

"A gun!" Someone shouted from nearby. "He has a gun!"

Henry reached for it only to feel a sharp jab in his side. The pain had him straightening as he looked for the cause.

"Stay where you are." Sloane's blue eyes gripped Henry's. "Back away from the gun."

He did as Sloane ordered and held up both hands before him, heart thumping. "Where's the girl?"

Sloane scowled. "We'll worry about her later. After this is done."

Was she still alive, then?

A few people nearby grasped what was happening and backed away. Murmurs of concern were quickly followed by shouts and cries of alarm, which increased as more of the onlookers realized the danger.

"He has a gun!" Several people moved back as Blackwell retrieved his gun, placing it back inside his jacket with a nervous glance around.

If only they were closer to the royal carriage, the guards might intervene—but Henry couldn't see them now that the crowd had circled around them.

"You don't want to do this, Blackwell." Henry returned his focus to him, though the way his side stung, he needed to watch Sloane as well.

"I do," he said. "I have to. Something must be done to save our country."

"England for all. Not just for the wealthy," Sloane murmured, turning the blade in his hand but ignoring those gathered nearby.

Henry remembered the landlady's comment that Sloane could hardly wait to use the blade. An icy chill ran along his spine. "This isn't the way to do it." If he kept them talking—

Cheers from the crowd near the train cut off the thought. The Queen would soon pass by. He had to act, despite the odds against him.

"Blackwell," he cried, only to kick Sloane's knee, hoping to throw him off balance.

The man snarled and the blade flashed, slicing Henry's coat sleeve. He remembered all too vividly the slices that had crisscrossed both of the victims and jumped back, trying to stay out of the path of the knife.

"Watch out!" Someone shouted from nearby. "This one has a knife."

Henry plowed his shoulder into Blackwell, hoping to knock him down, then spun to block Sloane's attack. The blade caught Henry on the forearm, and he hissed at the pain. Lunging for Sloane's hand holding the knife, Henry forced it upward then drove his knee into the man's middle. Sloane bent over, gasping at the pain but still refusing to release his weapon.

Henry risked a glance at Blackwell to see the man scrambling to his feet as he reached inside his jacket once again.

"No!" Henry shouted.

The royal carriage was nearing, and fear crawled along Henry's skin. He shoved Sloane back with everything he had and dove for Blackwell, tackling him to the ground.

A few men in the crowd seemed to grasp what was happening. A pair of them grabbed Blackwell and held him to the ground, the man still struggling.

The royal carriage passed by, and Henry caught a glimpse of Queen Victoria staring at the commotion and pointing in their direction.

Suddenly he had more help than he could've thought possible. The crowd at large had at last understood the situation and soon had Sloane disarmed and restrained as well.

Henry lay back, breathless. He'd done it.

Fletcher arrived with reinforcements and gathered the weapons, barking orders to have Blackwell and Sloane cuffed by uniformed constables.

"Where's Maeve?" Henry demanded of Sloane.

The man only smirked in response.

"Tell me, damn you!" Henry grabbed his lapels and shook him.

"I don't know what you're talking about."

"Let's finish this at the Yard," Fletcher advised as he glanced around the interested crowd.

Teeming with frustration, Henry reluctantly agreed, and the constables hauled the two men away. "Sloane needs to tell us where Maeve is."

Fletcher nodded, his expression somber. "And we need to send for a doctor," he said as he eyed Henry's wounds. "A few stitches seem to be in order."

Henry glanced at his forearm which trickled blood, well aware of the stickiness of his side, a sure sign it was bleeding as well—not to mention the painful sting. "Maeve comes first. We have to find her."

Less than ten minutes later, they strode into the Yard.

"Inspector Field," Johnson called from the desk. "A message arrived for you."

Henry read it quickly, then read it again in disbelief.

"What is it?" Fletcher asked.

"Maeve escaped on her own. She's with Mrs. Greystone and confirmed that Sloane is the one who took her."

Fletcher chuckled. "We should've known she'd manage. After all, she walked from the Tower to Mrs. Greystone's in the dark of night."

The next hour was a blur. They questioned Blackwell and Sloane, Reynolds was updated, and a doctor tended Henry's injuries, which unfortunately included stitches, much to his dismay. Samuel was located and also arrested. Dannon came into the Yard despite the bandage around his head, and the Home Secretary was informed, finally, that they had found their men. Henry sent a message to Amelia to advise her that both men had been arrested. Perdy was nowhere to be seen.

Sloane was less than cooperative. But when Henry recounted to Blackwell precisely what he thought had happened first to Pritchard and then to Mr. Elliott, the man confessed.

Darkness had fallen by the time Henry emerged from the Yard, and he was exhausted. But he had to see Amelia and Maeve, see for himself that they were both well.

He took a hansom cab, his body protesting with every movement. Luckily he'd had a spare jacket at the Yard so Maeve wouldn't have to see the slices in his.

Fernsby opened the door before he could knock. "Welcome, Inspector," he said with a broad smile.

"Thank you."

"Mrs. Greystone and Maeve are awaiting you in the drawing room, sir."

Henry looked up to see Amelia standing at the top of the stairs, clearly anxious to hear what had occurred. He did his best to hide his aches and pains as he walked up to her, but it felt as if each stitch pulled as he went.

"Good evening," he began.

"Henry," Amelia said breathlessly. "It's so good to see you." She smiled. "We understand congratulations are in order."

"Blackwell and Sloane are in custody."

"That is a relief." She grinned. "And you managed to save the Queen. You've had a busy day."

He chuckled only to grasp his side.

"And were evidently injured in the process." Amelia sighed. "A very busy day, indeed."

Maeve emerged from the drawing room and more of Henry's tension fell away. "Hello, Maeve."

She gave a single nod, but the smile curling her lips had him smiling in return.

How nice it was to have them so pleased to see him, because he felt the same.

Amelia put her hand on Maeve's shoulder but continued to hold his gaze. "We are so very proud of you, Henry."

"Thank you." He drew a long, slow breath. In truth, he was pleased with himself, too.

He had to hope his father—and grandfather—would be as well. To have solved the murders when everything seemed to be going against him was both a relief and an accomplishment. Seeing justice served for both Warder Pritchard and Mr. Elliott provided a certain satisfaction. While that in no way made up for their deaths, he hoped it allowed them to rest in peace and gave some comfort to their families.

Justice had prevailed. That was something he didn't take lightly since it didn't always happen.

As he shared a smile with Amelia, he couldn't help but wish he would eventually be able to provide it to her.

Epilogue

"Caw, caw..."

Henry turned to see a raven perched on a low branch not far from the grave site. The mournful sound echoed around the cemetery where Aberforth Pritchard was being laid to rest, beside his wife, with military honors.

Henry shared a puzzled look with Amelia. The bird couldn't possibly be from the Tower, but still, its presence made him wonder. By the look on her face, Amelia was of the same mind.

Wallace, Daniels, and the other yeomen warders he'd met over the past week were in attendance. He'd spoken with each of them briefly, pleased they could breathe a little easier knowing the guilty had been caught.

Maeve stood with her aunt and uncle who'd arrived two days previously. How much the girl understood was unclear, but she held her aunt's hand as she solemnly watched the coffin being lowered into the ground.

Her aunt bent to gesture to her.

Maeve released her hand and walked forward to take a white rose from a nearby basket and, after a moment's pause, tossed it on top of the coffin. Silent tears coursed down her cheeks, and she drew a shuddering breath before returning to her aunt's side.

Her uncle lifted the girl into his arms and held her as the service drew to a close. The couples' obvious affection for Maeve helped ease the ache in Henry's heart.

"Ashes to ashes and dust to dust."

Amelia lifted a gloved hand to wipe away a tear with her handkerchief, and Henry blew out a breath he hadn't known he'd been holding.

Grief was a tangible force, one that took some under and forever changed them. Others, like Amelia, found a resilient strength that kept them afloat despite the weight of tragedy and loss. He hoped Maeve managed to find that, too.

A short while later, they were saying their goodbyes to the girl and wishing her family well. Amelia held her tears in check, but Henry knew her well enough by now to see how distraught she was.

And he was, too. The ravenkeeper's daughter had become so much more than a witness. He had no doubt she would prove her strength and intelligence to everyone around her in the coming years. He only hoped he and Amelia had the chance to see it for themselves.

"Would it be permissible for me to visit Maeve?" Amelia asked Maeve's aunt. "I have come to care for her and would like to stay in touch."

The woman's kind smile and eager agreement helped to slow Amelia's tears. The two women quickly exchanged addresses, and then Maeve hugged Amelia once again.

He and Amelia waved goodbye to them, and then it was time to depart.

"May I escort you home?" Henry asked Amelia as those attending took their leave.

"Thank you."

Amelia was quiet on the short journey. He was too, unhappy to realize it was unlikely he'd see her in the coming weeks.

"I wonder if there is a school that would benefit Maeve," Amelia said. "A special one for those with similar challenges." She glanced at Henry. "Perhaps I could offer to pay for it if there is."

"I think there are, and that would be incredibly generous of you," Henry agreed. "She would have the chance to realize she isn't alone in her silent world."

"I shall see what I can discover."

The silence in the cab drew long, the clatter of the horse's hooves muffling their thoughts.

"I suppose you already have another case to occupy your time," Amelia said at length.

"Yes," he admitted. "A puzzling stolen jewelry case for one. I haven't had time to properly investigate the matter until now, but it deserves my attention."

"Oh?" Her hopeful look almost suggested she wanted to hear about it.

Doubtful, when she had a life of her own.

"Who will be your next interview?" he asked.

Her face lit with enthusiasm. "A sailing barge skipper. They hold a race each year. It should prove quite interesting."

"I look forward to hearing about it," he said, only to catch himself. His words suggested he would see her soon and she would tell him about it. How presumptive of him.

"I will hold you to that." She smiled as he handed her out of the cab. "Good afternoon, Henry."

"And to you." He appreciated that she didn't say goodbye. It made him hopeful he would, indeed, be seeing her again soon.

Ready for the next installment of The Field & Greystone Series? Order The Mudlark Murders, coming November 2024!

A young girl—a mudlark—is found dead on the muddy bank of the Thames in her best dress, a crystal perfume bottle clutched in her lifeless hand...

Fearing foul play, widow Amelia Greystone sends for Scotland Yard Inspector Henry Field—the man still haunted by his failure to solve her husband's murder. Though the trust between them is fragile, Amelia believes Henry is the only one capable of delivering justice.

Henry soon confirms Amelia's suspicion but is met with orders to abandon the case. He refuses to turn a blind eye and reluctantly agrees that Amelia aid him as he conducts a clandestine investigation.

As secrets unravel, a second body surfaces, and the pair unearth a plot with chilling ties to the government. When Amelia's personal demons threaten to drive her into the killer's path, Henry must confront his own fears to not only save her but stop the villain.

Order The Mudlark Murders today!

Author's Notes

T hank you for reading The Ravenkeeper's Daughter. This book was inspired by a newspaper article my sister sent me, which led me to another book, *The Ravenmaster: My Life with the Ravens* by Christopher Skaife. I highly recommend it if you're interested in learning more about the life of a yeoman warder and his charges.

I took a few liberties with the details of The Tower so I could fit in a murder and hope that doesn't detract from the story.

Charles Frederick Field, Henry's fictional grandfather, truly was an inspector and a friend of Charles Dickens. He was a colorful character, and it would have been a challenge to follow in his footsteps.

Thwaites & Reed is not only the oldest clockmaker in London but possibly the oldest in the world.

In 1878, the Detective Department of Scotland Yard was reorganized after a scandal when several detectives were convicted of accepting bribes. Mr. C.E. Howard Vincent became the Director of Criminal Investigations, having recently been enrolled at the University of Paris in law school where he studied the Parisian Police who developed a system for investigating crimes. Many of their techniques were implemented with Vincent, who reported to the Home Secretary rather than the Commissioner.

I hope you enjoyed the story. Look for *The Mudlark Murders*, the next book in the Field & Greystone series, coming soon.

Other Books by Lana Williams

Loving the Hawke, Book I

Charming the Scholar, Book II

Rescuing the Earl, Book III

Dancing Under the Mistletoe, a Novella, Book IV

Tempting the Scoundrel, a Novella, Book V

  Romancing the Rogue, A Regency Prequel

Falling For the Viscount, Book VI

Daring the Duke, Book VII

Wishing Upon A Christmas Star, a Novella, Book VIII

Ruby's Gamble, a Novella

Gambling for the Governess, Book IX

Redeeming the Lady, Book X

Enchanting the Duke, Book XI

The Seven Curses of London Boxset (Books 1-3)

The Duke's Lost Treasures:

Once Upon a Duke's Wish, Book 1

A Kiss from the Marquess, Book 2

If Not for the Duke, Book 3

The Secret Trilogy:

Unraveling Secrets, Book I

Passionate Secrets, Book II

Shattered Secrets, Book III

The Secret Trilogy Boxset(Books 1-3)

The Rogue Chronicles:

Romancing the Rogue, Book 1

A Rogue's Reputation, a Novella, Book 2

A Rogue No More, Book 3

A Rogue to the Rescue, Book 4

A Rogue and Some Mistletoe, a Novella, Book 5

To Dare A Rogue, Book 6

A Rogue Meets His Match, Book 7

The Rogue's Autumn Bride, Book 8

A Rogue's Christmas Kiss, a Novella, Book 9

A Rogue's Redemption, a short story, Book 10

A Match Made in the Highlands, a Novella

The Wicked Widows Collection:

To Bargain with a Rogue

Falling For A Knight Series:

A Knight's Christmas Wish, Novella, Book .5

A Knight's Quest, Book 1 (Also available in Audio)

A Knight's Temptation, Book 2 (Also available in Audio)

A Knight's Captive, Book 3 (Also available in Audio)

The Vengeance Trilogy:

A Vow To Keep, Book I
A Knight's Kiss, Novella, Book 1.5
Trust In Me, Book II
Believe In Me, Book III

Contemporary Romances

Yours for the Weekend, a Novella

If you liked this book, I invite you to sign up to my newsletter to find out when the next one is released.

Reviews help readers and authors, and I'd be honored if you'd write one, no matter how brief!

About the Author

Lana Williams is a USA Today Bestselling Author with 50 historical fiction novels filled with mystery, romance, adventure, and sometimes, a pinch of paranormal to stir things up. Her latest venture is with historical mysteries.

She spends her days in Victorian, Regency, and Medieval times, depending on her mood and current deadline. Lana calls the Rocky Mountains of Colorado home where she lives with her husband and a spoiled rescue dog named Sadie. Connect with her at https://lana williams.net/.

Printed in Great Britain
by Amazon